THE
TANGIBLES

NATALIE BLANK

Dedicated to my daughter.

one

NO ONE ASKED me to prom, so I asked Larry. And he responded *no*. Just like that, without explanation. I took it upon myself to ask him again and again until he gave me a legit answer. Finally, he said, "Rae-Rae, if you really want to go to prom, you'll have to go with yourself or ask someone tangible."

I wasn't actually being serious with him. What could I possibly gain from going to prom other than public humiliation? *Look, there's Rachel, dancing with her imaginary friends!* Even if Larry did agree to be my date, Larry doesn't dance, so I'd be awkwardly wobbling with myself. To terrible music no less.

So instead, I'll be sitting on the couch, watching Netflix with a bag of Doritos while everyone else gropes each other in overpriced dresses and tuxedos, wearing corsages that will die in a few days. What a *great* way to end junior year. At least Mom will be working, and I can hang out with Larry all night.

Larry is the perfect guy friend. And by perfect, I really mean perfect. He's my shoulder to cry on, my reading buddy, the guru of tidiness, and the brother I never had. He makes sure I'm dressed and ready for school, that my hair is combed, and my teeth are brushed. Sometimes I forget to do these things myself, so Larry reminds me.

"Rae-Rae, are you sure you want to wear that?" Larry asks Friday morning of prom. I'm wearing a new tank top, and it's a bit revealing. Or perhaps a bit too small.

1

"Is it my boobs, my butt, or my gut?" I ask, twirling around.

Larry scratches his chin, always stubble free, and says, "I think it's all three."

I groan and debate changing. "It fit fine a week ago."

"Just wear a cardigan on top," Larry says, pointing to the white one on the floor. It's short-sleeved, so at least I won't sweat. "And next time, don't eat a whole bag of hot tamale chips right before bed."

"Mmmm, but they were so good." I slip into the cardigan. "Crap. This makes my boobs look even bigger."

"Yes, but it slims everything else, so problem solved. You look great."

See what I mean by perfect? Larry always knows how to make me feel better without being creepy, perverted, or mean. He knows how self-conscious I am about my weight.

"Will you help with my makeup?" I ask. "Just the eyeliner."

"Of course."

I sit on the edge of my unmade bed while Larry kneels in front of me. His lips smell like bubblegum, courtesy of the ChapStick he applies every twenty minutes. Larry has cinnamon-colored skin and large eyes like melted chocolate. He's a beautiful hybrid, inheriting every stature benefit from his tall Norwegian dad and every exotic trait from his Ethiopian mom, most notably his sharp pointed nose. His parents are long deceased, taken captive by a desolate tribe in Africa. Larry, the sole survivor of his family, has found peace living with me. When I'm at school, he passes the time by reading or drawing in my notebook. His sketches are mostly of me, or at least what I would like to be. Tall, thin, and not crazy.

His devotion to me is unusual, but necessary. And if he wasn't gay, I would be attracted to him, possibly to the point of *liking* him. But that's impossible. None of my intangibles are ever straight, attractive, and into me like that.

He finishes one eye, then steps back to take a look at his work. Pleased, he continues with the other. "So, have you checked out the new neighbors yet?" he asks.

"No. But I'm sure they're perfectly normal."

"Maybe they'll have a daughter or son your age. Someone you could talk to at school."

"Yeah, and maybe we'll have sleepovers and be instant best friends."

Larry sighs and steps back, satisfied with his work, but not amused by my sarcasm. "I'm being serious."

I roll my eyes, not getting his point. "That's something *Mom* would suggest."

"Rae, that's something anyone would suggest."

I love it when he just calls me Rae. It makes everything he says afterward feel right, even if it's not.

After I check my makeup and my body one last time, I rest the back of my head against his lap while he massages my temples and brushes his fingers through my light-brown hair. We never rush the mornings, as it's my favorite time of day to be alone with Larry.

"I wish I could just stay home today."

"No, Rae-Rae. You don't want your mom to get suspicious."

"She's always suspicious."

"You know what I mean. If she finds out you're skipping, she'll start bringing Mrs. Martin around more. Or worse, she'll make you go on the shot."

"She won't put me on the shot. She knows how I feel about needles."

"Yes, but you still need to be careful. How many days has it been this week?"

"I can't remember."

"Oh, Rae-Rae."

"Oh, Larry."

"Oh, Mrs. Martin. How she smells like soup."

I cover my mouth to muffle my god-awful chuckles. "I know, right?"

Larry is always able to end a serious conversation with something randomly hysterical. But my laughter jolts to silence when Mom knocks on my door as though preparing for a police raid.

"Hey, what's going on in there?"

"Nothing," I say, quickly grabbing my phone. "Just watching a funny YouTube video."

She enters, even though she didn't ask permission. She's always trying to catch me in the act, openly conversing with Larry, but Larry usually warns me if someone is coming.

I lift my head off Larry's lap and quickly show Mom my saved "funny cat compilation" video. She smirks and rolls her eyes, always seemingly annoyed by anything that amuses me, from my phone in particular. I mean, who doesn't laugh at cats who jump away from cucumbers? She drops the laundry basket she's holding on the floor and proceeds to throw every piece of clothing into it.

"Hey, some of those clothes are clean."

"Then hang them up. And how about using your bookshelf for all these books instead of having them in piles everywhere?"

"I'll clean everything up later. School?"

"Yes, I know. I'm driving you."

"I can walk."

"Yes, but I don't have to work until noon today and I would really like to drive you so we can talk. Unless there's someone else you were planning to talk to?"

She looks around the room, obviously not noticing Larry, but still suspicious of his presence. I smile politely, grab my backpack, and walk to the door. "Nope, we can talk all you want."

"Did you take your medicine?"

"Yeah. You can check my pack again if you really want to." The skipped pills just end up flushed down the toilet.

"I don't need to check."

"Good. Now let's go so I can get through this stupid day."

"Why is it stupid?"

"Because it's prom tonight, and most girls are going to be leaving early to get their hair and nails done, so the whole second half of the day is pointless."

"Oh, honey, are you worried you're going to be the only junior at school this afternoon?"

"No. It's just dumb. All of it." I slink around her and jog down the stairs. Mom takes her time, always in observation mode. Always trying to find fault.

And me, I'm always searching for new ways to fake it. I've learned so much about my condition over the years that I know how to play the game and cheat if need be to live a somewhat normal life. It's the medicine. Whether I'm on or off. I don't like being on. It's a sad, mundane world when you've got a pole through your head, blocking out all the pretty people just dying to be your friend. While honest to the extreme, people like Larry are a crucial comfort when the tangibles don't want anything to do with you.

Do I hate them? No. I just can't relate to them. Or connect. The tangibles I deal with daily are quick to judge, and they make assumptions about me without taking the time to get to know me. So I do what I can to tolerate them. I have to live in their world. And in their world, having "imaginary friends" when you're seventeen is not acceptable. Even if your imaginary friends are better friends than they are.

My therapist once asked, if given a choice, would I live solely in the intangible world? I wouldn't answer the question because even with her, I have to cheat to stay in the game. But if I was forced to answer, I would say no. Because certain intangibles aren't super nice and friendly like Larry. And they could always come back if I were to go off my medicine for too long. Unlike Larry, they're not out to help me; they're out to hurt me.

And sometimes I forget to put my seat belt on.

"Seriously, Rachel?" Mom asks, reaching over to do it for me. Her dark brown hair wafts my face. Even though she showers twice a day, that antiseptic hospital smell seems to follow her everywhere.

"I was going to do it." I catch myself before I roll my eyes. "I was going over history questions in my head."

"Do you have a quiz today?"

"Yeah, on the dynasties of China."

"Sounds…"

"Boring."

She smiles, for the first time that morning, and puts the SUV into reverse. My mother is attractive despite the forehead wrinkles, probably caused by scowling so much, and random gray hairs she dyes away every six months or so. She has high cheekbones, animated blue eyes, good teeth minus the coffee stains, and a classic button nose, but she looks older than forty-five. More like fifty-five. Being an ER surgeon takes a toll on your skin when you don't see daylight enough, and your sleep schedule is a mess. She constantly laments about needing a face-lift. I think eight hours of sleep a day would work better. And maybe cut back on all the coffee and soda.

"You did an excellent job with your makeup today," Mom says. "Did someone from school teach you?"

"YouTube videos."

"Oh. Right. YouTube. Nowadays, you can learn anything from YouTube."

"Not everything."

"So, let's talk about prom."

"I'm not going."

"I know that. I didn't expect you to. I was just wondering if you wanted to do anything this weekend since I have Saturday and Sunday off."

"When does the pool open?"

"Not until Memorial Day weekend."

"Oh. Okay."

"We could drive up to your grandpa's lake house if you want to swim."

I shake my head. "I need to study this weekend. I have AP exams next week."

"Oh, yes, that's right." She taps her nails against the steering wheel while we wait at a red light. I turn to the right, noticing a man and his dog run by. Anytime I see a grown man with his dog, I get really sad.

"Anywho," Mom says, pulling me from my depressing thoughts. "I wanted to talk to you about the new neighbors. They're still settling in, but I met both the husband and wife. Very nice, respectable people, both lawyers. They work long hours."

"Great, so you'll never see each other."

"They have a teenage son. He's going to start school on Monday."

"Why bother? School is stupid after prom. Unless you have AP exams."

"It's important for him to feel welcomed and to get to know people."

"What does this have to do with me?"

"You should meet him."

"Why?"

"You could use this as an opportunity to work on your social skills."

"*Mom.*"

"He's not going to prom either, so maybe you could go over and introduce yourself and maybe play some basketball outside?"

"I don't play anymore."

"I wish you would. You were so talented."

"Yeah, until I started passing the ball to imaginary people."

"That was before you were medicated. I bet now you could—"

"I don't want to introduce myself to anyone! As soon as he, whoever he is, finds out I'm a freak, he'll either make fun of me or just ignore me like everyone else does."

"You don't know that. And you're not a freak."

"Whatever. Can't I just study this weekend?"

"If studying is all you want to do. I just thought it would be nice for you to talk to someone your own age."

"You sound like Larry."

"Larry?" Mom grips the steering wheel like she's trying to strangle it. "Larry? Have you been talking to Larry again?"

"No."

"You've been skipping, haven't you?"

"No, I haven't."

"I'm going to start monitoring you again."

"You don't need to do that."

"I will do whatever is necessary—"

"To make me feel like a freak? Because that's what it feels like when you interrogate me about my pills."

"I'm not interrogating you. I'm just asking questions."

"You're—"

I bite my lip, halting my next thought from slipping out. I want to tell her that she's wrong, that she's a control freak, and this is why Dad left. But it would hurt too deeply to hear me, her only daughter, say such things. But mean things and the truth can't always be separated.

"Okay, fine," she finally says. "You haven't mentioned Larry in awhile. That's all."

"You know the medicine doesn't make them go away completely. The medicine just keeps them from talking to me. From distracting me."

"We could put you back on a stronger dose."

"And turn me back into a zombie? Mom, please, I've been good all year. No episodes. Why can't you trust me?"

"I do trust you. I don't trust *them*."

"Don't worry about them. They don't control me."

7

Mom nods, trying to maintain her composure. She drops me off at school, says goodbye and good luck with the quiz. Poor woman won't shed a tear in front of anyone, not even me. Sometimes I think she needs therapy more than I do. She could use a real friend. Hard, though, working twelve-hour shifts.

Every day, when I enter my overcrowded, sports-loving high school, I lift my head high, not to feel proud, but to be aware of my surroundings. Most students are aware of my condition, and the majority of them simply do the "nice" thing and ignore me. Then there are a few girls in particular who like to torment me by either tripping me, pushing me, or making fun of me. I've been seemingly normal for the past few years, but they still remember eighth grade and find joy in humiliating me. Because of their personas and the way they dress, like hanging butt cheeks are in style, I've nicknamed them the "tangiwhores."

Today of all days, I can be thankful they're distracted by prom, so I walk by unnoticed to my locker. I have history first period. Once I get this quiz out of the way, the rest of the day should be pretty easy. That's until I see Mrs. Zuckerman, the school psychologist, coming toward me.

"Rachel, how good to see you today," she says, her overly stretched smile making me want to vomit. I can smell the coffee on her breath. And it never smells like good, fresh coffee, more like eight-day-old coffee that's been sitting in the sun, getting bathed in by birds and bugs.

"Hi, Mrs. Zuckerman," I reply less enthusiastically.

"I'm glad you're here a little early because we have a new school nurse, and I would like you to meet her."

"Mrs. Baker is gone?"

"She's on maternity leave, remember?"

"Oh, right."

"It's important you meet her substitute."

"Why?"

"I don't think I need to explain why."

"I take my medicine at home."

"Yes, but you come to the nurse quite frequently."

"For headaches."

"*Rachel.* Please."

Ugh. No point in arguing. I can always get a late pass to first period. But all this nonsense is messing up the study session I'm having in the back of my head.

I follow Mrs. Zuckerman to the nurse's office, avoiding the whispers from the tangiwhores. Anytime they see me with the psychologist, they instantly assume something is wrong. *Take her away. Lock her up. Dose her good.* Seriously, it never ends.

The near three-minute walk to the nurse's office is a complete waste of time because nobody is even there.

"She's stuck in traffic," the attendance secretary calls from the main office across the hall.

"Thank you," Mrs. Zuckerman says. "Alright, you'll have to meet her later."

The bell rings.

"Can I get a late pass?"

The secretary writes me the pass since Mrs. Zuckerman suddenly needs to be at a meeting. These women are always messing my day up. Larry would never make me late for class. Then again, Larry never comes to school with me. He never leaves the house.

"There you go," the secretary says, handing me a green slip.

"This is an unexcused late pass. I should get a pink one if it's excused."

"I'm sorry. I'll write you a new one."

As I wait for the correct pass, the principal's door opens, and out struts this stunning Native American woman dressed like a senator, but with the face of a Hollywood actress. She has beautiful flawless skin, luscious red lips, and shoulder-length black hair straightened to perfection. Even Larry, with all his artistic skills, couldn't make me look like that. He'd be like, *Rae-Rae, you need Jesus to look like that.*

She turns around, flipping hair like it's part of her movement pattern, and reaches a hand for a young man, who I assume is her son. She guides him out the door and then returns inside the room, shutting the door behind her to talk privately with the principal.

With long black hair shadowing the sides of his face, he takes a seat on the other side of the main office. My high school has a decent mix of ethnicities, but rarely do we see any Native Americans. I could be mistaken about his heritage, but even if I am, I'll just pretend he is what I want him to be. I do it all the time with my intangibles; I can certainly do it with the tangibles. Especially since I know he's not going to talk to me.

But we do have that moment. When he brushes the hair off his face and stretches his head back, he pauses and looks right at me. And like fire and snow, we don't know what to do with each other, and we definitely don't speak, but we can and will remember that we had a moment where we looked into each other's eyes and saw another person. I can't say what he saw in me, but I saw sadness in him. A longing to be understood. And while I wanted to see more, my late slip was finally prepared, and I had to go to class to fail a quiz because the minute I saw him, I forgot every single dynasty of China.

two

THE REST of the day goes by like any other school day, minus overhearing several guys brag about boning their prom dates. If I had anything to boast about, it would be my garden, but no one wants to hear about that.

While all the guys go home to put on tuxedos and fill their pockets with gum, cash, and condoms, I head straight to my backyard to do some weeding. I'm a perfectionist when it comes to my garden, and I take pride in my work. If it weren't for my fair skin, I would spend hours outside, digging my hands through the dirt. There's something oddly cleansing about soil. Almost to the point of healing.

When I was hospitalized, the nurses had trouble convincing me to participate in activities, such as board games, music, even television. Then one day, they asked if I wanted to plant flowers. It was the first time I was allowed to go outside, after weeks of indoor seclusion. Because I behaved so well and listened to the gardener's instructions, I was invited to plant the next day and the next. Eventually, the doctors started to have sessions with me outside in the garden rather than indoors. That was when I began to open up, vocally and mentally, and eventually was released. Mom believes in that "time heals all wounds" stuff. But it depends on what you're doing with your time.

Larry never comes outside. He blames the mosquitos, but really it's to avoid Breezy, who can be pretty dominant. Their clashing personalities drive me up a wall, so they each have their territories.

11

But they're still confined to home and nowhere else. That's their choice and mine. I can't handle them at school or anywhere public.

Breezy is a huge advocate for all things organic, but she hasn't been around much because of her spring allergies. When summer hits and the pollen settles down, she'll be livelier and help me to grow giant tomatoes and cucumbers. Larry and Breezy are the only intangibles I talk to these days. I used to have more, hanging together like one big group of friends, but I lost them after the hospitalization. After the meds. The high dosages. I'm glad Larry and Breezy were the only ones to come back, as they're the easiest to get along with, despite Breezy's occasional tantrum over the garden.

Her biggest complaint has been against this ugly red bush growing too close to the garden. I've been dying to chop it down too, but Mom likes it for some reason. I don't know why people born in the seventies like bushes. If you want privacy, build a fence. If you want something pretty to look at, plant flowers.

For the next half hour, I trim the bush and let my mind wander. The garden was my only happy memory of that hospital, minus the day I was allowed to leave. I remember conversations between the nurses. They thought while I stared into space, I wasn't listening or aware of their presence, but I heard everything: *"She's so young to have schizophrenia. It's so rare for children. I wonder who she inherited it from."* And that I'm not sure of. Genetics do play a role, but there's no way to prove anything, especially with how little I know about my dad's side of the family. Schizophrenia is too complex. Every case is different and unpredictable. People like Mrs. Zuckerman tend to generalize, and while I have the knowledge to shut her down, doing so would cause me more harm than good. Normal teenagers can get away with back talk. People like me have to swallow their pride, if they have any, and pretend everything is fine.

I'm chopping rather aggressively now. I pause to wipe the sweat off my forehead and notice that the neighbor's back door is open.

I can no longer hear the sweet sounds of spring. I can only hear the sound of my heart thumping against my chest so violently it feels like a Xenomorph might pop out. All thoughts of the hospital and Mrs. Zuckerman disappear. All focus is on the young man outside.

He walks a few feet across the grass and stretches his arms over his head. He has shoulder-length black hair, smooth dark skin, thick eyebrows, and eyes a deep earthy brown, radiating the warmth of a garden. Even Larry's perfect features can't compare. Because Larry doesn't walk with masculinity or muscles, and this guy walks with it like I don't even know.

It takes several seconds for me to make the connection that I am staring at the boy from school. But this time, his eyes are bulging in absolute horror. Am I that hideous? Or is he pointing at something else? I look down at my chest. No Xenomorph. But there is blood dripping from my fingers.

"Rae-Rae!" Larry yells from my bedroom window. "Are you alright? Come inside!"

"Rachel, you're bleeding everywhere." And now Breezy is there too. She wears a white mask to protect her from the pollen and a sombrero-like hat to shield her from the sun. "Rachel? Did you hear me?" Her head bobs back and forth. I take a step forward and fall sideways onto the grass. "My goodness, you're a mess!" I roll onto my back. Breezy looms over me. Her curly red hair looks like a ball of fire in the sun. My eyes roll back, darkness takes over, but her voice prattles on. "You need to be more careful. You should be using an electric blade for that bush, not those scissors. They're far too small, and you'll end up ruining them."

Please shut up, Breezy. *Please.*

When I open my eyes, Breezy and Larry are gone. And the guy next door is on his knees, wrapping my hand with gauze and tape. I open my mouth to say something, anything, but a faint croaking sound comes out instead.

He is a spectacular human being now that I'm seeing him up close and personal. He even smells nice, like Axe or whatever hot guys use these days as cologne. Then I notice four white marks across his neck. They look like scars. His hair is pulled back into a ponytail, even though it was down just a minute ago.

"Hey," he says. "You're awake. Can you sit up?" When I don't answer, he puts a hand behind my neck and gently lifts me up. "Can you hear me?" He waves his other hand in front of my face.

"Yes…I can."

"I wasn't sure if you fainted or what was going on."

"My…hand?"

"I wrapped it. But you need stitches. Are your parents home? I didn't see a car in the driveway."

"My mom." I close my eyes so I can focus on my articulation. "No dad."

"Are you light-headed? Should I call 911?"

"No. Don't call 911. I, ya…" I'm stuttering, not a good sign. "I n-n-need my medicine."

"Where is it? I'll get it for you."

"K-kitchen-n counter. It's in a p-p-packet."

He lowers my head carefully to the soft grass and runs inside my house. I don't hear from Breezy or Larry again, which is fine for now. I'm more concerned about the stuttering.

"How many?" he asks, returning with the packet and a glass of water.

I'm supposed to take one pill every morning at the same time, but my schedule has obviously gotten out of control. I usually don't have any withdrawal symptoms from skipping here and there, but today's a first. Today I feel a slippage. Or maybe it's just the blood loss. Or meeting my next-door neighbor like this. Whatever the cause, I need my brain, my whole body, to calm down.

"T-t-two."

He helps in every way possible, by holding my head up, dropping the pills inside my mouth, and pouring the water down my throat. It takes time for the medicine to kick in, but I feel better knowing it's in my system and the intangibles will stay quiet.

"Was that anxiety medicine or something?" He tries to read the side label, but it's been scratched off.

I take a deep breath and roll my tongue side to side before speaking again. "Sort of," I say, clear as day. Using my good hand, I push myself up to a sitting position. My new clothes are ruined unless I want to wear them for Halloween.

"Are you okay?" he asks, his one hand hovering behind my back in case I topple again.

"I think so." I fold my arms over my knees and gape at the blood-stained grass. "So much red. So much…" I look at him and notice there's blood all over his hands. He didn't put gloves on even though they come inside every first aid kit.

"It's okay," he says. "It'll wash off."

"I'm so sorry."

"It's really okay. Accidents happen." He looks at my pack again. "Your name is Rachel?"

"Yes. Rachel Andrews. Who…who are you? I mean, what's your name?"

"My name is Arnold. Arnold Begay."

Arnold. I don't know why I imagined something more *epic* for his first name. Like Xerxes or Achilles. He would fit into *The Iliad* world perfectly, while I would only suit the part of a handmaiden or slave.

"How are you feeling right now?" he asks. "How's your hand feel?"

"It hurts."

"No kidding?" He laughs at my sudden realization of pain. He has a near perfect smile, a sure sign that he had braces. I rock an okay smile for never having braces. My teeth are straight, but my gums stick out. So, best to avoid smiling, even when he does.

"Where did I cut it?" I ask.

"You nicked the skin right between your index and middle finger."

"Really?"

"Yes, and you still need to go to a hospital. We can call your mom if you want. I have my phone with me."

"My mom works in the ER. She's a surgeon. She won't answer her phone if she's in the middle of a surgery."

"Alright. Well, how far away is the nearest hospital?"

"The one my mom works at is in Germantown. Five, six miles, maybe?"

"Is there a bus that comes by here? I don't have my license yet."

"Same."

Pills delay everything.

Fifteen minutes later, we're on the bus, sitting in the far back to avoid attention. It looks like we're either going to a horror fest, or we just had a freak accident. I haven't sat next to a boy on a bus since middle school. But come to think of it, I haven't sat next to *anyone* on a bus since middle school. I prefer walking, my mom's SUV, or just not leaving the house.

"I'm sorry about your pants," I say after a few minutes of awkward silence.

"Hey, they're just jeans. I've got a dozen other pairs."

"And your shirt. There's a spot of red on your shoulder."

"This is a Sex Pistols T-shirt. Blood gives it more character, so thank you."

I don't bother to ask what Sex Pistols means. Instead, I study the floor, his mint-green sneakers, and my gray sneakers. My socks don't match. Thanks, Larry.

The bus driver knows we're going to the hospital, so he drops us off in front of the ER instead of making us walk from the bus stop. I'm hoping Mom is doing an extensive surgery, so she can't be bothered. I don't know how long it takes to get stitches. I've broken bones before, but no major cuts.

I sign myself in and hand the front desk lady my insurance card and ID; Arnold helps since I'm one-handed. I explain what happened, as vaguely as possible, and when they ask for a parent/guardian, I mention my mother.

"Oh, Dr. Andrews," the lady says. "She's in surgery right now. Do you want to wait for her to do your stitches?"

"I would prefer whoever is available."

"Okay, honey, no worries. Can you fill this out on your own? It's a touch-screen."

"I should be fine."

Arnold carries the iPad for me to the waiting area. He offers to hold it, but I assure him I'm okay using my leg to prop it up. I hope he doesn't stay hovered over me while I answer all these very private questions.

"This may take a while," I say. "You don't have to stay."

"I don't mind."

"If you have somewhere to be, I totally understand."

"I really have no place else to be. I'm new here, and you're the only person I know so far."

"You didn't meet anyone at school?"

"I wasn't there for very long. I just met the principal and the school psychologist."

"Oh, Mrs. Zuckerman. She's…great."

He smiles at my sarcasm. "Do you have to see Mrs. Zuckerman a lot?"

"Unfortunately."

"For your anxiety?"

"Yeah, for that and other stuff." I wiggle in my chair, trying to find a more comfortable position that gives me more space from him. Eventually, he stands and sort of wobbles from foot to foot as though playing soccer with an imaginary ball.

"Everyone seems cool so far," he says, kicking his foot out. The gentleman waiting nearby looks pissed and moves to another chair. "But it's too early to tell yet. They could just be putting on their 'nice to meet you, but I really don't care' faces right now. Back home, people just say what they think. Sometimes a good thing. Sometimes not."

"Where's home?"

"Santa Cruz. Born and raised. My folks are mostly Cherokee, with some Navajo thrown in, if you're at all curious about heritage, but I don't make a big deal of it."

"I think my family is mostly Norwegian."

"Ooo. That means you descended from the Vikings! You're a warrior at heart." He pretends to unleash a sword.

"I don't think I inherited any of the valor, just the pale skin."

"I wouldn't call it pale." He puts away his fake sword. "More like Snow White." He smiles, hinting at flirtation, or maybe he's teasing me. "Anywho, where are you from? Locally."

"I was born in Hagerstown, but we moved here when I was three."

"Garfield, Maryland." He emphasizes the G, almost like a pirate. "Does it ever make you think of the cat?"

"All the time. We have the highest population of cats in the whole county."

"Really?"

"There's no actual statistic that proves it. But we have a pet store, two veterinarians, and an adoption center, so you could say we're animal friendly here."

"And a small town," he says, dribbling his imaginary ball backward. "So, besides adopting a cat, what is there to do around here?"

"I'm not the best person to ask."

He stops his footwork. "Come on now, why say that?"

"I need to finish this."

"I know. I'm distracting you. I'll get some water. You need anything?"

"No, thanks."

While he's gone, I hurry through the questions, moving at lightning speed when I get to the part about medications and hospitalizations. I don't want to think about my stay in the mental hospital again. The gardening was a pleasant memory earlier, but now I'm thinking about the bad parts. The straitjacket. The examinations. Pills. Needles. Doctors and nurses watching my every move. I glance up, wondering if anyone is looking at me, but the nurse is now seeing the gentleman from before, so there's literally no one around.

After I return the iPad, it's another fifteen-minute wait. Arnold and I have a pretty easy time talking to one another, which surprises me, since I rarely talk to people my age. I'm calmer now that I feel my medicine, but in a few short hours, I'll be like a zombie due to drowsiness. I never take two pills at once. I'm not supposed to, ever, but today was an emergency.

"So, it's just you and your mom?" he asks. "For how long?"

"Since I was eight. My dad walked out on us."

"Like suddenly, or was it coming?"

"My mom knew it was coming, but for me, not so much. He left after breakfast one day. He even took our dog."

"That's awful. Some people just shouldn't be parents. They ought to be sterilized or something. They ought to—"

"Rachel Andrews?" the nurse calls, saving me from a sensitive topic best reserved for another time. Or never, actually.

"That's me." We stand simultaneously. "Are you sure you want to come back? It might make you…uncomfortable." *Me* uncomfortable.

"If I'm not mistaken, I was the one that wrapped up your hand initially."

So we follow the nurse into the nearest check-in room, where she takes my temperature, blood pressure, asks me my height (5'5") and then proceeds to weigh me. I, of course, think 145 pounds is a fat person's weight, even though Larry has tried to convince me it's in all the right places.

I have to explain again how I cut myself, how it was purely an accident, and then Arnold explains what he did for the wound and that there was a lot of blood but that I had lots of valor and stayed calm the entire time. If only he knew what a panic attack I was having inside my head.

The nurse proceeds to browse through my answers on her iPad, squinting over the section about medications and hospitalizations. I bite my bottom lip, hoping she doesn't say anything too revealing, but she seems more concerned about getting me to see the doctor than questioning me about my mental health.

"I'm Dr. Andrews' daughter, in case you're wondering," I finally say.

"Yes, I know." She sounds unimpressed. "Your mother is not going to be able to see you. She's doing a very extensive surgery right now. You'll probably be done and out before she's even halfway through with her work."

"That's okay." Really, it's okay.

My doctor comes in a few minutes later. Luckily I know him—Dr. Lewis. He's a good friend of my mother's, and while he's a very attractive, all-around great guy, he's a devout Catholic and has six kids with his wife.

"Rachel!" he exclaims after giving me a friendly tap on the back. "I haven't seen you since Christmas. How are things? Are you staying out of trouble?"

"I guess not today."

"And who is this?" He gestures to Arnold, who's been wavering in the corner, trying to stay out of the way.

"This is my neighbor, Arnold. He, uh, brought me here."

"How nice of him!" Dr. Lewis raises both arms like he's about to announce the winner of Miss America. "You must be her knight in shining armor!"

Dr. Lewis is slightly dramatic and comical, so he often treats kids and teenagers instead of grumpy adults.

After shaking hands with a slightly embarrassed Arnold, he washes his hands and snaps on a pair of blue gloves. "Let's see what we have here," he says as he removes the tape.

As more of my skin is exposed, I feel a regurgitating feeling in the back of my throat from the rusty smell of blood and the faint smell of alcohol. Or it could be that I'm thirsty and should have said yes when Arnold offered me a drink.

"It looks like the bleeding has died down," Dr. Lewis says after removing the gauze. "Whoever wrapped this for you did an excellent job." He winks at Arnold. Another awkward moment to add to the list. "You're going to need a few stitches. But first, I'll need to sanitize the wound and give you a shot of Novocaine."

I stand up, aimed to run. I don't know why I didn't make the connection earlier that needles would be involved with stitching.

"You'll need to sit down for this," Dr. Lewis says. "I know you don't like needles, but it's just one pinch, and then you won't feel anything else. You can look away the whole time."

Dr. Lewis eases me back onto the medical table. I hold my breath. Will I make it through this? Or will I end up getting restrained or sedated? Which could very well lead to a visit to the psych ward. Or worse.

Arnold comes to the rescue just when I'm about to break. He's by my side, holding my undamaged hand. "Look at me," he says, his deep-brown eyes alluring and kind. "Now's a good time for a distraction, right?"

I nod helplessly.

"I'll tell you a story, okay?"

I release my held breath. "Okay."

"One time when I was eight, I went camping with my Boy Scout troop. It was my first time being away from home for more than one night. Everyone thought I'd be the bravest and know all kinds of things about camping because of my heritage, but my mom and dad are rarely outdoors; I'm usually discovering things for myself. Anyway, after all the adults went to sleep, some of us snuck out for a late-night swim at the lake. There was a cliff you could jump from, but it wasn't safe to do at night when you couldn't see the rocks all that well."

My eyes sink. "Did anyone die?"

"No one died. Relax." He gives my hand an extra squeeze. "So, I was the first one to climb up to the top, but I never jumped off the cliff. Something was whimpering inside one of the nearby caverns, so I went inside to check it out, and it was a mama wolf and her pups.

"Now, mama wolves are super territorial and will attack anyone they see as a threat, but this mama wolf was injured. She had broken her leg somehow and could barely stand. She must have dragged herself back home to be with her pups. So naturally, she didn't pounce on me. She just growled and whined. Sort of begging me not to hurt her family. But I just wanted to help. So I went back to wake the adults, even though all my friends told me not to since we'd get in trouble for being out so late. But the troop leader was a veterinarian and could help. At first, he was reluctant to do anything, claiming nature had a way of balancing itself, but when I told him about the eight pups that would die without their mom, he decided to help.

"In the morning, he hiked a mile down to his car where he had an emergency medical kit and a non-lethal gun. He shot the wolf with a strong sedative, and while she slept, he reset her leg and wrapped it up. I got to play with all the pups while he did his work."

"Did she recover?"

"She rested for a few days inside the cave. We brought her fish and water from the lake, and her pups could still nurse from her. Toward the end of our trip, everyone warned me to leave her alone, now that she was moving better. Even though we had helped her, she could always turn on us."

He takes a deep breath and prepares for the epic conclusion.

"And?" I ask.

"Alright, you're all done," Dr. Lewis says.

I turn and look at my newly bandaged hand. I missed the whole thing, every single stitch, even the initial Novocaine shot.

"That's it?" I ask.

"Yep. They're the dissolvable kind. Should clear up in about two weeks, but in the meantime, try not to move it much or bathe with it for at least forty-eight hours. Then you can remove the bandage." He hands me a paper with the generic do/don't list for stitches. "Your mom will know what to do if it starts to look infected. You can take Tylenol if you have any pain tonight."

"Will there be a scar?"

"A small one. I only had to do four stitches. It was a clean cut." He tosses the disposables. "Let me see if your mother is out of surgery. I'm sure she's going to want to approve my work. You can wait here or outside if you need to walk or stretch." He's looking at Arnold, who is back to playing soccer. "You have a lot of energy, young man."

"This is nothing," Arnold says.

Dr. Lewis smiles and pats us both on the shoulder. "Take care, you two. Stay out of trouble." I thank him as he walks out the door.

When I scoot off the table, I fumble over my feet and instinctively reach for Arnold. He catches me by the arms, careful not to touch the stitched hand.

"You okay?" he asks, his eyes all over my face.

"I'm..." I look right at him. "I'm just thirsty."

"Here." Not taking his eyes off me, he pulls a water bottle from his back pocket and opens it for me.

"Thanks." I take a small sip and then another. "This is good water."

He laughs. "For two dollars, it better be."

I take another sip, but this time I cough, spitting water all over Arnold's poor T-shirt. I cover my mouth in horror. "I'm so sorry." I hiccup and cough some more.

He smiles and takes the bottle from me. "It's just water. You okay?" He pats me gently on the back, sending shivers up my spine like a high striker.

"I'm fine. I...I just..."

One hand is on my shoulder, the other is levitating near my waist. His eyes won't leave me alone. Something inside nudges me to close the gap between us, but I fight the strange urge and step back.

"We should go," I say. To which he nods, smiles, and opens the door for me.

We fly by the front desk, past the waiting room, and straight outside. I send Mom a quick text message letting her know I'm okay and that I'm going home on the bus. With Arnold's jitter feet and my detestation of hospitals, it's senseless to wait for her.

"Are you hungry?" Arnold asks on the bus.

"Not really. I'm kind of tired."

"Well, I've got two shoulders. Which one do you want?"

"What?"

"To rest on?"

I sit up straight. "Oh, no. That's okay. I'm fine."

The bus hits a speed bump, and my head lands right on Arnold's shoulder. I fully expect myself to leap back, apologize, and feel incredibly stupid, but I don't do anything. I keep my head on Arnold's shoulder and close my eyes. I could sleep, but Arnold's legs bounce like he's playing drums for a rock band.

When we get to our stop, Arnold has to help me off the bus. It's just a short walk home, but it feels like a marathon. To keep me from stumbling, he puts his arm around my waist, and I worry he'll think I'm too fat, especially since his body feels like steel. But how often is it that a tangible will ever come in contact with me like this? The intangibles touch me, but it's not that deep, earthy connection you have with someone real. You don't feel out of breath or scared to blink because you know they'll always be there, inside your head at least. Tangibles can leave whenever they want to. And not always give you fair warning.

"Does your medicine always make you this tired?" he asks as he assists me up the two stairs of my front porch.

"I took too much."

"You're not gonna OD on me, are you?"

"No. Just need to sleep..." I fumble with my keys. He unlocks the door for me and opens it. I stumble inside the house and head straight for the couch. The cold leather smell is soothing.

"You sure you're okay?" Arnold asks. "I could stay with you until your mom gets home." He spreads a blanket across my body and removes my shoes.

"You don't want to meet my mom."

He sighs. "I'll stay until you fall asleep."

three

"*RACHEL*! *WAKE UP*!"

Mom shakes me like I'm dead or overdosing. It takes several seconds to make sense of my surroundings since I'm not used to falling asleep in the living room. I catch a glimpse of Larry sitting by the window. He's reading *The Outsiders*, one of our all-time favorite books, and drinking a Starbucks latte. Won't say anything. Just smiles and waves, reassuring me that he's still there, just in silent mode while the meds do their job.

Mom is practically on top of me, screaming like she's in a Tennessee Williams play. "If you don't say something, I'll—"

"I'm awake." I push her away and scoot to the far side of the couch. "Calm down."

"Calm down? I've been trying to call for hours. Dr. Lewis said you left without waiting for me to see you."

"I didn't want to wait. I was so tired." I pull the blanket from her, but it's difficult with one hand. She helps, but not before looking over the stitches.

"Why were you so tired? Did they give you a sedative or something?"

"No, I just accidentally took two pills today."

"What? How? The pills are marked, so you don't do that."

"I know. I'm sorry."

"Rachel, you have to be more careful. Do we need to start doing a chart again?"

"No."

"It's vital the pill is taken every day at the same time. No exceptions. Do you want to have a relapse and ruin everything we've worked toward?"

"It won't happen again."

"Dr. Lewis also said some boy was with you."

"Yeah, some boy. He helped get me to the hospital."

"I need more details than that."

"Tomorrow. Please. I'm so tired. And sorry. I need to sleep. Please, just let me sleep."

"Fine. Tomorrow, I want you to tell me everything."

Everything minus the truth.

I arise to the smell of bacon. Not a bad way to wake up, unless you're a vegan, but it can only mean one thing in this house.

Mrs. Martin is hard on the eyes. She's got flabby skin, clumpy gray hair, and an extra-large nose, capable of swatting down horseflies. But besides her unfortunate looks and consistently smelling like soup, she is the nicest lady in the world, and she's one hell of a cook. She comes once a week to tidy up the house, make meals, and "babysit" me, if need be.

"Hello, love," Mrs. Martin says, entering the living room with a hearty plate of breakfast. "Your mom got called in a few hours ago."

"I didn't know she was on call this weekend." I eagerly take the plate from her and bite into a crisp piece of maple bacon. "For how long?"

"I think she said it's only a half-shift, so that's six hours? She said she would be back in the afternoon sometime."

"Dang. That's too bad." I'm not too disappointed, considering I get to postpone talking about yesterday's mishap.

"You need to take your medication now. It's past your usual time," Mrs. Martin says, setting a glass of water and my pill on top of the coffee table.

"I can take it on my own."

"Your mother asked that I watch you take it today."

"But we haven't done that in over a year. Is this going to be a regular thing?"

"She didn't say."

Mrs. Martin takes the plate from me so I can hold the glass. She doesn't know how late I took my medication yesterday. I still feel its effects. But I can't let her know, so I comply and swallow. Then I return to eating more bacon while she continues to meal prep.

Larry fades into the wall, his presence becoming more like a shadow. I should have just let the pill slide under my tongue and then spit it out, but Mrs. Martin knows to watch out for that. I sigh and think about how bleak the day will be with no one to talk to.

I place my empty plate in the sink and linger by the window. When I think about yesterday, it plays back like a dream. Like it never really happened. Because things like that just don't happen to people like me.

And for someone who hallucinates, I have a lot of trouble believing someone like Arnold actually exists.

After a long bath and an even longer time trying to do my makeup, which I eventually give up on, not having Larry's help, I'm left with clumpy mascara and smeared eyeliner. Maybe if I wear all black today, it'll look appropriate. Then again, who am I trying to impress other than Mrs. Martin, who wears frumpy turtlenecks even in the summer?

It's seventy-five degrees outside, and if I had two working hands, I'd be back in my garden, tackling that stupid bush again. I was supposed to spend the day with Mom, and now I have to cope with Mrs. Martin who keeps trying to feed me. Can't she see I'm already in enough turmoil with my body? I don't need six breakfasts to get through the day.

After three blueberry muffins, the guilt of overeating sinks in, so I go outside to shoot hoops. Mom is constantly pressuring me to play again, even if it's just on the driveway, but it's not easy with one hand. I can dribble and shoot but passing would be difficult. Passing has *always* been difficult. After a few shots, I stand in place and debate going over to thank Arnold. That would be the right thing to do. But I'm not sure if I have it in me to be social again. And what if his parents answer the door?

I bounce the ball high and yawn as I catch it with one hand in the air. This is why I detest my medicine. It's like being on a sugar low all day. I try to do something, like exercise, but fail to commit. It's depressing.

I sometimes read about other people's experiences with schizophrenia online. The most common forum is always about medication. What are you taking, and is it helping you or making your life unbearable? And it depends on your symptoms and, if you hallucinate, what you hear or perceive. If my intangibles were clowns and monsters, I'd probably ask for Clozapine, which is the most effective antipsychotic but risky on your immune system, so it's the last resort for kids. I responded best to Seroquel, having to take three pills a day, and now down to one pill a day for "maintenance."

But rarely do I read about people actually being cured by their pills.

With my last bit of energy, I go to the end of the driveway and attempt to do a one-handed three-pointer. I miss and the ball rolls into the neighbor's yard, right under the front porch. This would be an excellent time to go back inside and never play basketball again, but then Arnold comes outside as if summoned to ruin my plan.

He's shirtless. *Perfect.*

"Hey, Rachel!"

I try to say hello but waving works just as well.

"How's your hand?" he asks.

"It's fine. How are you?"

"I'm good." He twists side to side, cracking his back. "I was just about to go for a run. Do you want to come?"

"Thanks, but I can't right now. My ball rolled under your porch." *That's my excuse?*

He crouches, like he's modeling for the Olympics, and peers under the white porch. "I don't see it. It may have rolled to the other side of the yard." He walks around and finds it. "You can come over. My house won't bite."

"I'm good. I should go back inside."

"Okay." He rolls the ball toward me. "I guess I'll see you later." He jogs to the sidewalk and sprints away.

Now that was stupid and rude of me. He was just trying to be nice, and I shut him down like a tangiwhore. I suppose it's easier to let him slip away and pretend like yesterday never happened. Then I look at my hand and think of the scar I might have. A constant reminder that yesterday did happen, and I'm childish for believing otherwise.

I'd speak more clearly if I wasn't on my stupid pill. How long has it been since I took it? Forty-five minutes perhaps? There's still a tiny chance I could get some of it out. My metabolism isn't what you would call fast these days.

After I check in with Mrs. Martin, I start my run. I'm not trying to catch up with Arnold. I'm running so I can go throw up. If it means throwing up that delicious breakfast, so be it. I need to wake up and make sense of my life. I need to feel something.

I run to the lake, which is only a quarter-mile away, and hide behind a bush. I fall to my knees, ready to use my finger, when someone creeps up from behind.

"What are you doing?"

It's Arnold again. I shouldn't be surprised at this point.

"I thought you didn't want to run?" he asks.

"I was just trying to get away." I look at the ground, at the saliva on my finger. "I was trying to throw up."

"Here? That's strange. What's wrong with your toilet?"

I can't do this. Not with him, all sweaty and gorgeous, and me all sweaty and gross. I stand from my silly puking position and start to walk away.

"Hey, wait." He literally leaps in front of me. I almost collide into his chest, jolting back at the very last second. "I didn't mean to hurt your feelings. I didn't mean strange in a bad way. I just…" He exhales noisily. "I'm just trying to get to know you. And you seem turned off by the idea."

"It's not a good idea."

"Why not? Did I do something wrong?"

"No, you didn't. It's not you. It's me." I rub my forehead, despising my excuse. "I'm sorry. It's my medication. It makes me tired and say asshole things sometimes."

"Yeah, I remember that from yesterday. You said it was for anxiety or something?"

"Sort of. It's complicated."

"That's okay. Complicated isn't always such a bad thing."

"It is when you skip. But I have to." I shake my head and turn away from him. "I'm sorry. I shouldn't have said that. You wouldn't understand."

"No, I do understand." He steps in front of me, his hands hovering over my shoulders even though I have no intention of stumbling again. "The side effects suck. Drowsiness. Numbness. Overall feeling of I don't care?"

"That and more. But yes, you're on the right track."

He relaxes his arms and steps back. "So that's why you were trying to throw up? To get it out of your system?"

"Yes. And I'm sorry if that made you uncomfortable. And I'm sorry I'm not as thankful as I should be for everything you did yesterday. No one's ever done something like that for me. No one even really talks to me like you did. No one tangible, that is."

"Tangible?" His eyebrows furrow. "What's that supposed to mean?"

I rub the back of my neck. "I'm sorry. I said too much."

"It's okay. You don't have to apologize so much. We all got issues. I have to take pills five days a week for ADHD. On the weekends, I get a break. That's the deal I made with my parents."

"You have ADHD?"

"Yeah. What do you have if you don't mind me asking?"

"I'd rather not say."

"Why not?"

"Because I don't think you'll want to talk to me anymore if I say."

"You think so?" He raises his eyebrows and folds both arms across his immaculate chest. "You should give me a chance. I'm open-minded."

"Minded. Yeah, no, I think I'll wait. Or rather, you'll find out soon enough."

"How am I going to find out if you don't tell me?"

"You go to my school now. You'll know. Everyone knows."

"Sounds like you should just tell me yourself."

"What I have is very…" I bite my lip. "It's extremely rare for young people to have what I have."

"Which is…telekinesis?"

"No!" I can't help but laugh. "No, definitely not."

"Then tell me."

"How about you tell me the end of your camping trip story? You never finished it. Are the scars on your neck from the wolf?"

"Yes. Mama Wolf scratched me. Almost killed me." He leans forward, so we're almost touching; I can feel the heat radiating off his skin. "Are you untrusting because of your dad abandoning you?"

I step back, the heat overwhelming. "How do you know he abandoned me?"

"It's just something I read into. After what little you told me about him, I could only assume he never came back."

"What else did you read into or assume?"

"That you hate him and you never want to see him again."

"I don't hate him."

"I see. Fair enough." He uncrosses his arms. "Well, I don't feel like running anymore. Do you like walking?"

"Yeah."

"Then walk with me. Talk to me. What about this? You let me get to know you as much as possible this weekend. And Monday, I promise you, no matter what I find out, it won't change anything between us. We'll still be friends, okay?"

"Friends?"

"Or whatever. Something else. I don't know. Just let me have the weekend. Okay?"

"The whole weekend?"

"Or whatever you can spare."

Suddenly, having that pill in my system isn't such a big deal. I have someone to talk to that actually wants to talk to me, and furthermore, he's real, attractive, and seemingly straight. Plus, he's getting me to walk and talk, two things I rarely do at the same time. I feel a little more energized already.

"So, do you play on a team?" he asks. "For basketball?"

"I used to. In middle school."

"What position did you play?"

"Point guard. I could shoot three-pointers. I just had trouble with passing. What about you?"

"I used to play soccer." He kicks the imaginary ball to me, but it rolls by. "But now I'm more into solo sports like weightlifting and running. We're building a gym in the basement right now, so I'll always have a place to let loose some energy. You should check it out. Girls should lift too."

"Yeah, maybe." Sounds extreme. "Why did you and your family move here? Did your parents get a better job or something?"

"An opportunity came up that they didn't have to take, but I needed a fresh start somewhere else, so they took it."

"Why did you need a fresh start?"

"I had some trouble at my old school, and it just wasn't working out for me anymore, living there."

"What kind of trouble?"

"I don't think I should tell you yet." He smirks, as though he does want to tell me. "I'll tell you on Monday, okay?"

"Alright. Well, this is going to be hard to get to know one another if we have so many secrets."

"Let's come up with something fun to do instead. We could go to a skate park. Do you like to skate?"

"There aren't any skate parks around here."

"Really? That sucks. They're everywhere in Santa Cruz. What do people do around here? Play with their cats all day?"

"No." I laugh. "We have…well, there's a music café. People hang there, listen to music, and drink coffee and tea."

"Nice, let's go there."

"Uh, well, if you're into music, I…" I do not want to go somewhere so public with him. "I have an old record player in my room."

"Really?"

"Yeah, I have tons of albums too."

"Great! Let's go listen to them."

"In my room?"

"Yeah, if that's cool with your mom?"

"She's not home right now. But Mrs. Martin, our, uh, housekeeper, is. And she might…"

"So you're going to have to sneak me in?"

"I guess so."

"Great! Let's go!"

His energy is ridiculous, but it's Saturday, he's free of his medication, and he seems open to any idea I throw at him. I should've thought twice though before suggesting my bedroom, but it was either that or public humiliation. Tangiwhores and jocks hang out at the music café. Not the right crowd for people like us.

People like *us*?

four

I ENTER through the front door while Arnold sneaks through the back. He knows the first-floor layout, and I've already told him how to get to my bedroom. It's just a matter of distracting Mrs. Martin long enough.

She's in the laundry room, adjacent to the kitchen, folding some clothes. The washer is on, making a wonderfully loud noise, but I don't want her to leave the room until I know Arnold is upstairs.

"Do you need any help?" I ask.

"Goodness gracious, you scared me!" Mrs. Martin exclaims, nearly hitting me with a towel.

"Sorry. I just wanted to help carry the laundry up for you."

"You shouldn't be doing anything strenuous until your hand heals."

"Yeah, but it's a lot of stairs."

Mrs. Martin huffs and waves a sock at me. "I'm not that old! My children are still in college, and I still don't qualify for senior citizen discounts yet, thank you very much."

"I just wanted to help."

"That's generous of you. But I'll leave these baskets here for your mother to carry up later since those stairs are so *hard,* and I've got a few more meals to prepare before I leave."

I'm sure Arnold has found his way to my room by now, so I leave Mrs. Martin to finish the laundry and skip up the stairs. I pause when

I reach the top, overwhelmed by the thought of a boy being in my bedroom. A real boy. Larry is almost always around, in some form or another, but he won't make an effort to distract me if there's a tangible present.

When I open my bedroom door, Arnold is standing next to the bay window, holding the beaded curtains off to one side. My room has two windows: the big bay window faces Arnold's house, and the little square one faces the backyard.

I close the door behind me. "We have to whisper. Just in case."

"No problem." He points out the bay window. "My room is across from yours."

I tiptoe across the manila carpet, wishing I didn't have piles of books and junk everywhere, and stand next to him. This strange, tingly feeling creeps down my throat, nearly choking me.

"My room is through the window with the black curtains," he says.

I swallow hard to clear my throat. "Do you always keep them shut?"

"Most of the time. But I'll have to keep them open from now on." He lets go of my beaded curtains. The rattly noise nearly jolts me off my feet. "So we can talk with two cans and a string."

"Like our grandparents did?"

"Or we could just text each other." He smiles and runs his hands across the beads.

I smile and nod, but then I notice Larry sitting across the room with his latte. He looks extremely uncomfortable and keeps reapplying his ChapStick, a somewhat nervous tick of his. I raise my eyebrows at him, hoping he'll just leave the room. But he keeps making movements, very distracting ones, like fiddling with his shirt collar. He's not supposed to act like this when I have a tangible around. He knows the rules. And I'm on my pill. So what the hell is this?

Obviously, I'm staring in Larry's direction, but thankfully, my record player is right next to him. I cross over, as if that's what I was planning to do, and open it. The record inside is *Let It Be*, The Beatles' last major album before they broke up. Probably my favorite, but full of sad, depressing songs, so I change it out for something more upbeat.

"Hey, I like that album," Arnold says, looking over my shoulder.

"You do? Most people say it's their worst album."

"Most people are idiots."

My lips curve to one side. "What song do you want to hear?"

"'The Long and Winding Road' is pretty good."

"That's my favorite."

"Then what are you waiting for? Play it so we can get this party started." Arnold shakes his hips like we're about to jam out, but he switches to a more avant-garde style when the song plays. He swims his arms through the air and tries bending backward, only to find he has little mobility in that direction. So he bends forward and tries to pull me in to dance with him, but I keep my distance while enjoying his routine all the same.

Larry yawns, seemingly unimpressed with the performance, and finally fades away. Arnold's dance comes to an end, and he takes a big Broadway bow.

"Sorry," he says. "I didn't mean to ruin the song."

"You didn't."

"Let's play it again."

I turn the needle back, and this time we stand in silence to listen to the first few lines. Arnold's stillness eventually breaks, and he looks around for somewhere to sit instead, but every option is a mess. So I quickly make my bed and toss my books to one side.

"You read a lot." He gestures to the piles all around the room. I have a bookshelf, but I like re-categorizing with Larry. "Oooo, *Lord of the Rings*. *The Secret Garden*. And…*Calculus*?" Arnold picks up one of the textbooks. "That's pretty advanced. What grade are you in?"

"I'm a junior."

"Same. Is this AP level?" He sets the book on top of my nightstand.

"Yeah. I have exams next week."

"Wow. AP classes too? You must be pretty smart."

"I guess so. My mom pushes the harder classes, not me. The better I do, the less likely I'm…" To have to take classes with the emotionally disturbed students again.

"Your mom expects a lot from you?"

"Yes and no. She wants me to do well in school, no matter my setbacks. Academically, I do. I even have enough credits to graduate early, but she won't let me."

"When do you turn eighteen?"

"December. I wish it was sooner."

"I'll be eighteen in January."

"We're both winter babies."

He sits down on the edge of the bed and rubs the back of his neck, now damp from dancing. "I'm sorry if I smell at all. I sweat a lot."

"Oh, no. You smell great. I mean...you just...you don't smell bad."

Smiling, he loosens the tie holding his hair back and lets down his hair. He shakes it and then braids it, something I've never seen a guy do. The braid is uneven, and I could fix it for him, but then I'd be touching him. And while the idea intrigues me, the song playing is sad and depressing, and I can't help but feel a bit more sad and depressed when it finally ends. It makes part of me want to run away because all of me knows this moment is temporary. He's never going to be in my room after Monday. He'll never come near me.

I stop the needle before the next song plays. "Do you want to listen to something else?"

He shakes his head. "Come sit next to me."

With a single nod, I tiptoe across the room and sit two feet away from him. The bed creaks, and while we both laugh, I'm concerned it might make too much noise for Mrs. Martin not to hear.

"Is this the first time you've had a guy in your room?" Arnold asks.

"No," I say. Larry counts as a guy, so technically, I'm not lying.

"Then is it safe to do this?" He edges his hand toward mine ever so slowly until I feel his fingerprints brush against my skin. My whole body tenses.

"I've never had a guy in my room before." Larry *doesn't* count.

Arnold starts to pull his hand away, but then I do something unexpected. I unfurl my fingers and allow his to slip around mine. Arnold smiles and rubs his thumb against my wrist, right over my heartbeat.

We stay like that for the next half-hour, just holding hands, making small talk. I could spend all day with him, and if I had that chance, I would. I would try to spend as much time with him as possible.

Even more, I wish I could take Arnold into my imaginary world to keep him a secret from the real world. Because the real world would never accept us. Or maybe they would. Maybe it's just me, deep down, who cannot grasp that a moment like this is possible. And could happen again. It doesn't have to be temporary.

After Mrs. Martin leaves, I take Arnold outside to show him my garden. I explain where I will plant certain vegetables and why they have to be in a specific order. Potatoes and tomatoes hate being next-door neighbors, so best keep them apart. Plant marigolds around the perimeter to repel insects. Always lock the gate to keep the groundhog away. And so forth.

"So, is this going to be your profession?" Arnold asks.

"What? A professional gardener?"

"You could study horticulture in college. I know they have lots of programs in California for that, but I'm sure there's some at UMD or wherever you decide to go."

"I'll probably just go to the community college."

"Why? You don't want to live on campus somewhere?"

"It's better to stay home, at least for the first year. In case something happened, I'd be near my mom."

"In case what?"

"You'll know on Monday."

"I'm really looking forward to Monday."

Mom's SUV pulls into the driveway, and instantly I want to throw Arnold behind that hideous red bush, so she won't see us together. Because her seeing me in open conversation with an actual human being would drive her to new levels of zeal that no one needs to witness.

"Rachel?" she calls out. "Rachel, who's that with you?"

"Crap." Too late to hide.

"Is this my cue to go?" Arnold laughs.

Mom is still in her scrubs. Her hair looks unwashed, and I'm pretty sure she hasn't slept more than a few hours in the last two days. But her eyes light up like the Fourth of July when Arnold steps forward to introduce himself.

"Hi, Dr. Andrews. I'm Arnold Begay, your new neighbor. It's nice to meet you."

She doesn't seem at all bothered by his shirtless appearance. She smiles and shakes his hand when he presents it to her.

"A pleasure," Mom says. "I met your parents, Joslyn and Crew. You're all from California. Must be lovely."

"Yeah, it's pretty sweet."

"The weather here is all over the place. In Maryland, we're supposed to have four seasons, but in reality, we have around ten."

"Really?"

"Yes." Mom continues to smile. "Anyway, I'm sorry to interrupt, but I haven't had a real chance to talk to my daughter since yesterday morning, and a lot has happened since then."

"I was with Rachel yesterday afternoon when she hurt herself."

"Oh!" Mom gasps and presses a hand against her chest. "Then you're the one that helped her get to the hospital?"

"Yes."

"Thank you so much for doing that. Rachel sometimes needs a lot of—"

"Mom, didn't you say you needed to talk to me alone?" Seriously, stop talking to him before you ruin everything.

"Yes. Let's go inside. Thank you again, Arnold. It was wonderful to meet you. We should have you and your parents over for dinner sometime. We haven't had anyone over for dinner in years. We've just been so busy!"

Liar. We haven't had anyone over for dinner in years because the last time we did, I almost killed the guy.

"Well, you must have been outside with that young man for hours from how sunburned you are," Mom says as she digs through the refrigerator for breakfast leftovers.

"Yeah, I know. I should've worn sunscreen."

"He probably doesn't have to worry about getting sunburn." She shoves a cold piece of pancake into her mouth before using the microwave. "So, Dr. Lewis said that you cut yourself trying to trim that bush. For heaven's sake, if you hate that bush so much, I'll just pay someone to have it professionally removed. I don't want you getting stitches every time you garden."

"It was an accident."

"It probably didn't help that you nearly overdosed on Seroquel either."

"I didn't nearly overdose. I went from 400 to 800 milligrams. That's not even close to being dangerous. They had me on 1000 milligrams a day when I was at the hospital."

"That was different. Doctors and nurses were monitoring you. At home, anything could happen. That extra 400 milligrams made you extremely drowsy. Could you imagine if you were behind the wheel of a car?"

"Don't know, Mom. I've never been behind the wheel of a car."

Mom smirks as she opens a can of diet soda. "Well, it's a good thing Arnold was there to help you. Though I wish you had stayed at the hospital so I could have seen you. You have no idea how worried I was when I found out. I wanted to come home right away, but you know how it is at work. It's one emergency right after the other."

"It's fine. It'll heal in a couple of weeks."

"Yes, but I don't want people at school making comments."

"The bandage can come off before Monday, so no one will even notice. By the way, why did you ask Mrs. Martin to watch me take my medicine this morning? Please tell me we're not going back to *that*."

"It was just for today. Since you were so tired yesterday, I didn't want you to forget."

"I never forget." To take it or flush it.

"And what about Arnold? What does he think?"

"What does he think of what?"

The microwave beeps. The plate is hot, but she grabs it anyway and tosses it onto the counter. "What does he think of you and your condition?"

"He doesn't know."

"You didn't tell him?"

"Mom, I don't talk to anyone. The first person that shows any interest in me, do you really think I'm going to be like, oh, by the way, I take antipsychotics for schizophrenia?"

"Mental disorders are not taboo subjects anymore." She dives into her late breakfast, covering her mouth while she chews.

"He's going to find out on Monday, just by word of mouth, so I doubt he'll talk to me after that."

"Maybe you should tell him now."

"I'm not going to. I hope you didn't tell his parents about me."

"No, I didn't. We only talked for a few minutes. Just enough to get the basic, hello, what do you do for a living, where are you from, sort of business."

"Good."

"Why? Were you planning on seeing him again this weekend?"

"I didn't make any official plans with him, but I might see him, considering we live next door to one another."

"Well, I was hoping we could spend some time together this weekend, but I need to catch up on sleep. However, it is important for you to see him again."

"For real? You're not worried?"

"Rachel, he's a real person. Seeing you talk to real people and only real people means the world to me."

"Even if it's only for the weekend?"

"At least you'll know it's possible to connect with the living."

"I know it's possible. But it's not always safe. Real people can hurt me. My other friends can't."

"Except for Mary."

"I haven't seen Mary since the night she went crazy. Not even a glimpse. I don't even remember what she looks like."

"Well, if you do ever start seeing her again, even a glimpse, you have to tell me immediately. You know what Mary is capable of doing."

"Yeah, I know."

We all know.

After lunch, Mom retires to her bedroom while I attempt to study for my AP Calculus exam. I already know more than enough to pass, but Mom expects (or hopes for, as she says) a high score, not mediocre. It baffles me how I have no major trouble learning Calculus, but it's like bending steel to have a normal conversation with someone my age. On or off the pill, I always sound so stupid when I talk out loud.

Almost like there's another Rachel taking hold of the mic, and she won't let the real Rachel speak up. Yet Arnold doesn't seem confused or put off by it. Maybe his ADHD keeps him from catching my glitches.

I study in the living room until late afternoon. That's until I'm bothered by a bouncing sound coming from outside. Sure enough, it's Arnold, winning my attention yet again. He has my basketball, and he's shooting hoops in our driveway. This time he has a shirt on.

"Hey, Rachel," he calls when I step outside. "Hope you don't mind me borrowing your ball for a bit."

"No, I don't mind. I was just studying. My mom's asleep. We're supposed to watch a movie later, but I have a feeling she's going to sleep all day and night."

"So that means you get to hang out with me again?"

"I should study more. But tomorrow?"

"Tomorrow works. What's your number?"

I hardly ever use my phone to call or text people. It's mainly just for YouTube and random Internet searches. It seems odd giving my number away. I have less than ten contacts in my phone, and three of them are for takeout orders.

I return to the living room while Arnold continues to shoot hoops. Not even a minute after sitting down, my phone vibrates against the coffee table. It's my first text message from Arnold. From anyone under the age of eighteen.

A: **How's the studying?**
R: **Boring. How's basketball?**
A: **Hard to do alone.**
R: **I'm one handed right now so can't help much.**
A: **You can still shoot.**
R: **Kind of.**
A: **Your mom seems nice.**
R: **She likes you.**
A: **Yay!**
R: **She thinks you're ice.**
A: **What?**
R: **Sorry meant to type nice.**
A: **That's better!**

R: :)
A: **We should start running together.**
R: **I'd slow you down.**
A: **No you won't.**
R: **I gotta lose a few pounds first.**
A: **Don't lose anything.**
R: **Lol yeah right.**
A: **You're perfect just the way you are.**

I look up from my textbook and phone. Larry is sitting in the armchair across from me, shaking his head. I run to the kitchen to open my Seroquel pack. I study the pills carefully, check the expiration date, and so forth. Larry's random appearances have been bewildering. I think I may just be experiencing a mental hiccup, with all the ups and downs with dosages this week.

I return to the couch and attempt to study again, but Larry's smirk is too diverting. Communication with the intangibles is near impossible when I'm on Seroquel, but something has changed in me, something I can't fully comprehend. It happened in the bedroom with Arnold. A feeling of letting go. Of trusting.

The pole inside my head tilts to one side, allowing Larry to speak.

"Rae-Rae."

"Larry?"

"*Rae.*" He nods his head toward the front of the house.

"What?"

"I don't want you to get hurt."

"I'm not."

"He's different, I know. You're intrigued. But you don't know who he is. And he doesn't know you like I know you."

"Okay, then." I toss my book onto the coffee table, making a loud noise. "If you know me so well, then tell me, what's the better choice? To continue talking to people that don't exist, or talk to someone real? What's the bigger risk? If I get caught talking to you, Mom will up my dosages again, and then you'll disappear completely."

"Rae." He kneels in front of me and places his cinnamon-colored hands on top of mine. I see his hands, those perfectly trimmed nails and cuticles. I see the rise and fall of his chest and the crinkles under his eyes when he smiles at me. But I don't feel his flesh; I don't smell anything beyond his bubblegum ChapStick, and even then, it feels more like a memory of the smell.

"What, Larry?"

"You need me. And you need Breezy. You know what happens when you're consistent with your medication. You get overly tired. Numb. You stop doing your makeup. You stop caring. When you let go and let us in, we make you smile." He runs his fingers through my hair, but I don't feel anything. "We make you happy."

"Are you worried I'm going to numb you all out to be with Arnold? Because that's not what I'm going to do. I'm still going to live in the gray, just as I've always been doing. Because I can't survive on either side completely. And it doesn't even matter because Arnold won't want to be a part of any side when he finds out I'm crazy."

"I think he may want in no matter what."

"Why would you think that?"

"You're perfect just the way you are?" He rolls his eyes at my phone, nestled between my thighs.

"It's just a text message. If he says it in person, then I might believe him."

"You didn't respond." Larry sits on the couch next to me. He leans his chin over my shoulder. "What's he saying now?"

A: **Sorry if that was the wrong thing to say. Talk to you tomorrow?**

"See?" I say. "He's not even convinced it was the right thing to text."

"Don't text him back."

"I should at least say goodbye."

"Don't do it. Always make him be the last one to text. It gives you more power."

"Since when have you cared about power?"

"Since you started talking to him."

"You're the one who suggested it from the start."

"I was hoping for friendship. Not courtship."

"Courtship?" I laugh. "Larry, what the hell have you been reading?"

"Everything you read. You know what I mean though."

43

"Okay." I re-read Arnold's last text about six times. "So he may like me, a little. Why do I have to care about power?"

"You should always care about power. You don't have any in the real world. You got your mom and teachers and doctors telling you what to do all the time. You don't want this boy taking any part in that."

"Larry, stop."

"You wanted to talk. You pushed through for me."

"I know. But you need to shut up now."

"*Rachel.*"

Larry never calls me by my real name. And that's because my dad never called me by my real name. He always called me Rae-Rae or just Rae. Until the morning he left. During breakfast, he said, "Rachel, pass the syrup," and that's when I knew something was wrong. Throughout the meal, I kept thinking I had done something terrible. Or my mother had because she wasn't speaking. Even the dog was acting weird.

"Rae." Larry corrects himself, but the damage has been done.

"Please stop talking." I rub my palms against my forehead. "Please. I just need you to lay low for a few more days. Then we can have fun again."

"You'll have fun with Arnold. And you'll like him more."

"Don't be jealous. Please?"

"You're my family. You're all I have."

Larry fades into the couch, leaving nothing behind, not even his bubblegum scent. We never argue, but then again, we never speak to each other when I'm on my pill. Today I pushed through to reach Larry. How? I really don't know. Some people believe schizophrenics operate at a higher level of intelligence because they can tap into deeper parts of their brains. If everyone could do that, would Larry be real?

If everyone were like me, I'd have no reason to hide.

But ever since Arnold stepped into my world, I can't hide.

five

I **FALL** asleep on the couch again. It's more comfortable than my bed, which is in dire need of replacement. We're not rich, and we're not poor, but Mom is overly cautious about what she spends her money on. Except for this humongous couch, for some bizarre reason. She sat on this couch one day while we were out shopping, and the following week it was in our living room. The old couch my dad used to sleep on when she would kick him out of their bedroom was gone. Maybe there was a real reason after all. She just wanted something better.

I wake up around 7:30, shower, and dress, while Mom attempts to make breakfast. She burns the bacon, so we go out to our favorite diner, Willie's Waffles. We both go for the classic two eggs, two slices of meat, and two pieces of toast meal. I drink orange juice and water; Mom puts down three cups of vanilla coffee.

Food tastes better when I'm off my medication. I didn't plan on skipping today, not when I'm going to be hanging with Mom, who is always suspicious of my behavior. The pill fell into the sink when I opened the pack. And something inside me said *let it go*. So I did.

At the table, I peel off the crust to my toast and set it aside for Mom, who can eat gluten to her heart's content without gaining a pound. I think about Arnold, shirtless in the sun, and how I would look shirtless next to him. A hard piece of chocolate alongside a flabby egg white. Man, oh man, why did he have to be so gorgeous? And why did I have to think about him at freaking breakfast? Why couldn't I just *let him go*?

"Something wrong?" Mom asks.

"No. Why?" I quickly take a bite of toast.

"You look upset. What were you thinking about?"

I shrug my shoulders. "The ending of *Grapes of Wrath*."

"Oh. Hmm." Mom raises her eyebrows and taps her fingernails against her coffee mug. I should have come up with a better lie. "Are you sure?"

"I'm fine." I chew into the other piece of toast without delay. "Really."

"Does your hand still hurt?"

"Barely."

"Are you disappointed you can't work in your garden this weekend?"

"No. I can work on it next weekend. I need to focus on my exams anyway."

"That's probably hard to do when you have Mister Dreamboat next door."

I practically choke on my next bite of bread. "Mom!" When I reach for my glass of water, I knock over the saltshaker. Now it's obvious something is wrong.

"What did I say?" she asks, moving the saltshaker to her side of the table.

I lean back into my chair and fold my arms across my chest. Forget trying to eat now that Arnold has wiggled his way into the conversation. "You talk like he's going to become my boyfriend. You do realize that's impossible. Me ever having a boyfriend."

"It's not impossible. Just because you have a mental condition does not mean you're handicapped from having a normal life. Besides, most of your symptoms have been treated or gone away on their own."

"If normal is being medicated for the rest of my life, then yeah, okay, I guess I'm normal."

"The Seroquel is key to keeping you on the right track. You haven't had any episodes. You haven't talked to any of them, have you?"

"No." I grab a piece of crisp bacon and bite the tip off.

"But you still see them? Larry and Breezy?"

"Yeah." I bite again, determined to finish this meal. "But they're like shadows. They don't do much."

"I still think if we upped your dose for a short while, it would get rid of them completely. We could try 600 milligrams again. You were on 600 when you were a freshman."

"Is that when I took two pills a day?"

"Yes, you took the two 300mg pills. One in the morning and one before bed."

I pinch my lips together and nod my head three times while I pretend to consider her proposal. "That's a lot of remembering."

"I would help with that." Her eyes light up like a Christmas tree. Crap, she's being serious. "But first, we'd have to talk to Melinda and get her approval."

"No, Mom."

"It would only be for a short while. Maybe we could do it over summer break so it wouldn't interfere too much with school. I know how tired you get. And you've been doing so well this year. I wouldn't want to ruin any chances of you—"

"Not getting into the community college with a 3.70 GPA?"

Mom sighs. "Please consider it? You know I value your input."

I trace my finger around my glass and imagine myself as a tiny ant falling into the orange juice. Would I swim, or would the sourness consume me? Would I morph into a more powerful ant or simply die?

"No," I finally say, shaking the thought away. "I'm okay living this way. Always a tad here, and not here." I give the glass a little squeeze, wondering how strong I'd have to be to break it. "I just wish you would be okay with that."

The light fades from her eyes. "As long as you're taking your pill and doing well in school, I guess that's all I can ever hope for. Though it would be nice to have…" She shakes her head and reaches for her coffee mug.

"To have what?"

"Never mind." She takes a sip of her coffee, then another.

"To have what?" I ask louder.

She sets her mug down. Her whole face squints together as though she's already apologizing. "Grandchildren one day."

"Oh geez." I roll my eyes. Not this again. "I'll adopt if it makes you happy."

"No, forget it. It was selfish and inconsiderate of me to say something like that. Especially when you're so young."

I think about that ant again and finish my orange juice in one gulp.

After breakfast, we go to the mall. I need a new bathing suit, and I'm only into one-pieces. Mom, having a flat stomach the majority of her life, is only into bikinis. So we shop on opposite ends of the store.

I choose two to try on, one black and one red. I'm a pretty fast shopper, unlike Mom, who will search hours for one specific item.

As I'm slipping into the formfitting nightmare, I stop midway to look at my protruding waistline. I was never like this before eighth grade. I was always lean. Nothing jiggled. Nothing got in the way. The doctors warned me of Seroquel's side effects, weight gain being one of them. And sure enough, between eighth and eleventh grade, I gained thirty pounds despite not growing an inch taller.

Mom blames puberty. I blame the pill. I *always* blame the pill.

I snap the straps over my shoulders. It's a bright red bathing suit, not an ideal color for someone so pale. I turn sideways to survey the back. When I look up at the mirror, I am joggled by an awful sight. One of my intangibles is standing right next to me. Someone I haven't seen in years.

Mary.

I don't know what part of my mind birthed Mary. She's like a ghost from a horror movie. She appears as a little, pale girl with tangled dark hair and long fingernails. About eight or nine years old. She wears a simple gray dress, torn stockings, and black clumpy shoes. She always makes the room feel cold, even if it's a hundred degrees. In eighth grade, before the hospitalization, she was the most vocal and dominating of the intangibles. But the Seroquel wiped her out. Or at least I thought it did.

She lifts one finger to her mouth, warning me to be quiet. Then in slow motion, she reaches an arm toward my face like she wants to pet me. I tense every bone in my body.

Instead, she slaps me.

"Rachel? How's everything fit?" Mom calls from outside the door.

"Uh, I'm fine." Ouch, I'm not fine. "I don't like the way this one fits, so I'm going to try on the other one."

"Can I see? It probably fits you fine." She tries to open the door, but it's locked, of course. "Rachel? Open up."

Mary is gone, but the hand mark across my face is legit. If Mom were to see it, she would suspect that I had slapped myself. Why, of all days, did Mary have to show up?

I don't have my medicine with me. I don't have my makeup with me. I have seconds to figure out what to do about the mark on my face. But what if there is no mark? What if I just imagined Mary slapped me?

In a panic, I grab a scarf that just so happened to be left inside the dressing room and wrap it around my head like those old ladies do to keep from getting sunburned. It covers the mark just enough.

"Rachel?"

I open the door. "It's way too tight in my butt."

"It's adorable! It fits perfectly. I love it. But what's with the scarf? You look like my Aunt Sandy."

I smile politely. "If you think this one is good enough, I'll get it. I don't feel like trying on the other one."

"Are you comfortable in it?"

"I'm never comfortable in a bathing suit, but whatever. I can't swim without one."

———

Thank God the slap mark is on the right side of my face, so Mom doesn't notice it on the drive home. She's too busy talking about an episode of *House Hunters* and what she would like to do with our kitchen should she ever have the time or money. I space out since I don't care about the kitchen so long as it's functional. We have granite countertops and high cabinets, so what if we don't have the double oven and LED lights? How about we buy a new mattress for my room instead?

As soon as we get home, I excuse myself to study in my bedroom. Really, I need to talk to Larry pronto. He is fully prepared to listen to every word that comes out of my mouth, even though I basically told him to get lost the day before.

I shut the door behind me, toss my new bathing suit across the room, and shake the jitters out of my hands.

"Rae?" Larry doesn't even have to ask. He knows something crazy just happened because I'm pacing, and I only pace when I'm hysteric or near hysteric.

I feel like a piñata about to flood the room with candy. I have to play a record to muffle our sounds, or at least my own.

"Rae-Rae, sit down. You're making me nervous. What just happened?"

I sit on the bed with Larry and swallow hard. "She came back."

"Mary?"

I nod my head. "She didn't say anything. Just smacked me across the face. Or maybe she didn't. I don't know. My mom didn't notice any mark. Do you?"

"I don't see a slap mark. But your one cheek looks a little red. Like sunburn maybe? Or too much blush?"

"She did hit me."

"This is not good. Mary's the reason you got locked up."

"And kicked off the basketball team. And everything else. She's evil. Pure evil. And she's back. I don't understand why. Do you think it's because I've skipped my medicine too much the last month? I mean, maybe I shouldn't skip so much. Maybe I should only skip once a week or do what Arnold does and only take it during the school week."

"Okay, calm down." Larry puts his hands on my shoulders, but the tangibility isn't there again. "There's no need to go to the extreme for this. I can protect you from Mary."

"You didn't that one time. None of you did."

"That was a long time ago when things were out of control. Michelle and Donovan were always around, distracting me. I'm all yours now."

"Even still, I only see you when I'm home. I see Breezy when I'm outside, in my own yard. When I leave my house, I'm open to attack. She could get me at school, at therapy, anywhere. And if she attacks me in front of people, they're all going to think I'm relapsing. It'll be a disaster. I don't want to get sent away again. And I don't want to have to take *more* medicine. Mom talked about upping me to 600mg. You and Breezy will disappear completely if I go that high."

"Don't worry about us. Just…" Larry takes a deep breath and taps his thumb against his chin. "Stay home today. And tomorrow, take your medicine. Take your medicine all week since you have to go to school. And then once the weekend comes, go off your medicine and see what happens."

"So do what Arnold does?"

"Yes. I think that's a smart idea. It gives you a little bit of freedom, without the worries."

"But who's going to help me with my makeup in the morning?"

"I can help a little bit before you take your pill."

"You still won't be able to talk. Unless I do what I did before and push through, but that was very stressful. You acted weird when I did that. You were very persistent. Dominant, almost."

"I know. I was. But I was also just looking out for you. I'm always looking out for you." He brushes his fingers across my eyebrows. "And you're pretty. With or without makeup."

"Pretty? Ha. Very funny."

"You are. Arnold wouldn't be trying so hard to see you if he wasn't attracted to you."

"He's not attracted to me. Guys like him do not go after girls like me. I have ugly brown hair and a weird smile and—"

"Beautiful lips, stunning brown eyes, attractive curves. You're smart, you read a lot, you know your music, you grow an amazing garden every year. You're unique. You're not the typical girl around here. And he likes that."

"How do you know?"

"Rae-Rae, I know because deep down, you know."

I walk over to the bay window and run my fingers across the purple beads. Arnold isn't outside, and his black curtains are shut. I wonder what he's doing. Maybe he's working out in his gym. Or maybe he's out exploring.

I see my reflection through the window and note some of the highlights Larry mentioned. Are my eyes stunning? Are my curves attractive or just blobs of fat? And my lips? How are my lips beautiful? The bottom lip is bigger than the top, but I bite it so much, the skin is always chapped or split. Larry's are moist. Because Larry is flawless, and I am not.

Larry shows me his latest drawing. It's a sketch of both me and Arnold, side by side, holding hands. Arnold looks just as he does in real life, and so do I. Larry drew me as I am.

But next to Arnold, I don't nitpick my imperfections. Because I am with Arnold, and that makes everything strangely and imperfectly better.

"Do you miss him already?" Larry asks.

"Maybe."

"You like him."

"I don't know. Kind of. I…I just know I have to see him. At least once more. Should I text?"

"Has it been twenty-four hours?"

"Almost."

Larry smiles. "I know I was pretty blunt with you yesterday about the whole texting thing. But if you want to text Arnold, you should. You should do what feels right."

I nod my head and study the sketch one last time. Larry's never drawn anyone but me. If this isn't a sign I should try once more with Arnold, I don't know what is.

"Alright," I say, trying to focus on my phone instead. "Here goes nothing."

R: **Hey. I'm sorry I never replied.**
A: **Yo! It's cool. What are you up to?**
R: **I was going to study more but I don't want to.**
A: **I'm working out. Should be done soon.**
R: **Cool.**
A: **Do you want to come over and watch a movie?**
R: **Are your parents home?**
A: **They're out shopping for new furniture.**
R: **Gtg ask my mom.**

"You should invite him over here to watch the movie," Larry says. "It's safer here. I can watch over you."

"I feel safe with Arnold."

"He can't protect you from Mary. What if she jumps out in front of you when you're watching the movie? Unless you're watching a horror, your scream would seem a tad out of place."

"Crap."

"Rachel?" Mom knocks on the door, then barges in. "Hey, are you okay?" She sees the phone in my hands. "Were you talking to Arnold?"

"Yeah, he wants to hang out again." I silence my record player, so we don't have to shout. "Is that okay?"

"That's perfect because I have to drive up to see your grandpa."

"What's wrong?"

"He's having trouble with the AC again. He keeps turning the heat on by mistake."

"Oh, dang."

"He needs to be in a nursing home, but the stubborn fool refuses to leave his house."

"No one wants to be locked up."

"He wouldn't be locked up. He would be supervised and taken care of."

"Same thing."

Mom rolls her eyes. "Anyway, do you want to come? Oh, wait. Arnold. Never mind. Just be safe with him. What are you all going to do?"

"Watch a movie."

"Watch a movie? Rachel, you know what that means when a guy wants to watch a movie with you?"

"It means he wants to watch a movie with me?"

"It means..." She sighs. "Look, just do me a favor and have him come here. And watch the movie in the living room. Not in your bedroom. And keep your phone nearby."

"Jesus. Nothing is going to happen. It's not like he's going to take advantage of me."

"I don't know him well enough to make an accurate analysis of his character. But he's shown nothing but kindness and respect to you, so I can't judge him so poorly. Just be safe. And don't eat too many snacks tonight."

R: **My mom is leaving soon. Can you come over here?**
A: **Sure!**

R: **We have Netflix. Tons of movies.**
A: **Nice. I gtg shower. See you in 30?**
R: **Cool.**

Thirty minutes gives me plenty of time to tidy up, brush my hair, and convince myself that I don't need makeup to feel attractive. Larry insists on choosing an outfit for me to wear, but everything he suggests is way too dressy. In the end, I settle on a pair of baggy jeans and a gray T-shirt. If Arnold is really into me like Larry says he is, I don't need to overdo the appearance factor to win his attention. I just have to be myself.

Arnold doesn't seem to feel the need to dress up either. He leaves his hair long. His clothes are simple and clean: blue jeans and a black V-neck shirt. He brings a bag of freshly made popcorn and two cans of Diet Pepsi, which I have to reject since I never drink caffeine, or anything carbonated. The kettle corn, however, I gladly accept.

Finding a movie on Netflix could take ages, but everything is categorized, and Arnold doesn't seem to be in any hurry. I leave him in charge of the remote while I pour myself a glass of water. Larry hides in the laundry room with a stack of books; he's on to reading *The Perks of Being a Wallflower*, another of our favorites. He's promised to stay put unless there's trouble from Mary.

"What are you in the mood for?" Arnold asks from the couch.

"Uh, I don't care. I could watch anything."

"What's your favorite movie ever?"

"Promise you won't laugh?"

"Promise."

"I have a thing for Disney movies, so right now, it's *Moana*."

He laughs anyway. "What's your favorite non-Disney movie?"

"I don't know."

"What's your favorite genre? Besides Disney."

"Dramas, I guess."

"Are you going to sit down?" He turns around and catches me loitering in the kitchen with my water.

"Uh, yes, I'm coming."

Holding my glass like holy water, I sit on the far-right side of the couch and lean into the armrest. Arnold is in the middle with both legs spread, his right foot tapping against the coffee table. Parts of his body relax, while other parts are always active. It seems like most of his energy gets trapped in his lower body. It doesn't make sense that he would quit playing soccer.

"Drama, drama, drama." He searches through the endless list. "These are all so sad and depressing. Are you sure you don't want to watch a comedy instead?"

"I really don't care what we watch. You pick."

"Okay. Let's watch porn."

"Uh…"

"Just kidding!" He guffaws and pauses his search directly on the one movie that could ruin the evening. "Ooo!" he says, standing up to stretch and cheer. "Russell Crowe! My man!"

I take a huge sip of water. I'd rather watch porn than *this* movie.

"I watched this movie last year for psych class," Arnold says. "Have you seen it before?"

"Yes."

He sits down, closer to me this time. "Did you like it?"

"No, not really."

"Why not? You said you liked dramas."

"I just…I felt bad for the wife. It wasn't fair for her."

"Oh, yeah. She had to deal with a lot."

"And they had a kid together too."

"But they fell in love and got married before she found out. It didn't change how she felt toward him. She still stayed married to him."

"Yeah, but she was miserable."

"Hmmm, okay." He clicks on the following list, comedies. "We probably shouldn't watch it if it makes you so upset."

"No, if you really want to watch it, we can." I grit my teeth and hope he chooses something else.

"No, it's cool. I just wanted to hear your opinion of it. I'm surprised you didn't show any empathy toward the husband. I mean, he's the one who has to live with…I can't remember what it's called. What's the disease called when you see imaginary people?"

I swallow hard. "Schizophrenia."

"Yeah, that one. Why wouldn't you feel bad for him?"

"I guess I just…" I pause, trying to formulate my thoughts logically and empathetically, so I don't sound like a heartless bitch.

"When I watch a movie, I always put myself in the main character's spot. So I do feel empathy, but only for the people affected by the main character, not the main character himself. Does that make sense?"

"Yeah, it does, sort of."

"Why sort of?"

"As the main character, you should always make sure you're taken care of first. If you're not happy, how can those you love be happy?"

I bite my lip and nod. "I agree." Somewhat.

He releases a heavy breath and smiles anyway. "So, we should probably just watch *Moana*?"

We settle on an episode of *Doctor Who* instead.

The couch can "comfortably" seat up to six people, but Arnold has a way of making it feel much smaller. When I watch a movie, I typically sprawl out, but with Arnold next to me, smelling like he just walked out of a Mount Olympus shower, I feel more inclined to sit rigid and poised.

But every time Arnold gets up to move or stretch, he takes another opportunity to sit closer to me. Eventually, I retreat for more water and sit on the opposite side of the couch, where there's still plenty of room.

"If you want to play musical chairs, let's at least put some music on," Arnold laughs.

"I don't want to play musical chairs. I just want some space."

"I'm sorry." He scoots onto the floor. "That better?"

"You can still sit on the couch."

"Okay then." He jumps up and sits right next to me, so close that I would have to elbow him to stand up. "That better?"

I try to keep a straight face. "Just keep your hands to yourself, mister."

"Yes, ma'am!"

Now I'm laughing. I turn and seriously almost butt heads with him. He moves his arm away to create a temporary space and then lies it across the back of the couch, right behind my head. His body curves slightly toward mine, his one foot tapping against the floor like a little drum solo. I remain forward and rigid, with both eyes on Dr. Who. I may have zero experience with guys and couches, but Larry and I have talked about body language. Larry says guys will always invade your space if they're really into you. Always sounds a bit much to me.

Arnold isn't touching me, not at all, but I feel tickled all over. For a moment, I imagine what it would be like to kiss him, but I've never kissed anyone before. I asked Larry once if he would kiss me, just so I could have practice, but the idea grossed him out.

"Do you want to watch another episode?" Arnold asks when the credits play.

"Oh, uh…"

His phone buzzes like an alarm clock inside his pants. He stands to check the message. I release an epic breath of air.

"I'm sorry," he says. "It's my parents. They're home, and they want to talk about school. We can watch another episode later, or maybe tomorrow, if you want?"

"Tomorrow is Monday."

"So?"

"You'll know my secret tomorrow."

"You talk like it's the end of the world." He circles the coffee table twice and walks to the window and back. Then he takes a good, hard look at me, with his lips twisted to one side. I don't know what he's thinking or doing, so I look directly at my feet to avoid any chance of finding out.

"Come here," he says.

"What? Why?"

"I want to hug you before I leave. If that's okay?"

The amount of time it takes for me to stand up makes it seem like I'm a hundred years old. The amount of time it takes for me to walk over to Arnold makes it seem like I'm purposely trying to avoid him.

I pause two feet away from him, and with one step, he closes the space between us and wraps his arms around me. My arms stiffen at first but eventually make their way around his torso. His abs are rock solid, and our height difference makes his chest the perfect resting spot for my head.

"I'm glad I met you, Rachel."

I don't know what to say. Making so much physical contact all at once has diluted my ability to speak. It takes me out of the gray, away from the dark and light, and centers me in stillness. It's such a strange place to be, but it feels balanced.

After Arnold leaves, I return to the couch and watch the Russell Crowe movie. About the schizophrenic husband and his poor wife. I imagine myself as the main character, and it's not that hard to do, considering we have so much in common.

When the movie is over, Larry joins me on the couch. "I don't like that movie," he says.

"I don't either."

"Then why did you watch it?"

I rub the bridge of my nose with two fingers. "Sometimes, I need a reminder of what is real and what is not."

"Oh." Larry lowers his head. "I see."

"That hug was real."

"Did you like it?"

"Too much." I stand and look down at Larry. He's diluted in appearance and looking sad and weak. "I wish we could hug like that."

"We do."

"No. We don't. Not ever."

We don't say anything else. Larry eventually gets up and hides away somewhere with his books while I just stare across the room, too immobile to go to bed just yet. After everything that happened today, I am left with an empty, desolate feeling. I have no desire for Monday to ever come. Just give me the weekend again. Give me Arnold. In the words of Paul McCartney, "Lead me to your door."

six

I REFUSE to go to school. Exams aren't until Tuesday. I'm missing review day, but I can review on my own. I don't need to go to school to hear about prom. And I don't want to see Arnold. Because the minute he talks to me, someone will warn him to stay away from me. And then Arnold will want to know why. And then they'll tell him. Everything.

"She's schizophrenic."

"She put a guy in the hospital once. If you value your life, you'll keep your distance."

"She's really smart because she's secretly planning to take over the world with her imaginary friends. Don't let the quiet face fool you."

And then Arnold will never speak to me again.

So if I avoid seeing Arnold at school, I prolong the inevitable. Childish, I know. But I need another day. Just one more day to process everything.

"You spent too much time in the sun this weekend. That's why you have a migraine now," Mom says after taking my temperature. "You still need to go to your therapy appointment later if you're feeling better."

"Yeah, I know. I just need to sleep." I pull the covers over my head. Mom leaves my pack on my nightstand. I take my pill and sleep away the morning. When I wake up in the afternoon, I feel groggy and downright miserable. Arnold will be wondering why I'm not at school, and if he has any sense, he'll figure it out on his own.

I eat a sandwich and stare at the couch, thinking of what might have happened had Arnold stayed last night. I keep imagining him kissing me, and it's a thought I don't want to be having. The uncertainty of it all makes me want to pull my skin off.

My brain on fire, I call Melinda and ask if I can come in early. She gladly sees me at 1:30. Her office is two miles away, but the idea of being on a crowded bus with Mary a possibility, I walk the entire way.

Her full name is Dr. Melinda Elizabeth Brackett, and she's a child psychiatrist specializing in severe mental disorders. She sees the multiple personality kids, the OCD kids, the anorexics, and me, her lone schizo. I've been seeing her for about three years now, and she is the only tangible I trust, more so than my own mother. She knows all about my intangibles: their names, what they wear, how they talk, and where I usually see them. The only thing she doesn't know is how much I've been skipping my pill, for almost a year now, to talk to Larry and Breezy.

"Rachel, welcome," Melinda says, opening the door to her beautiful, blue office. It's like a beach house. The aquamarine walls are decorated with seashells, anchors, fishing rods, and photographs of the deep blue sea. There are plenty of places to recline or sit, from the fluffy green couch to the leather armchair to the wooden stool next to the open window. I choose the couch today to sprawl out. Melinda takes a seat in her rocking chair, where she usually resides unless she's doing hypnosis.

Melinda is almost fifty years old, but she looks like she's thirty. She's the healthiest eater I know, she's never been married or had any children, and she always wears sunscreen when she goes outside. Her strawberry-blonde hair is neatly pinned up. Her cheeks are rosy and freckled, and her attire is always beachy and serene, even in the winter. Today she wears a white blouse and a long teal skirt.

"You missed school today."

"I told my mom I had a migraine." The lie slips out, smooth and easy, like caramel sauce running down an ice-cream sundae.

"Did you?" Her paper-thin eyebrows raise ever so slightly.

"I had a *headache*. But really, I just didn't want to go to school today."

"Why is that?"

Ugh. I might have a migraine if I let the whole truth out, aka Arnold, so I start with the little stuff. "Well, prom was Friday, so that's all everyone's going to be talking about today."

"Does it bother you that you didn't go to prom?"

I sit up and lean forward, noticing that my socks don't match yet again. Navy blue and black, no big deal, but it annoys me, nonetheless. "God, no," I say, imagining myself walking into prom in an ugly Cinderella dress with mismatched shoes. "It would have been worse if I had gone. I would have gone by myself. And everyone would have made fun of me."

"Rachel, when you say *everyone*, do you really mean everyone? From what you've expressed before, it only seems like a few girls tease you these days."

"I know. It just feels like everyone is still talking about me behind my back."

"What do you suppose they're saying about you?"

"That I'm a monster. I shouldn't be allowed to attend public school. I should never be trusted with any object because I might throw it at someone."

"Have you thrown anything at anyone since middle school?"

"No."

"And you've done well in school since?"

"Yeah. Very well. Better than anyone predicted I would. Even myself."

"Do you think the students want to harm you?"

When Melinda says it like that, I think of that scene from *Carrie*, when she's being attacked in the locker room. Not physically harmed, but morbidly embarrassed. In my case, instead of tampons and pads flung at my head, the girls would throw basketballs. Tons and tons of basketballs. I can hear them in my head shouting, "Throw the ball, Rachel! Throw the ball!"

My cheeks boil at the thought, but Melinda waits patiently for my answer, never in a rush, and never out to catch the flaw, like Mom. Only the truth.

"I don't know," I finally say. "Sometimes." I scratch around my ankles, the carpet looking mighty comfortable compared to the debriefing couch. "I just…" When I sit up, the blood rushes to my forehead like a tidal wave. I pinch my lips together and exhale through my nose. Steady now. It's just Melinda. You don't have to hide. "I still don't trust them." Bingo. "That's all I got."

Melinda usually praises me for pushing through a blockage, but instead, she goes right on to the next question. "Have any of the students, other than the few girls you've mentioned before, ever tried to harm you?"

"No."

"Do you think if you had gone to prom that you would have been in any danger?"

Danger? God, no. No one would have dumped animal blood on me. My life is a drama, not a horror.

I shake my head, trying to extract the Steven King stuff; I don't even like his novels. "I wouldn't have had a good time at prom. That's what it comes down to. I would have been alone, dateless, looking like a loser. No one asked me to prom. No one ever will. Because they're all still scared of me."

"Many of them witnessed your breakdown in eighth grade, which upset your teammates."

"Yeah, we lost a lot of games because of my mistakes." And pregame panic attacks.

"But that was before you were diagnosed and medicated. You're a completely different person now. You no longer have any speech problems. You are aware of what is real and what is not. And most importantly, you're open to discussing these things with me. You're open to change."

"Yeah, but no matter how hard I try, I'm never going to be completely normal."

"And how do you feel about that?"

Well, I know how my mother feels. She makes it clear almost daily, even without words. Disappointment. Discontent. Always searching for a rebuttal. A way to turn it all around. But I just want to move forward. Even if it's not in the same direction as everyone else. That's what I *want*. But how do I feel?

"It makes me sad," I say.

"Sad?" Melinda sounds surprised. Well, no wonder. I don't think I've ever uttered the phrase before.

"It makes a part of me sad, knowing that I'll probably never get married or have kids. I'll be alone the rest of my life. And the other part of me feels relieved I won't have to deal with that. I'll just have to take care of myself. And maybe that's a better life after all. I mean, you've been successful all on your own. And happy."

"Yes, I am very much happy with my life. But just because I never got married or had any children doesn't mean I never experienced love."

"Did you ever want to get married, though?"

"Maybe I still do." Melinda smiles to one side. "But this is about you, Rachel. How do you feel about love?"

"Love?" Why does Arnold, holding red roses and dancing shirtless in my front yard, suddenly come to mind? "Uh, it's complicated."

"How so?"

"It's hard to explain. I could give you an example."

"Sure."

I lie back down for this one. "Okay, so the movie, *A Beautiful Mind*. This girl falls in love with her professor. They get married, have a kid. And then his schizophrenia gets out of control, and he has to be so medicated that he doesn't even want to have sex with his wife anymore. She's depressed, hating her life, and yet everyone who watches it admires her for being so brave, continuing to love her husband even though he's out of his mind. I just don't think I could, if I were the husband, be able to love anyone or want anyone to love me. I would want to give up and die at that point. Or just be allowed to go off my meds completely and let the other world consume me like he eventually did by the end."

Melinda blinks several times, which means she needs extra time to process my words. I've never talked about going off Seroquel and living in absolution with the intangibles. I've always been okay and accepting of my gray reality. That's how I survive. How I find balance. But is that how I find happiness and meaning in life?

She leans forward in her rocking chair and smiles sweetly, always reassuring me she's not out to judge. "I'm glad you shared your thoughts with me. However, I do need to make sure you are not considering going off your medication. That is something we would need to discuss first. With your mother as well."

"No, no worries of that."

"Do you ever forget to take your pill?"

Time for a dozen half-lies. "We label the pills, so I don't forget."

"Have you had any unusual interactions with your intangibles? How are Larry and Breezy?"

"If I see Larry, he's usually just drinking a latte or reading a book. Sometimes he sketches. And Breezy is always in the backyard."

"And what does she do?"

"She hangs around the garden, picking flowers or playing with animals. The squirrels and birds aren't afraid of her."

"That's because the squirrels and birds have no awareness of Breezy."

"Oh, yeah." I laugh and roll my eyes.

"Have they spoken to you?"

I hate that question. "Nope."

"Nothing at all?"

"They'll gesture at me, but they never talk."

"What about the others? Michelle and Donovan?"

"Still haven't seen them since middle school."

"And what about Mary?"

I clench my teeth together. Melinda rarely brings up Mary these days. To hell with this session. "What about her?" I ask.

"No sightings?"

I swallow hard. Goose bumps prickle across my arms. It may just be paranoia, but the room feels colder. I picture Mary creeping up behind Melinda's rocking chair, but Melinda sways back just at the right time, crushing the image.

"Rachel, do you see her?"

"No." I shake my head and rub my arms. "But the thought of seeing her again…scares me." And it's already happened.

"You know what to do if she ever shows up, even for a mere second," Melinda says.

"I know."

"You may not want to tell anyone because you're afraid we'll up your dosage to keep her away, but she is the only intangible that causes harm."

"I know. And I haven't seen her."

"Very well then." Melinda crosses one foot in front of the other and clears her throat with a gentle *ahem*. "Let's go back to not wanting to go to school. You had a headache and a strong desire to avoid hearing about prom. Are you nervous about your exams this week?"

"No." I rub my arms again; the goose bumps have vanished, but I still feel anxious.

"Is there any other reason why you might be avoiding school?"

"There is, but it's stupid."

"Please share."

"Okay." I take several deep breaths. This session is a waste if I don't face up to the real problem at stake. "I'll give you the short version of a very long story." I don't know why I feel so embarrassed that I have to cover my face with both hands. "So I met this guy; he's my next-door neighbor. He has no clue that I have schizophrenia, but he knows I have something, maybe anxiety, but he still wanted to hang out with me all weekend. He's really sweet, but I told him he wouldn't want to hang out with me anymore once he went to school today and heard all the crazy stories from everyone. So, I guess you could say the *real* reason I stayed home today is because I couldn't stand the thought of him not wanting to hang out with me anymore. And I know that must sound immature and stupid, but nothing like this has ever happened before, so I'm not entirely sure how to deal with it."

I peek through my fingers. Melinda's lips press together; she's either very concerned about my problem, or she's trying not to laugh. She takes a sip of water before asking, "And what is this boy's name?"

"Arnold. Arnold Begay. He's Native American. Cherokee, he said. And he's really good-looking. Like insanely good-looking."

"Do you like Arnold?"

"Um, oh...I think so."

"You say he's sweet to you. In what way?"

"Well, he took care of me when I had to go to the hospital for my hand."

"Your mother mentioned on the phone earlier that you had a small accident with a pair of scissors."

"Yeah, I had to get stitches." I hold up my hand. The bandage is off, and the stitches are hardly noticeable. The skin is still a tad puffy and red, but painless unless I touch it. "Did she tell you about Arnold?"

"No, she did not. I guess she wanted to see if you would tell me first."

"That's a relief."

"You know she's just looking out for you." Melinda pours me a glass of water. "Tell me more about Arnold."

"There's not much more to tell." Even though the simple thought of him makes it hard to breathe.

"Really?"

I sit up and take the glass from her. "He's polite. Kind. Funny. And I don't think I should ever go near him again." I take a mouthful of water.

"Rachel, it sounds like this could be the perfect opportunity for you to let go of your fears and allow someone real to be your friend again."

I stare at the condensation around my glass. I think about that ant again, crawling into my glass. It would have a better chance of surviving in the water than in the orange juice. But there'd be little chance of it morphing without the acidity of the juice. Is Arnold a cup of water or a cup of juice?

"Rachel?"

"I'm not thirsty." Not anymore. I hand her back the glass. "Thanks, though."

"Did you hear what I said before? About Arnold becoming your friend?"

"My friend?" I laugh at the thought and pine at the reality. "It's more complicated than that. I don't think Arnold just wants to be my friend. He gives the impression that he wants more. And I don't even know or remember what it means to be someone's friend, let alone..." I shake my head. "It doesn't matter. Whatever he's feeling, or whatever I'm imagining he's feeling, it's all going to end as soon as he finds out about me. I'm just avoiding the inevitable. I'm just being a coward as usual."

"Rachel, you need to see Arnold again. You need to tell yourself about your condition. That's the only way you're going to know how he truly feels."

"Oh, but he's seen *A Beautiful Mind*. I'm pretty sure if the wife knew her professor was crazy, she never would have married him."

"Are you sure?"

"If I knew, I wouldn't marry him."

"Hmm." Melinda raises one of her teeny eyebrows. "Well, let's take things in reverse a bit. Imagine that Arnold is the one with schizophrenia. And you find this out after you just had a wonderful weekend together. Would you ignore him? Make fun of him? Never want to see him again?"

"Oh, no. I would never make fun of him. Especially after he was so kind to me." Even when I was rude to him. "But I know everything there is to know about schizophrenia, so I wouldn't be afraid of him. I would be more intrigued to get to know him at that point. I mean, just think of the things we could talk about."

Melinda beams. "Yes, and even if you yourself were not schizophrenic, it doesn't mean that you couldn't talk to him anymore. Just like your classmates. There may be someone suffering from something else, maybe depression or bipolar disorder. Wouldn't it be nice if they had a friend like you to talk to?"

Hell, no.

Resting my elbows against my knees, I place my head in my hands and tap the sides of my face. "You mean the emotionally disturbed kids that are isolated to one classroom all day? No, thank you. I spent the first half of ninth grade with them, and I have no desire to go back."

"Some of those students were kind to you."

I groan, not wanting to revisit the days of Cindy Martin scratching her skin off in class and Lee Henderson whipping his penis out in front of my desk. I behaved perfectly and earned straight As, studying into the dark hours of the night to ensure I placed out by second semester.

I sound like an asshole now. I should have empathy for those kids, especially Lee, who was abused as a toddler, but being placed with them, even for a semester, has forever labeled me emotionally unstable.

"What about the students in your classes now?" Melinda asks.

I take a deep breath. "It sounds possible. It does. Me talking to other students. Making a friend. But I overthink things, and the way I talk is weird. I'm not always *linear*."

"Arnold doesn't think so if he wanted to hang out with you so much."

Over the weekend, I had several strange moments with Arnold, from awkward hand-holding to awkward conversations. But he didn't run away. He stayed. He asked questions. He genuinely wanted to know me. And from what I can remember, he seemed to enjoy my company. Every bit of it.

And despite all my fears and uncertainties, I enjoyed his.

"I opened up to him," I finally say. "I never do that. I…" I jump off the couch, nearly tripping over my own feet. "I do need to talk to him. Like right now."

Melinda chuckles and motions for me to sit back down. "Okay, well, before you do that, let's make a *linear* plan for what you're going to say to him."

Melinda convinces me to finish our session, but I've already made up my mind that I will talk to Arnold as soon as we're done. I'm going to tell him what I am and that he can take it or leave it. *"But remember to show empathy,"* Melinda encourages. *"He has feelings too."*

I can't go to school. It would be suspicious of me to show up at the end of the day, merely to speak to Arnold, when I'm supposed to be home sick. Mrs. Zuckerman would surely demand an explanation and then call Mom.

So I text Arnold from my front porch.

R: **How was school?**
A: **Lame. How come you weren't there?**
R: **Doctor's appointment.**
A: **I'm sorry. Hope you feel better soon.**
R: **I'm not sick or anything.**

I wait several minutes for him to text back, but nothing happens. I have a dreadful feeling in the back of my head that he already knows, and he's decided to avoid me from now on. Of course, he'll be friendly and polite when he sees me. He's not an asshole. But he won't go out of his way to hang out with me.

I'm too paranoid. I have to stay calm. Everything in my head is only speculation. I won't know the truth until I see Arnold again.

R: **Are you on your way home?**
A: **Yeah. Walking home with some guys.**

The only guys that live on our street are Tommy and Ale Mason, fraternal twins who are into punk rock, skateboards, and motorbikes. Ideal friends for someone like Arnold. I used to play with Tommy and Ale when we were all kids, but once middle school came, we didn't talk much since I was more into basketball. After eighth grade, I never spoke to them again. No need to explain that.

I hear chattering, followed by the sounds of a skateboard. Tommy, the curly blond, pops an ollie right in the middle of the street. The tail of his skateboard snaps against the black tarmac, making an incredibly loud noise.

"Oh yeah, man," Tommy calls. "You only live like six houses down from us. But you live next door to the schizo girl."

Ale and Arnold appear just in time to see my startled reaction. Now would be an excellent opportunity to stay calm, to demonstrate I'm not the stuttering psycho from eighth grade who throws balls at imaginary people. That I'm a mature, composed young woman now.

But Tommy's words have ruined any chance of that. Unable to handle this choking burst of embarrassment, I run inside my house and shut the door.

My chest tightens up, and I pant as though I've been running with tape over my mouth. Larry sees me from the couch, but I took my pill today, so he's muted. And while I could push down the pole to let him in, I don't want his help or even his concern. I want to feel this pain all on my own, so I remember it. So I know in the future what will happen should I ever try to connect with a tangible again.

I had such high hopes after my hour with Melinda. But in the end, it doesn't matter what cup I jump into. I drown in both.

The doorbell rings three times. I run to my bedroom and shut my curtains, just in case Arnold tries to get my attention the old-fashioned way.

Ding. Ding. Ding. Text messages galore.

A: **Come outside. We need to talk.**
A: **I'm sorry for what Tommy said.**
A: **Please come talk to me. They're gone now.**

No. No. And no. Go away, Arnold. Go far, far away.

seven

IT'S TUESDAY. I have to go to school. AP Calculus exam in the morning, followed by AP World Studies in the afternoon. I eat breakfast, pop a pill, and scamper out of the house a half hour early. There's a note on the front porch. Scared Arnold might be lurking around or ready to bounce out the door to see me, I grab the paper and hustle to school. By the time I get there, I'm covered in sweat and hungry again. Since I'm early, I go to the nearby music café to grab a bagel. When I see the whole cheerleading squad inside, I turn right back around and go to the 7-Eleven instead. I eat a donut, a terrible choice for energy, and read the note:

The long and winding road that leads to your door will never disappear. I've seen that road before...

Paul McCartney. Arnold wrote all the lyrics down with a red pen. I should be flattered. I should just melt all over and run to him. Run right to his door, just like the song.

But this is reality. And I need to pass my exams first.

I hurry to school, dodging Mrs. Zuckerman and her coffee breath, and find the exam room. I'm the first person there besides the teacher. I close my eyes and think about the problems ahead of me. The one thing I like about math is there are real and unreal numbers, and both are accepted universally. Imaginary numbers are used to solve real-life problems.

If only they could be used to solve all problems.

The exam is more challenging than I anticipated, but I'm one of five kids to complete the entire thing under the time cap. I'm confident I passed, maybe not the highest score, but as long as I earn college credits, mission accomplished. Maybe next year, I can have an abbreviated schedule and only attend high school half a day.

Anyone taking two exams gets a double lunch today. And because I'm a junior, I could go out to eat at the nearby Chipotle or Subway. But the bathroom stall is safer. I don't think I'll run into Arnold there.

For an hour, I sit and watch YouTube. Mostly music videos, some cat compilations, and one random video about cactus soup. A few minutes before the bell, I hear the chatter of two girls doing their makeup together. I peek through the stall door and tense up. It's Alexia and Tonya, two of the tangiwhores.

Alexia and I used to be on the same basketball team until I was *removed*. The last game was a disaster, and she still has hard feelings about it. We were down by two points with a minute left to score. I had the ball. Alexia was wide open, but Michelle was on the court, dressed to play. Mary was also there, popping in and out like a ghost. I couldn't make sense of who was on my team, who was on the other team, what was real, what was in my head. This was before I even knew I had schizophrenia. But everyone, real or not, wanted me to throw the ball. So I did. To Michelle. But of course, she didn't catch it. The ball went flying into the bleachers, hitting a seven-year-old boy right in the head.

"So, did you see the new guy? The Indian?" Alexia asks, tearing me from the awful memory.

"You mean Native American?" Tonya clarifies, a bit more sophisticated of the two.

"Yeah, whatever, the Native American. What do you think of him? Doesn't he seem rather odd?"

"No, he seems rather hot, if you ask me. Why do you think he's odd?"

"He was just moving his leg so much in art class. It was driving me insane."

"Oh, well, maybe he's medicated, you know? My little brother gets leg tremors because of his asthma medication."

"Yeah, maybe. It's still annoying. I'll make sure not to sit next to him tomorrow. He's not my type anyway."

The bell rings. My next exam is on the other side of the building, but Alexia and Tonya don't have to rush to any exam, so they continue to chat. Maybe if I move quickly, I won't be noticed.

When I open the stall door to sneak out, Alexia grabs it from the other side and screams when she sees me. "Jesus! Why are you trying to scare me?"

I look down, allowing my ugly brown hair to spill across my face like a curtain. My response should be, "You should always knock before opening a bathroom stall, so it's your fault, asshole." But I keep my head down and say nothing.

"Hello?" Alexia waves a hand in front of my face. "Aren't you going to apologize?"

I move around her, sucking in my stomach to avoid any physical contact. She rolls her eyes at me.

"Why don't you ever say anything?" Alexia asks. "You talk to teachers, but you never talk to any of us. You know, maybe we wouldn't make fun of you if you just acted normal. Do you even know what normal is?"

My forehead furrows, and the desire to slap some sense across her face has never been so high. Alexia is your typical over-privileged, dumb white girl who happens to play basketball very well. And Tonya is her Asian sidekick she keeps around, so she doesn't seem racist. But even I, the outcast, can see right through her.

I open my mouth and release a small sound. "I…"

"Yeah?" Alexia says, smacking her overly glossed lips together. "You got something you want to say, freak?"

"I…" My voice cracks, but I recover volume. "I don't talk to you because you're a mean person. You don't just make fun of me. You make fun of anyone different. If acting normal is what it takes to make you a decent human being, I'd rather be a freak the rest of my life."

Alexia doesn't have a rebuttal. Tonya opens her mouth to say something, but the silent arrow has struck her too.

"And while I'm on a roll here, I think you're annoyed that Arnold, who is Cherokee, by the way, didn't pay any attention to you in class, so now you want to put him down. Which is very childish and immature and..." The late bell rings.

Rather than finish my sentence or make any closing remark, I jolt out the door. I have a short burst of adrenaline in my system, and it's enough to get me to the other side of the school just as the examiner is closing the testing door.

Mom, having the day off, picks me up from school, so there are no worries of running into Arnold on the way home. For the rest of the week, I do whatever it takes to avoid him, even if it means having lunch in the bathroom. In between classes, I hide behind someone tall to avoid being spotted in the halls. And as soon as the day is over, I bolt out the door and run home. Arnold has slowed down in his attempts to reach out via text, phone calls, and notes, making life considerably less hectic but considerably more depressing since I'm on my pill and have no one to talk to. Larry and Breezy barely exist when I'm consistent. By Friday, I don't even see their shadows.

And this is why I can't be medicated all the time. Because I get to that point where I really am alone. And no matter how many times I stare out my window, just wishing for the loneliness to end, I know it won't. At least with Larry, I can mask the pain. I can have friendship and comfort, even if it's only in my head. Even if it's only a few days a week, or just for the early morning hours, I'll take it.

Mom has to work 6:00 to 6:00, the worst possible shift because people like to let loose on Friday nights and do stupid things that put them in the ER. After we have a quick dinner, she bids me farewell and warns me not to take a shower if it starts to rain. Supposedly a huge thunderstorm is coming, and the power might go out. Great. Just what I need. Loneliness and no Netflix.

Around 8:00, it starts to rain. I'm tired enough to go to sleep, but I want to talk to someone first. Anyone. I could call Melinda. She always answers her phone but expects it to be an emergency. I could call my grandfather, but I don't like him one bit. So why even consider it?

Because I don't have anyone else to call.

"Larry?" I call out across the empty living room. "Larry, are you there?"

I try hard to break through for him, but the pole is too heavy. I can't find Larry anywhere. Five days of consistency. And *boom*, my intangible world is on shutdown.

"Larry, I need you. I'm sorry if I hurt your feelings the other day when—"

The doorbell rings like a gunshot in my ear. I wish I could rewire it so it would shriek, "Go away!" instead. It rings again, seemingly louder this time. I creep across the carpet and look through the peephole. It's Arnold, trying one last time to reach out to me. His clothes and hair are soaking wet from the rain. He looks so sad. And then I remember what Melinda said: *"Remember to show empathy. He has feelings too."*

I haven't considered Arnold's feelings at all this week. I've only been thinking about myself. I've been sticking up to tangiwhores but acting just like them.

A flash of lightning, the power goes out and then comes the crash of thunder. My heart pounds violently against my chest. Arnold bangs on the door. My heart leaps into my throat.

"Rachel!" he calls. "Come on. I know you're in there. I need to talk to you. Please."

I press my forehead against the door and feel the vibrations as he bangs again. The intangibles have begged for my attention but never a tangible. Not once. Not even my mother would work this hard to connect with me. She would leave or call Melinda.

"Okay, Rachel. If you don't want to talk to me anymore, I get that. I just thought you should know that I…"

He doesn't finish his sentence. He's going to leave me there, not knowing? My hand shakes, reaching for the doorknob. I expect to see him walking away when I open the door, but he lingers on the front porch, facing the stairs. His hair falls below his shoulders, dripping water onto the welcome mat. He turns around slowly. My hand grips the doorknob like a stress ball; I'm too nervous to let go. Too nervous to run. Too nervous to do anything but stand there and gawp.

"Hi," he says. "Can I come in?"

"The power went out."

"That's okay. Do you have a flashlight or any candles?"

"They're in the kitchen."

He reaches for my hand. My fingers unpeel, one at a time from the doorknob, but I keep my hand to myself and make room for him to enter. Once we make it safely to the kitchen, I open the drawer hosting all the emergency lights. We light several candles, and each take a flashlight.

"Would you like a towel?" I ask. "We have a few in the laundry room that should be clean."

"Sure, thank you."

He takes off his shirt and wrings it out over the sink. I turn the other direction, finding his movements to be entirely too distracting. He takes his shoes and socks off next. I'm terrified he'll take everything off, but he leaves his pants on.

"So," he finally says, drying his hair with the towel.

"So." I lean against the counter, my eyes on the sink. There are a few dishes that need to be washed. I could do that to avoid eye contact. I could...

"Why have you been avoiding me?" He slips in front of me, blocking my reach of the sink.

"I haven't. I've just been busy."

He tosses the towel on top of the counter. "Don't lie. I saw you run to school the other day, and I know you don't like to run."

"I had exams this week. I wanted to get there early."

"This was Wednesday. You didn't have an exam on Wednesday. I also overheard some girls saying that you've been eating lunch in the bathroom all week. So, yes, you are avoiding me. Unless there's some other guy you're afraid to go near?"

I shake my head. I'm afraid of all guys, but especially Arnold right now because he knows the truth.

"It's better this way," I say.

"Better? No, it's not better. It sucks. You haven't talked to me. You've just made this awful assumption that I don't like you anymore. Or worse, that I think you're some kind of freak. Right?"

"Yeah…"

"And that sucks you would assume that about me."

I lower my head, feeling like the worst person in the universe. I really did mess this whole situation up. I didn't consider how bad my silence would affect him.

"Did I do anything wrong?" he asks. "I'm still trying to figure that out. Was I too forward with you?"

"No."

"Have you heard a single bad word come out of my mouth about you?"

"No."

"So, really, you should have no reason to be avoiding me."

"Monday, you—"

"I didn't say anything. Tommy did. And I ditched him and his brother right away to talk to you, but you wouldn't let me in. You shut me out, Rachel."

"I'm sorry. That was a mistake. I assumed…" I raise my eyes to his level. "I shouldn't assume anything."

"That's right."

"But you know, don't you? Tommy and Ale told you about me, right?"

"They told me the short version of what happened to you in eighth grade. And guess what, Rachel? It doesn't matter. You're still a cool person. At least that's what I felt last weekend with you. Tommy and Ale were shocked you took the time to hang out with me. Because apparently, you don't talk to anyone at school."

"I can't. Everyone is—"

"Out to get you? That's paranoia. And frankly, well…"

"What?"

"I was going to say immature. But I know how rough it is to have a mental condition. So I am understanding. Supportive. And I'm here for you."

He opens his arms ever so slightly, and I instantly turn away and press my hips against the counter. I'm cuing I need space, but I don't object when his hand grazes the tip of my shoulder. His body is like a blanket ready to envelop me, and while I initially think of suffocation, I also feel warmth and protection.

Yet when his other hand tries to wrap itself around my shoulders, I dip under his arms and retreat three steps. I'm not buying it. He can't be that supportive of me; he barely knows me. This is just a pity act if anything.

I grab a candle. Holding something fragile will keep me from pacing. "You feel sorry for me. I don't want you to hang out with me because you feel sorry for me."

Arnold's thick eyebrows pinch together. His lips curl to one side, and he chortles, even though his eyes are sullen.

"I'm sorry," I say, setting down the candle before I catch the house on fire. "I shouldn't have said that."

He shakes his head. If he can handle this much crap from me already, maybe he is legit. And I'm just a fool for thinking otherwise.

"What makes you think I don't want to hang out with you simply because I like you and want to hang out with you?" he asks.

Despite my nerves, I can't help but smile, even if it's all mushed to one side of my mouth. When he smiles back, completely, I allow the rest of me to smile, gums and all.

But every up has its down, and I go back to the drawing board, determined to find the flaw, just like my damn mother.

"Did they tell you exactly what I did in eighth grade? Did they tell you how I got locked up?"

"That was a long time ago," Arnold counters. "And I bet if you told me your version of the story, it would help to clarify things."

"Arnold. I don't clarify things for anyone except my therapist, and even then, I have to lie sometimes because the truth is I'm not always with it. I don't always take my medication when I should. Because I still need my crazy world to be real sometimes. So I…" I clasp my hands together to stop myself from shaking. It feels like I'm on the verge of a cliff, and if I say one more word, I'll fall.

"So you what?" Arnold's sweet voice is the hand that pulls me away from the cliff, back to safe grounds.

I look up, letting out what pains me the most. "So I don't always have to feel so alone."

His eyes soften. "I know what that feels like."

"How?"

"Trust me. If you think your past is messed up. Mine is too."

"But I did terrible things. You don't want to know."

"I do want to know." He takes a step forward.

And damn it if I don't take one too. Right toward him. "No, you really don't. The less you know, the better."

"Well, I can always just go ask people about you and hear their exaggerated stories."

I nearly choke on my own breath.

"Or you could just tell me yourself," he adds.

I cross my arms, feeling chills in every direction. Therapy is only once a week for a reason. "I don't want to tell you. Not right now. I'm not trying to be rude, I just…"

"Okay, not right now. I get it. We can take things slow. We should take things slow."

I exhale little by little, trying to steady my pounding heart. Arnold hasn't moved his eyes off me. It's like he's trying to break through me, to reach places inside my mind that I can't even get to. But he's also trying to reach another place, more distant and cold.

My heart.

The Seroquel shoves a pole through my head, but whatever I've got locked around my heart, I've put there myself.

"So, what does this mean exactly?" I ask. "Do you still want to be my friend, or did I ruin any chance of that?"

"Friends forgive each other."

"I'm sorry. I'm sorry for everything. I didn't mean to hurt your feelings."

He smiles and reaches a hand toward my face. Hesitant this time, he waits for my permission, and when I nod, he brushes the loose brown hairs behind my ears, then cups the back of my neck and massages it. I tense at first, but when I realize how good it feels, I release my apprehension and close my eyes.

I imagine a world beyond what we see. A world where only Arnold and I can be. Where nothing can distract us and we have all the time in the world to be present with each other and ourselves. A utopia for two minds and one heart.

When I open my eyes, he moves his other hand around my waist and pulls me in close. He tilts my head back, bends his knees ever so slightly, and lowers his head toward mine. I can feel the air moving in and out of his mouth and nose. I can feel the pounding of his heart, almost as turbulent as my own. I can feel his hesitation, his uncertainty, his fear. But I can also feel his overwhelming desire to kiss me.

It's hardly a kiss. It's the bare minimum of contact between lips. He immediately moves his head back, searching for any reaction on my face, but I am immobile. I don't know what to do or how to feel about any of this. A part of me wonders if this is even right. Him, being here, holding me, kissing me. Am I ready for this?

"Are you okay?" he asks after several long seconds of silence.

"I think so." I run my teeth across my bottom lip. It tingles. "I thought we were just friends though."

"I never said *just*. But if you don't want this, tell me."

"No."

"No, what?"

"I've just..."

"Never been kissed before?"

"Is it obvious?"

He wets his lips and asks, "Would you like to try again?"

I nod, and his lips brush mine. Not innocently this time, but hot and fiery. I wouldn't call it fireworks, like in films or books. It's better than that. It's a wave of warmth that rushes to every corner of my body, making me feel complete and whole again. Every inch of me saturates with the awakening of long, lost desires.

When I press my hands and arms against his bare chest, he hoists me off the ground like I'm ninety pounds and sets me on top of the kitchen counter, away from the burning candles. My legs wrap around his torso as if I would collapse without him. My senses dilute, and I can no longer think straight. I'm living in the present, in a hybrid world with Arnold that no other tangible can touch.

It hasn't even been a minute, and already my shirt is coming off. But it's not him pulling it off. It's me.

"Rachel," he says, breathless between kisses. "Rachel, I don't want us to do anything you're not ready for."

"I don't care," I say, grabbing the back of his neck and diving my mouth further into his.

He gently takes my hand and pulls it away from his body. "Rachel. You just said that was your first kiss."

"Don't let go of me."

"Rachel." He cups my chin into his hands. I want so badly for this to escalate. I need to feel more. I've been numb for too long.

"Arnold, please."

Our lips join together, softly and sweet. With another blast of thunder and lightning, the power comes back. My bra is about to fall off, and my stomach looks like a blob of fat. I want to hold onto him, but I'm exposed now, and the desire to shield myself takes over. I wrap my arms around my waist and look down, embarrassed by my body.

"You're beautiful, Rachel."

He's not looking at my body when he says it. He's looking right into my eyes. I bite down on my bottom lip and smile just a little.

"You are," he says again.

He pulls my hands away from my stomach and wraps his arms around my waist. He lifts me off the counter, so I'm standing next to him. Once my shirt is back on, he takes my hand and walks me to the living room. We sit on the couch, but this time there is no space between us. He rubs his thumb against the little puncture marks on my hand. I don't mind there being a scar once the stitches dissolve. It's like having a memory of Arnold with me everywhere I go.

"Arnold?"

"Yeah?"

"That was really nice. I liked doing that. I mean…" I shake my head. "Sorry. I can be awkward sometimes. Sometimes when I talk, it's like I'm thinking out loud, and my thoughts can be pretty crazy."

"You don't have to be sorry for that. You can trust me."

I close my eyes and think about my first time meeting Melinda at the hospital. She came out to see me when I was planting flowers. I didn't know she was a doctor because of the way she was dressed, with a long blue skirt, gloves, and hat, much like a gardener. She asked me basic questions about planting flowers and vegetables, what I liked to eat, and so forth. I opened up to her slowly, but it took months for Melinda to break through to me. To establish any sort of trust.

With Arnold, it feels like no time is needed.

"I do trust you," I say. "But when it comes to words, I mean sharing things, I don't want to share everything all at once."

"Why don't you just pick one thing to share about?"

"That sounds fair. What should I share first?"

"Tell me about basketball. Tell me all the good things you remember about basketball."

"The good things." I usually only reflect on the bad. "It started early. I started dribbling and shooting when I was in preschool. I couldn't play on a team until I was eight, but my dad would teach me things, and we'd watch NBA and do brackets together for the college

81

teams. I played one season, and he was there for every game. And then…"

"He left?"

"Yeah. But that didn't stop me from playing. I started to play more because he wasn't there. I did summer basketball camps. I played at recess. After school. I made the school team in sixth grade, and I was captain of the team in seventh grade."

"You must have been really good."

"It was all I ever wanted to do. Basketball made me happy. But things changed during eighth grade. I started to have these headaches, which led to panic attacks before games. I couldn't focus. It was getting harder and harder to tell who my teammates were from the other team. Everything started to blend, and I kept hearing these voices in my head, telling me what to do. Pass here, throw there. And then those voices evolved into people. And some of those people wanted to play too."

"That must have been hard for you to deal with."

"It was. And at first, my mom was convinced that I just needed glasses, but my vision has always been perfect. It was just the intangibles."

"The what?"

"The intangibles. It's what I've always called them."

"People that aren't real?"

I nod. "They all started to show up at my games. And while most of them were friendly and nice, there was one. One that hurt me."

I shiver, goose bumps rising everywhere. On my arms, the back of my neck. And then I imagine Mary again, creeping up behind Arnold with that crazed look in her eyes. Radiating destruction, chaos, and misery.

Arnold holds me closer, crushing the awful image. "Are you okay?"

I rest my head on his shoulder. "I don't want to talk about it anymore. Please? That's all I'm going to share tonight if that's alright."

"Rachel, it's okay. I only wanted to hear the good things anyway."

"Can you stay with me? My mom won't be home until morning. Could you stay?"

"My parents would notice."

"Oh. Right." How stupid of me to forget that most parents work during the day and sleep at night.

"Or maybe they wouldn't. Who knows?" Arnold rolls his eyes and huffs. "But it's probably best if I go home soon. Are you okay? How are you feeling?"

Extremely warm and cozy, and not wanting to move from this couch ever again so long as Arnold is on it too.

"I feel good now," I answer.

"But you weren't earlier?"

I shake my head, exhausted by the trials of the week. I cover my mouth to muffle a yawn and lean back to stretch a bit. Arnold grabs me by both arms, kissing me in the process.

"Tell me more," he says, parting from my lips entirely too soon. "If you're up for it, I want to know more."

I'd rather just kiss him and run my hands across his chest again, but it's important he knows what this week was like for me.

"I've been very consistent with my medicine, so life has been pretty lonely. When I go off, even for a day, they talk to me again. My intangibles. It's so weird how I react to the pill. Some people have huge withdrawal or relapses within hours of not taking their medicine. But for me, I usually feel fine. I feel better because I'm not so tired. And my intangibles help me to be stable, as weird as that may sound."

"I'd like to meet them someday."

"Ha, well, good luck with that."

"Will you tell me about them?"

"I could. Tomorrow, if I skip my medication, I could introduce you to them, technically. You just wouldn't be able to see them. But I could ask them questions for you. Unless...oh my God. Are you freaked out right now?" I scoot back to study his face, but he shows no signs of shock or revulsion.

"No, not at all."

"Any other person would be freaked out."

He smirks. "I'm not like any other person."

"No, you're not." I relax and reach for his hands. "You're different."

Arnold stays with me on that couch until midnight. That's his curfew, and even though he's only next door, he still needs to be home on time. While the house feels incredibly barren after his departure, I have no trouble falling asleep. I wrap myself up in my comforter like a cocoon and lounge by the bay window. Arnold's curtains are wide open. With little effort, he moves his bed, so it's next to the window instead. He lies down and blows me a kiss. Even though we're separated, I close my eyes and imagine that he's lying right next to me. And maybe soon, I won't have to imagine at all.

eight

I'M NOT ALONE when I wake up. Larry is sitting on the floor, looking through all our books, reorganizing them yet again. He's probably just bored or anxious for me to wake up and not take my pill, so he can talk to me. His body comes in and out of view, like a ghost in a curtain. He disappears for a few minutes while I go downstairs for a glass of orange juice and to flush my pill down the toilet. I never know when Mom will check the pack. When I return, he's more visible, but still unable to talk. I close my eyes and locate the pole. I have just enough strength to push it over. Now the day can begin.

"Rae-Rae," he says, his smile twitching side to side. "You are glowing this morning." He hands me a copy of *Wuthering Heights*, our favorite romance novel.

"Glowing?" I laugh, hugging the book once before tossing it aside. "I look like crap in the morning."

"No, you look radiant. Like Catherine when she first meets Heathcliff."

"More like Catherine when she's dead."

"Oh, Rae-Rae. We get to hang out today, right?"

"Yeah. Sure." I yawn and stretch my arms overhead, not as excited by that idea.

"Or do you have plans with your new boyfriend?"

I look out the window. Arnold is still sleeping. "He's not my…is he?"

"He's *something*."

I tear myself from the lovely view and join Larry on the floor. The books are categorized by genre, and Larry seems most fixated on romance. Most of these novels end tragically, except for dear *Pride and Prejudice*. Now that's a novel I can relate to. And the one I locate first, buried at the bottom of Larry's pile.

"I haven't read that one in a while," Larry says.

"Yeah, same." I set the book on top of the others. "I've been behind in my reading these last few weeks."

"I wonder why?" Larry arches his eyebrows at the window.

"Yeah. About that." I bite my lip and look down, feeling my cheeks turn red.

"I wasn't around last night."

"You didn't hear me calling at all?"

"I was completely blocked out."

"You always come through when I need you."

"Five days in a row did some major damage. Or maybe you were just too distracted this week to even notice I was gone." I can't tell if he's being serious or sarcastic. Usually, I can tell.

"No, I noticed."

"Maybe you took too many pills by mistake?"

"No, I definitely did not. If I had, I wouldn't have been so…" My cheeks burn at the remembrance of Arnold shirtless in my kitchen, holding me, kissing me, making every part of me melt like a candle.

"Oh, no. What happened?" Larry's eyes are bulging with both excitement and concern. "Did you kiss?"

"A little."

"A little?"

"A lot. We kissed a lot." I bite my lip, thinking Larry will flip, but his grin stretches like an accordion.

"I'm happy for you," he says.

"Really?"

"Yes, of course! It's about time you let loose. You don't even drink caffeine."

"It makes my stomach hurt!" I laugh.

"Oh, Rae-Rae." Larry jolts to his feet and takes two big steps toward the window. "I know I had my doubts about Arnold, but now

I'm super excited for you. I think you should totally indulge yourself with him."

"You do?"

"Yes."

"Wow. I never thought you would be so supportive of this."

"I guess I'm a hopeless romantic at heart." He runs his fingers across the windowpane and sighs deeply. "But to be completely honest, a part of me is jealous."

"Jealous?"

"Because I can't." He pauses and looks back at me. "I really can't be a part of it."

"A part of me and Arnold?"

Larry nods and leans against the window, too dramatically to be considered normal behavior from him.

"But I would like to be able to watch," he says, his voice rising in pitch.

"Watch? What do you mean, watch? Watch us kiss? Watch us *do stuff together?*"

"I wouldn't be looking at you."

"No, you'd be looking at him. Oh, God." I knock the pile of romance novels over when I try to stand up; one of my legs has fallen asleep. I kick like the devil to wake it up, but my discomfort now amuses Larry, which pisses me off even more. "I don't have to share Arnold with you. He's mine."

Larry folds his arms across his chest and raises both eyebrows. "He's yours now? Well, you better go over there and make sure you two are indeed each other's. Make it official."

"I can't just…"

I don't want to go over to his house. What if his parents are home and want to meet me?

"You can't just what?"

I huff and throw my hair back into a messy ponytail. "I need to talk to Breezy."

Larry's mouth drops open. "You can't talk to me about this?"

"Not right now."

"But you talk to me about everything."

"Well, I'm sorry, but it's too weird right now after what you said about wanting to *watch* me and Arnold. It also makes me jealous and worried and all sorts of things I can't understand. And it's ridiculous because Arnold will never, ever be able to talk to you or even see you. No guy will. Because you don't exist!"

Larry lowers his head, and for the first time in a long time, his feelings have genuinely been slaughtered. So much that he can't even apply his ChapStick without shaking. I reach for his hand, but my fingers phase through his flesh as if he were a ghost.

"I'm sorry," I finally say. "I shouldn't have said that. That was really mean."

But mean things and the truth can't always be separated. A harsh slap of reality right there. With Mom, I censor myself because she is real. And her feelings matter. Larry is a creation, sculpted so stunningly, he should belong to some other schizo.

"You're here for me." I look up into his watery brown eyes. "You're here for me, and really you shouldn't be here. You should be somewhere else, with someone else. Someone who can give you what you want."

"Rae." He smiles just a bit and shakes away his freckled emotions. "It's never been about what I want. It's always been about you. I'm here for you. But I'll never be able to give you what you really want."

Touché.

I've been playing make-believe for way too long.

———

Mom is still sleeping, so I make a piece of toast and wait in the backyard for Breezy to arrive. She doesn't come when I summon her, like Larry. She comes when she feels like it. And usually, it's dependent on the weather, my state of mind, and the garden's condition.

Eventually, she appears next to the ugly bush, shaking her head at the neglected weeds. Her red curls bob. "If you're going to plant soon, these weeds need to be pulled."

I join her, pulling only with my right hand since my stitches still haven't fully dissolved. The sun is barely alive, and I'm already sweating.

"You should plant more tomatoes this year," Breezy says. "They grew so well last year."

"Sure."

"But you need to stay focused. Every day you need to be out here. Make sure everything is growing properly, no weeds, and especially be on the lookout for that groundhog if he comes around. He ate all the lettuce last year."

"Focused. Right." I look directly at Arnold's bedroom window.

"Already you're distracted." Breezy has the face of a child but the outlook of a forty-year-old woman. She is always so matter-of-fact.

"He could help dig the holes. I'm sure he would help me with anything at this point."

"Rachel, you can do a lot of things on your own."

I wave my hand to remind her of the stitches. "Uh, no, I can't actually."

"If you hadn't been so distracted by him, you wouldn't have cut yourself."

"That was a freak accident."

"You need to be more careful."

"Are you going to tell me to stay away from him, too?"

"No. I'm not."

"Really?" Another surprise. "Then are you supportive of us? Being together? Me and Arnold?"

"You know how I feel about men."

"You don't get along with Larry, that's all. And that's why you never come inside the house."

Breezy simpers and shakes her head. "It's not Larry that keeps me away."

"Is it my mom?"

"No. And you should already know the reason."

"I'd like you to tell me. Please."

"Well." She wipes her hands against the grass and takes a deep breath. "My parents used to fight all the time, so I would go outside to get away from it all. And now I'm outside all the time because it's where I feel safe and at peace. It's where I can forget about my dad, especially. Right here, with the flowers and trees. Everything alive and growing. It's the right place for me. And it's where you can always find me."

"Oh, now I see." I close my eyes and recollect what it was like as a child. How I would escape to the backyard whenever my parents fought. I would spend hours curled in the grass, picking at dandelions, just waiting for silence. Waiting for peace. Waiting for my reality to disappear.

When I open my eyes, Breezy is right in front of me, her face even more youthful. I feel the pressing desire to hug her, but she senses my longing and leans away. "It won't make you feel better," she says. "I'm not real, Rachel."

"I know."

"But my feelings are real."

"Yes. They are."

"Because you feel them too."

"Yes. I feel the same. I would go outside to get away from it all. But I never stayed outside forever, like you. I went back eventually. To my room. My books."

"And you found peace. In your books. In your mind. But never here." She points to the center of my chest. "That's where things got really messed up."

"Yes." I close my eyes again, remembering what I did on the days it rained and I couldn't go outside. I would crawl under my bed with my books and dolls. And I would pretend I was somewhere else, with a whole new group of people.

I open my eyes and smile, even though it hurts.

"I had a Ken doll named Larry. And he…"

"He became your best friend."

I blink several times, recalling how I would apply bubblegum ChapStick to "Larry" the doll. How I dressed him in nice clothing and cut out paper books for him to read. How I colored his skin with Magic Marker to make him darker. To make him the Larry he is today.

"I never really thought of it that way," I say. "It's like I invented him." But is it going to change anything?

It changes my perception, not my situation. My intangibles will never be more than dolls I used to play with or books I read. All fiction. Breezy evolved from my love of *The Secret Garden* and *Anne of Green Gables*. She's a hybrid, just like Larry. But what about Mary? Where did she sprout from? I never read horrors. I rarely watch scary movies. I don't even get excited over Halloween.

"Breezy, I saw *her*."

Breezy nods her head, clearly not as distraught as Larry was over the announcement. "I always knew she'd come back."

"What do you think she wants? And why is she back?"

"I don't know. But just be safe, okay? Don't go anywhere by yourself. You know Larry and I can't follow you to school, but Arnold can. Stick by him, and you'll be okay."

"You really think so?"

"Yeah. Arnold is different."

"He's accepting."

"It's not just that. He has a sadness in him. A deep one."

"What? Why do you think he's sad?"

"You'll know soon enough. And you may be upset at first. But you should try to listen to him. Really listen to him. If you accept him, as he accepts you, it will open up a lot of doors. A lot of possibilities. Stay on the right path with him. Don't veer off with people you don't know. It's only going to cause trouble."

"What people? What trouble? You're not making any sense." Breezy can be highly intellectual, but she doesn't always finish her thoughts. Nor does she feel obligated to answer my questions.

"Finish weeding and then go do something fun with Arnold."

"What kind of fun?"

"Whatever you desire. Just make sure it's what you want to do."

What do I want to do with Arnold? Well, for one thing, I'd like to kiss him again. And for longer this time, with no pauses to talk about anything serious. I'd like him to touch me, his bare skin rubbing against mine, his hands in my hair, his tongue down my mouth. Not in my living room, despite the serenity of the couch, but somewhere private, where Larry can't find us.

"Damn." I fan myself; my face is on fire again. "I'm not sure if I can trust myself around Arnold. Last night, I was the one pushing things, not him."

"It's okay to push a little. Just remember who you are."

"That's not always the easiest thing to do." It's near impossible.

"You also said that about your first garden. Now, look how far you've come."

"Still fighting weeds."

"Weeds will always grow. So?"

"So...?"

She smiles, at last a dash of benevolence. "Just keep pulling."

Forty-five minutes later, with focus, hard work, and one strong hand, my garden is free of weeds. I could plant today, but I need to go to the store, and like Breezy said, I shouldn't go alone. Mom will sleep into the afternoon, so my only and best choice for help is Arnold.

R: **Are you awake?**
A: **Yeah. I see you gardening.**
R: **I want to plant today.**
A: **Sweet. Need help?**
R: **Yes! But first I need to go to the store to get the plants.**
A: **Don't we need a car for that?**
R: **Yeah...**
A: **I have a wagon.**
R: **Perfect!**

We look ridiculous, pulling a child's-size red wagon across town to buy plants and flowers, but who cares? When I'm with Arnold, I'm invulnerable to the whispers and stares, even if they're all inside my head. Hand in hand, we could pull that wagon to the end of the Earth.

Breezy observes us but stays muted while we plant. I don't mind her eavesdropping, but I don't appreciate Larry watching us like a surveillance system from my window. The last time we were all together, I was bleeding and nearing a meltdown. No one would shut up. Today is a much calmer gathering. Arnold digs and helps put each plant in place, since I can't do much with one hand. It takes about an hour to fill up the entire garden. Afterward, we spread fresh soil across the ground, water, and ensure the gate is shut and locked. I swear the groundhog last year knew how to pick locks.

"So, how long will we have to wait before we can make a salad?" Arnold asks, wiping the dirt off his jeans.

"About a month. Depends mostly on the weather. Sometimes we get random cold days at the end of May."

"The ten seasons of Maryland?"

"Yep."

"Well, I look forward to eating many salads with you." He stretches his arms back and twists side to side, giving me a lovely view of his protruding abs. "So, what do you want to do now? Do you want to come over to my house?"

"Are your parents home?"

"Yeah, but they won't bother us."

"Okay…"

"They'll like you. Don't worry."

I run my dirty fingers through my hair and look down at my soiled clothing, feeling entirely too gross and underdressed to meet lawyers. "Can I go shower first?"

I scrub every inch of my body, even the most neglectful places, like behind my ears and in between my toes. I shave my armpits, legs, and bikini area. It's not like I'm meeting his parents at the pool, but it feels better being completely groomed. I brush and blow-dry my hair, spray myself with perfume, throw on some cheap earrings, and even pluck between my eyebrows.

Larry doesn't say a word when I wear a yellow summer dress instead of the typical shorts and tee. He's usually the one encouraging me to wear more feminine clothing. But things are still weird between us, and I'm not sure when we'll reconcile.

Arnold has probably been waiting forever for me, but he has a big smile on his face when I come outside.

He takes my hand and leads me to his house. I swallow the lump in the back of my throat, but it slides right into my stomach, curling into a pretzel. It feels like I'm about to meet a whole room of lawyers rather than two parents. I don't have as many social issues talking to adults as I do with people my age. This should be a piece of cake, but it's not.

The layout of their house is similar to ours, but they haven't fully settled in. The furniture is all arranged, and the TV is set up, but the various paintings, photographs, and Cherokee artifacts piled up in the corner of the living room look desperate to be hung. Arnold's mom is in the adjacent kitchen, cutting up fruit for a smoothie. The last time

I saw her, she looked beautiful in her work suit and heels, ready to take on the runway or a courtroom. Today she has her hair pulled back, very little makeup, and yoga pants on. She still looks stunning.

Arnold's dad is sitting on the couch with his iPad and a can of Diet Pepsi. He looks about ten years older than his wife, still in excellent shape, but his short dark hair is starting to gray.

As soon as they take notice of us, they immediately stop what they're doing and walk over to introduce themselves.

"Arnold!" his mom exclaims, quickly drying her hands with a towel. "You've brought a friend over."

"Mom, Dad, this is Rachel Andrews. She's Dr. Andrews' daughter."

"So good to meet you," Mrs. Begay says, reaching out to shake my hand.

"Nice to meet you," I nearly whisper, shaking her tiny hand. We are about the same height, but I probably outweigh her by twenty pounds.

"Nice to meet you, Rachel," Mr. Begay says, standing behind his wife, not as interested in the whole hand-shaking thing. He must be at least six and a half feet tall. He even makes Arnold look small.

"We met Beth, your mother, last week," Mrs. Begay says. "It's good to know we have a doctor living next door in case of an emergency."

Arnold's stone-cold face doesn't seem very happy with her comment. "Anyway," he says. "I was just going to show Rachel the basement."

"Oh, are you into weights, Rachel?" Mrs. Begay asks.

"Rachel plays basketball," Arnold answers for me. "I think she might enjoy some powerlifting on the side."

"Well, that's wonderful. Just be safe. Make sure you put the safety handles up if you bench or squat."

"I don't think I'm really dressed for that," I say.

"No, dear, you look like you're ready to sit outside and have a smoothie. I can make you all some drinks if you would like? We can put out the patio furniture today."

"No, Mom, we're good. Thanks, though."

Arnold takes my hand in front of his parents and leads me to the stairs. Their basement is one gigantic room, whereas ours has been framed out and finished. I look around, noting all the weight plates, exercise machines, and unopened boxes. I've never had to move before, but I can imagine it takes a long time to unpack.

"So, this is it," he says. "It'll be a great place to hang out once everything is rearranged and we get some furniture down here. It's nice and private. No big windows anywhere. There's a guest room over here." He points to a door. "It's just a bed right now, but my parents plan to have someone paint and install carpet. Do you want to see?"

I follow him into the bedroom, which seems somewhat out of place in this man cave of a basement. The room is small, with a single window facing the backyard. The bed only has a fitted white sheet on top, no pillows or comforter yet.

Arnold wraps his hands around my waist, and I feel the heat immediately. I'm off my Seroquel today, so anything could happen. I'm not at home, so there's no worry of Larry eavesdropping, and Arnold's parents don't seem like the kind to bother their son when he has a girl over. But I could always be wrong.

Arnold motions for me to lie on the bed with him, which I do without any delay or hesitation. My back against the soft mattress, he lies sideways against me and gently runs his fingers across my face and down the outskirts of my body.

"What are you thinking about right now?" he asks.

I bite my lip. "I'm thinking that kind of tickles but kind of feels nice, what you're doing."

"I like you, Rachel." He kisses my cheek. "But I know how new this must be for you. I don't want to make you feel uncomfortable."

"I'm not. I'm totally fine. I like it when you touch me. I like knowing you're here. That you're real. I want to know you more." Larry's enthusiasm for physical contact and Breezy's zeal for listening seem to go hand in hand. I feel more connected with Arnold every time we touch and with every word.

"I want to know you too," he whispers into my ear. "Every part."

He smiles and brushes his lips across my forehead. He trickles his fingers down the middle of my face and touches my upper body, outlining the curves and all my imperfections. I try to breathe normally, but it's hard to maintain an ounce of stillness when he's caressing me like this.

He reaches a hand under my dress and traces my underwear, every brush sending me a little over the edge of being able to contain myself.

"Is this okay?" he asks.

I nod because I don't think I'm capable of words anymore.

It's just his hand, but it feels like he's holding onto my soul when he moves it against me. I can't keep silent any longer, so I wrap my arms around his neck and bury my face into his shoulder, allowing his T-shirt to swallow my sounds.

nine

WHILE HIS PARENTS RUN ERRANDS, Arnold takes me upstairs to his bedroom. It isn't entirely unpacked or presentable, but I note that he likes to surf and play video games and owns more concert T-shirts than I can count. He has his own desk and computer setup with three monitors.

"I'm into programming," he says, noting the pile of Java and C# textbooks. "I think that's what I'm going to study in college. Thought it would be cool to design video games someday but more interactive ones where you really feel like you're in the game and are actually moving while you play."

"Virtual reality?"

"Yeah, but imagine your whole body stimulated. Like even your sense of smell."

"That would be pretty intense."

"I know, right?"

I wander around with my arms folded across my chest, not sure where to go or what to do. Like me, Arnold doesn't make his bed regularly, so he tidies up, so we both have a place to sit.

"Your bed is nice," I say, running my hands across the silky black sheets. "This mattress is really comfortable."

"It's one of those therapeutic ones."

"I could definitely use something like this in my room. My mattress is as old as I am."

"Then you are overdue for a new one."

He lays back, pulling me with him. I rest my head against his chest and fold my arm across his stomach. Lounging right where he sleeps, his aroma is even more intense.

"Your parents seem nice," I say.

"Yeah, they're alright. Even after all the shit that happened. It's probably because they're lawyers and deal with way worse cases."

"You're a case?"

"I was. Sort of."

"Will you tell me?"

"I guess I should." His right leg starts to tremor. "If you're going to open up, then I should too."

"Yeah, that's usually how it's done, right? When people are—"

"Boyfriend and girlfriend?"

I press my hand against his thigh to impede the shaking. My lips curve to one side. "Are we?"

He lays his hands on top of mine. "We better be. Cause I don't do friends with benefits. Do you?"

"I don't know what I do."

"I'm sorry. I didn't mean to say it like that. I've only had one other girlfriend. Awhile back, but it was nothing serious."

"Just fun?"

"I wouldn't call it fun. She was trouble, all on her own."

"Tell me?"

"I'll tell you about *my* trouble."

He takes a deep breath and rearranges his position, so he's sitting up. I roll over and lay the back of my head across his lap. Both legs are shaking now, but I don't mind the tremors if it helps him open up.

"Where to start? Okay, so childhood, nothing remotely exciting happened. My parents were always working and still are. I never got into much trouble, never hung out with the wrong crowds. Besides soccer and Boy Scouts, life was pretty boring."

"What about the wolf?"

"That was one exception. I never really pushed the limits after that, not until high school. Maybe it was puberty, or maybe it was losing interest in soccer, but overall I was having a hard time focusing, couldn't sit still, had trouble making and keeping friends, and so on. I just felt lost. And then, I was diagnosed with ADHD and put on Adderall. I'm still on it, but I only take it during the school week."

"What about summertime?"

"My parents haven't decided what to do about this summer. It depends on whether or not they make me get a job."

"You can help me garden. It's a big job, and it pays in health benefits."

"That sounds awesome. But they'll probably make me take the pills, regardless." He runs his fingers through my hair, just like Larry does, but the stimulation can't compete. "Anyway, at the end of ninth grade, I was pissed at my parents for medicating me. So I retaliated a bit and started hanging out with older crowds. Juniors, seniors, even some college kids. I went to their parties. I drank with them. I smoked with them. I liked it so much it became my life. I skipped my pills and ate gummies in the morning instead. It was a different kind of stimulator, more chill and natural. I liked it way better than the Adderall."

"I'm sorry, but what are gummies? You mean, like gummy bears?"

"Similar. But they're laced with THC. Marijuana."

"Oh." Oh indeed.

"Anywho, one day I messed up and took too many gummies, so it was pretty obvious I was on something. I denied it to the principal, but my parents made me do a drug test when I got home. Having no warning, I failed. My parents were upset and did the typical 'you're grounded' sort of thing, but it didn't change anything. I still did what I wanted to do. I liked being high. I liked floating away from reality a bit. I liked living on the edge. Life was more interesting that way. It made sense.

"Then a few months went by, and nothing changed. I'd sneak out to parties or get high by myself. My parents threatened to call the police on me, which was crazy considering they're lawyers. When they realized that wasn't such a great idea, they did the next crazy thing. They had me homeschooled. If I was home all the time, how could I get my drugs? So they kept me home for almost a year, back on Adderall, being homeschooled by this smelly old man since my parents continued to work all the time. And then I got depressed. Real depressed. Wouldn't leave the house, even when I was allowed to.

Wouldn't eat. Wouldn't work out. It got so bad that one night I gave up."

He rubs his fingers against his neck, and suddenly I make the horrific connection about his scars.

I lift my head off his lap and turn so we're facing one another. "It wasn't the wolf?"

"No, the wolf scratched me. And scarred me."

"Oh." I release a held breath. "I thought you were going to say…"

"But I did try to open them up."

"You…you mean…you tried to kill yourself?"

"I did a horrible job." Arnold smirks, as if it's not that serious. "But it was enough for my parents to see *some* of the truth."

I swallow hard. This can't be real. I can't be hearing this. Arnold, so happy and sweet, trying to kill himself? The thought makes me want to scream at him. How dare he even think of taking away his precious life? Doesn't he know how important he is? How much he means to me?

And then I have to remember that he's speaking in the past tense. This all happened before I met him. I take a deep breath to cast away my initial reaction of disgust. I, of all people, should be able to relate and sympathize. There were times in the hospital I felt like giving up. There were even times afterward I felt it too. The desire for everything to end.

"I'm so sorry," I finally say. "That's so sad. No one reached out? None of your friends came to see you?"

He shakes his head.

"How long ago was this?"

"It happened a few days after Christmas. I spent a week in a mental hospital to test out any other possible illnesses, but it just came down to clinical depression. Which they prescribed another fucking pill for." Arnold rolls his eyes. "It was a shit show, living in Santa Cruz, with all my old friends wondering what the hell happened to me. How I could go from seemingly normal to stoner to suicidal in just a few years. I refused any kind of therapy, so my parents started looking for ways just to leave it all behind, start over fresh. That led us here. And so far, I'm okay with their decision. Everyone thinks California is this great, laid-back place where everyone is happy and high all the time, but it's not."

"So, that's what you meant before when you said you could relate to me. How you could understand."

"Yes. Because I've been at rock bottom before. And I don't ever want to be there again. I just want to be free and happy. And I want to have lots of fun. I want to let loose and just be myself, whatever that may be."

"Let loose. Yeah, I like that idea of letting loose. You know, we could do that together. School gets out in a few weeks. We could have a crazy fun time this summer. We could go camping or climb a mountain or…"

"Get high together?"

At first, I think he's joking. "For real?"

"Yeah."

I laugh because I still can't believe he's being serious. After all the trouble he got into with his parents? And then moving across the country for a fresh start? I don't think getting high helps one to start over. Sounds more like relapsing to me. Then again, I talk to imaginary people. Who am I to judge?

"You okay?" he asks, rubbing his fingers against my clenched hands.

I try to relax, but it's near impossible when I have a truckload of questions running through my head. "I thought you…you mean you still do that? Get high?"

"I haven't. Not since last summer." Phew, now I can breathe again. "It's different here in Maryland. You guys are kind of uptight about it. The citations are worse if you're underage and get caught, but at least you've legalized medical marijuana."

I shake my head, the panic button pressed again. "I don't know if doing any kind of drugs like that would be good for me. Combined with my medication. Combined with your medication? Are you only on Adderall?"

"And Lexapro. It's an antidepressant. I don't like it. I still need to be able to enjoy life, to feel something. I hate being numb. Don't you?"

"Well, yeah. It's not what I would call fun."

"Exactly! It sucks." But is being depressed and suicidal supposed to be better?

This is a lot to process. So Arnold takes two pills a day, but he gets a break from the Adderall on the weekends. What about the Lexapro?

"Have you done anything else besides marijuana?" I ask instead.

"Would you be upset if I said yes?"

"I don't know. I've never done drugs before, so I can't relate. I mean..." Breathe and speak, Rachel. It's okay. "I can't understand why you'd want to go back to it. After everything that happened to you." But I can sympathize with wanting an escape from reality.

"It was just an idea," he says, shaking his head. "How do you feel about everything I've shared? Like, you're not gonna run for the door, are you?"

"No."

"Because if you ever feel like running, you need to let me know. I'll run with you."

"Sounds like a plan."

"Good." He jumps off the bed and stretches in every possible direction. "Why don't we take a break from all this serious stuff and go make some lunch? Are you hungry?"

"Yes, starving."

Arnold doesn't want to wait for his parents to return home with groceries, so he suggests we go out to lunch. Afraid of running into classmates or worse, I offer up my kitchen. Mom is awake and groggy, but rather thrilled that Arnold is over again. She tries to make us sandwiches, but soon gets the hint that we are seventeen and prefer to do such things independently.

We sit outside to eat since there's a breeze today. Breezy reclines near a tree, making a wreath out of grass and flowers.

"One of my intangibles is nearby."

"Really?" Arnold looks side to side, thinking she's sitting next to him.

"Her name is Breezy. She's younger than us, but she's very smart."

Breezy looks up for a second, surprised, but smiles.

"Breezy," Arnold says. "What is she like? What is she into?"

"She helps me with my garden, mostly. We talk sometimes, but not as much as Larry."

"Is Larry out here too?"

"He's inside the house."

"Is he always inside the house?"

"Just about."

Arnold's eyes narrow. "Does he follow you around?"

"Sometimes. But not in a weird, stalker way. He's like a big brother to me."

"What else is he?"

"He's smart like Breezy. But he's more reserved, more artistic, and into books. We read together. He's also gay, but he hasn't had a boyfriend since middle school."

"Whoa. So they all have storylines?"

"Yes. Is that freaking you out?"

"No. It's interesting. Very interesting. Wow. Is it just them? Or do you see more people?"

"It's just them now. I used to have more, but they all disappeared after I was medicated."

"Two is good. Hi, Breezy! What's up, Larry?"

Arnold waves his arms in every direction and blows each of them a kiss. Breezy rolls her eyes. If Larry is still surveying us from the window, he's rolling his eyes, too.

The sliding door to the kitchen opens, and Mom peeks her head outside. "Rachel? Hey, sorry to bother you, but I have to run up to your grandpa's."

"Again?"

"Would you like to come this time?"

"No, I'm good."

"Are you sure? You haven't seen him in over a month."

"I'll go next time."

"Alright. Well, I won't be back until late. I'll leave some money on the counter if you want to order pizza."

"Thanks, Mom."

She lingers in the doorway, looking like she wants to hug me, but it's not something we do anymore. Physical embraces stopped after I was medicated. Melinda thinks it's because I'm still angry at my mother for sending me away. Still angry at her for the divorce. Nowadays, I don't feel much anger toward her. Just annoyance.

"So, you're not a fan of your grandfather?" Arnold asks after my mom leaves.

"No. He's not a nice person. He lives by himself at the foot of a mountain. He's been rich all his life and never once offered to help when my dad left or when my mom needed money to finish school."

"Is it just him? Or is your grandma…?"

"I never met my grandmother. She died when my mom was a teenager. And my other grandparents, I haven't seen since I was a little kid."

"Cause of your dad leaving?"

"Probably. I don't know. My mom never reaches out to them. And they never reach out to us. For all we know, they're dead."

"I'm sorry."

"It's okay."

"Do you hate them?"

"Hate." I bite into the word like I'm biting into a nail. "It's hard to hate someone. I mean, you can dislike someone, but hate just makes me think of violence. Like all the stuff you see on the news."

"You can hate someone without wishing them dead."

"I don't see it like that."

"Well, what about love? Do you understand that?"

"Are we talking about general love or a specific kind of love?"

"Love is love."

I chuckle nervously and run my teeth across my bottom lip. It's about to split again. "Love," I say, trying to feel something, anything. But Arnold asked if I understood love, not felt love.

"You okay?" Arnold asks.

"Fine. I'm just…" I take a deep breath. "Do I understand love? Well, if I'm honest, my answer is no. I don't understand love, not completely. It's not that I'm stubborn or lazy; there are certain things I just can't understand. And I feel like it's because I haven't been given much of a chance to experience things the way I ought to."

"You've been held back?"

"Yeah, emotionally, that is. And it's because of my medication. It messes with me. Kind of like what you were saying earlier; it numbs out a lot. Which is both a good and bad thing for people like me. There's a lot of bad stuff I have to keep blocked out for my protection and others. But there's a lot more that I want, that I can't have."

"Why can't you have it? What's stopping you?"

I point to my head. "My brain. The way it's wired. Centuries ago, I would have been burned at the stake or locked up forever. They didn't tolerate mental disorders back then. If you heard voices, you were considered a witch. Nowadays, it's like, okay, we'll let you live, but you have to do everything we say, or we'll lock you up. You don't have any freedom."

"Because they think we can't handle ourselves?"

"Basically."

"That's why we have to rebel sometimes if we want to experience anything."

"The only rebelling I do is skipping my meds a couple of times a week, so I have someone to talk to. And one time, I stole a hot sauce bottle from Chipotle. I don't do anything else. I haven't been to a party since middle school. And those were always supervised."

"We could have our own party. Just you and me."

"No, I wouldn't want my mom to find out."

"She wouldn't. We'll do it sometime when she's at work. Doesn't she do night shifts a lot?"

And add another thing to hide from my mother? No, thank you.

I answer his question anyway. "She does three to four twelve-hour shifts a week, and they're either noon to midnight or 6:00 to 6:00 in the morning."

"That sounds brutal."

"She makes more money working night shifts."

"We'll have to plan it for a night when she's on the 6:00 to 6:00 schedule."

"Hmm." I scratch my chin and wonder if this party is just another "idea" or is Arnold serious?

"So, what do you think?" he asks.

"What about your parents?"

"You don't have to worry about them."

"Okay. But what exactly do you mean by party? Like when I think of a high school party, I think of loud music and beer." And I do not drink anything except for water, juice, and the occasional glass of chocolate almond milk.

"We could do that." He nods his head several times. "We could do a lot of things."

"But where are we going to get the stuff to party with? My mom would notice if I took anything from the liquor cabinet."

"Don't worry about that. I'll get everything we need."

"Okay." I scratch my arms even though they're not itchy. "This makes me nervous. Like I'm freaking out just thinking about it. I mean...what if something bad were to happen? Or what if we got caught?"

"Nothing bad will happen." He rests his hands on top of mine, so I don't itch my skin off. "I promise I'll look after you. Besides, it's not like I want to throw a party right this second. It's best to wait until summer. When we get to know each other better, and we don't have to worry about school. Right?"

I rub the back of my neck. It feels like I've been stung by a mosquito. More like stung with anxiety. For the first time since kissing Arnold, I have that anxious, panicked feeling that something might go wrong. I've been told all my life that drugs are bad. Alcohol is bad. *Don't do them!* By the same people who want to force pills down my throat every day. It's a contradiction, right? Where is the fine line? Why are some drugs okay and others not?

But it's enticing to Arnold. He was happy when he ate gummies every day. But he was all alone, with no one to monitor him. Maybe if he had someone to balance him, someone he could trust, he'd find a happy place in the gray, slightly in and slightly out, just like me.

Fortunately, we let the "idea" slip by us and spend the rest of the afternoon talking more about our childhoods. I never expected it to happen this way, but everything spills out. My dad's abandonment. Getting kicked off the basketball team. Mumbling and forgetting to do things, like take a shower or comb my hair. And then my final episode, the one that got me sent away for several months.

Arnold and I face one another, not touching, but our knees are only an inch apart. He's listening to me with his whole body, just like Melinda does, minus the tremors.

"So my mom was dating this guy named Irwin. A nice guy. Attractive. Successful. All those things single moms go for. But I felt like there was something off about him. I didn't trust him. Didn't want to talk to him, ever. It could have been paranoia fueled by my intangibles, who felt the same way, but there was one intangible who wanted him gone. Like permanently.

"Her name was Mary. She was never nice to me. Always messing with me, trying to distract me. At times, I felt like she was honestly trying to get me to hurt myself or hurt someone else. She was the main reason I got kicked off the basketball team. And all the while, my mom continued to date this weirdo. I lost a lot of friends during that time as well. It was just building up.

"And then one night, Irwin came over for dinner, and Mary decided to come along too. I never told anyone at the time about the intangibles because Mary warned me not to. So I had to suffer through the whole dinner, listening to Mary's nasty side comments while trying to maintain a normal conversation with Irwin and my mom. After dinner, my mom got sick, some kind of stomach bug, so Irwin offered to clean the dishes. I was all alone with him and Mary for just a few minutes. But that's all it took for Mary to go nuts. She started screaming and throwing dishes at Irwin. I tried to stop her. I really did.

"I can't remember what happened after that. Later, my mom said I wouldn't stop throwing things until I knocked myself out by running into the wall several times. I woke up in a mental hospital, worried I had broken my head. I never saw Irwin again, which was a good thing, I guess, because I never saw Mary again either. The drugs they put me on blocked her out, blocked everyone out.

"I was there for four months. They kept me so sedated and medicated, I had no desire to do anything. I wouldn't even tie my shoes. My mom couldn't stand to see me like that, so they lowered my dosages, gave me permission to go outside and work in the garden, and when I appeared to demonstrate some normalcy, I was allowed to go home.

"But I knew I couldn't mess up. I had to be consistent with my medication, stay calm and collected. All eyes would be on me at school. Ninth grade was pretty miserable, considering I didn't finish the second half of eighth, but I was a good student, so there was no reason to hold me back. I hardly said a word, even to my teachers, but I did well in all my classes. Always got good grades. Always did what I was supposed to do. But I was very lonely."

"Depressed?" Arnold asks.

"I don't know. I just felt empty. Not really there. But there enough. It was some time during tenth grade when my mom decided it was time to give me some freedom, as she called it. Meaning she wasn't going to watch me take my pill every day. I could be trusted to do it on my own. And I did for a while, and then one day I forgot, and Larry came back as this strange shadow. He didn't speak to me, not at first. It wasn't until the second day, when I skipped again, that he came into full view and spoke to me. We had such a good conversation, I wanted to skip again, but even Larry, as much as he wanted to see me too, warned me not to skip too much. So I waited a few days, skipped again, and so forth. Breezy came back eventually, but no one else. And it's been like that, on and off, until now."

"Are you worried what might happen if you ever truly go off?"

"Yes. I worry a lot about that. I worry about Mary coming back and doing something awful. When the doctors asked me why I attacked Irwin, I said I didn't. I said that Mary did it. It was the worst possible answer I could have given. Because when your imaginary friends start controlling you, then you become a danger to yourself and others. I can't risk going there."

"But you risk a little for Larry and Breezy?"

"Yes, but I trust them. They're my friends."

"Hmm." Arnold scratches his chin. "This Mary sounds like a real bitch."

"Big time."

"And you never got a chance to stand up to her?"

I blink about a dozen times. Is he for real? You don't just fight demonic hallucinations. My best line of defense with Mary is to ignore her, so she can't control me. That's what I learned in therapy anyway.

"What do you mean?" I ask.

"Push her back yourself. She's there for a reason. You just have to figure out why, and only then can you defeat her."

"What makes you think that? You don't know her. She could just be evil."

"She can't be evil because that would make you evil. Everything you perceive outside the real world, it's a part of you. A part of your mind. Your imagination."

I huff and turn away from him. "You sound like my therapist."

"I know a lot about this stuff." He rubs his hand against my knee, and while I enjoyed his touch earlier, now I'm just annoyed.

"You don't know schizophrenia." I wiggle away from him and fold my arms across my knees. "Not like I do." He couldn't even remember the term when we were talking about the Russell Crowe movie.

"I'm just trying to show you a different perspective. I'm not claiming to be an expert. And I'm not trying to be your therapist. I don't like therapists at all. I'm a little more unorthodox when it comes to treating the most important organ of the body."

"I just..." I exhale like I'm trying to blow out a hundred birthday candles. "On a scale of one to ten, schizophrenia is like an eleven."

"You can't use a scale to measure someone's state of mind. It's too complex. I could say what I went through felt like an eleven, but it's not the same. It's personal. You should know that."

"I do know. I just..." I bite my tongue, catching myself before I say something ignorant, unclear, or downright insensitive. Really, I'm just exhausted and need a break from the conversation. I stand and pace across the lawn. Breezy jumps out of the way, feeling my animosity. She doesn't like it when people are upset.

"Are you okay?" Arnold asks, following me, but maintaining some distance. "Are you angry or something?"

"I'm not angry. I'm just tired. We've been talking nonstop for hours." I try to steady my breathing, so I don't sound like I'm hyperventilating. "I haven't had any time to think about all this."

"Okay. I get it. I'm sorry." He takes one step back, his eyes lingering toward his bedroom window. "Maybe I should just go home now and give you some space."

I don't want him to feel like I'm pushing him away, but I feel the need to get away from him. Our mental conditions can't be measured, true, but can they be compatible with one another? Are we going to butt heads too often? And if so, will that ruin our relationship? Or will we learn to compromise?

Arnold turns around. His parents are home. Mrs. Begay pulls four shopping bags from the trunk while Mr. Begay holds a single can of Diet something. She waves for us to come over, but I feel a pounding in the front of my head. The start of a migraine. Too much sun or anxiety?

"I should go," he says. "Are you okay if I leave?"

"I'm fine." I walk toward the kitchen, grabbing our empty lunch plates along the way. "I just need to lie down for a bit." I linger in the doorway. "Will you call me later? Or text me?"

"Sure. I can do that." He places a hand on my shoulder. "Bye."

I look into his eyes and try to smile, but all I see is the same sadness I saw the first day we met outside the principal's office. Today, he reached out to me and shared some of his sadness, but I'm not sure if I reciprocated as well as I should have. I'm not even sure if he even likes me anymore. I'm not sure of anything right now.

Maybe I just need to take a nap. Or check my reality. My unreality. Whatever this is.

ten

I SLEEP AWAY the rest of the afternoon, thankfully bypassing a migraine. For dinner, I make a salad instead of ordering pizza. After an extra-hot bath, I put on my comfiest robe and lounge with Larry on my creaky bed. I stare at the ceiling and notice the tiny imperfections, the baby cracks. Larry is onto another book, *War and Peace*, which is surprising since we don't like that one. We don't say much to each other. I'm not mad at him anymore, but he knows I'm overwhelmed in thoughts, so he gives me space to think.

I suppose the only real question I need to answer is, not what Arnold wants, but what do *I* want? *As the main character, you should always make sure you're taken care of first. If you're not happy, how can those you love be happy?* While I didn't agree with him at the time, I'm starting to understand why it's so important. If I don't know who I am, I'll never be able to connect with Arnold. I'll never be able to feel for him truly. Because I'll be too caught up in myself. And I've been caught up in my world for way too long. It's time to face the truth. Or at least some of it.

What do I want?

What does anyone want in life?

I want to play basketball again. I want to get my driver's license. I want to see the ocean again. I want to climb mountains. I want to have a dog again. I want people to look at me and like me for who I am. I want to be able to speak to anyone, anywhere, with confidence and maturity. I want to be in control of my life.

I'm writing a list now. After I fill up an entire page, I notice I haven't mentioned anything about love, marriage, or children. When you're a kid, your parents feed you this idea that when you grow up, you'll fall in love, get married, and have children. What they don't mention is the fourth part of that series. You'll fall in love, get married, have children, and then there's a fifty-fifty chance you'll get a divorce and be miserable for a while or possibly the rest of your life. So, "happiness" with one person is like flipping a coin. Add a mental illness and the chances are even lower.

So forget the classic happily ever after for me. I think more than anything, I want experiences. Good or bad. I just want more out of life. I want to feel more. Be more of a complete person. Do things that put me outside my comfort zone. Make me go beyond the shore, like Moana. She never found any answers stuck on one island.

I look over at Larry, gazing out the bay window with his book folded over his chest. Arnold's curtains are shut, so there's not much of a view. I fold my list in half and tuck it between the books on my nightstand.

Larry continues to stare so nostalgically it almost makes me sad. He's usually so chipper and vibrant. But my mood isn't radiating much light to his persona.

"You never go anywhere," I say. "You're just here all the time. And Breezy never leaves the backyard."

He sighs and shrugs his shoulders. "This is where I belong. I only thrive when I'm with you. You're my battery."

"That makes it sound like you feed off me."

"Rae-Rae, you feed off me too. You gravitate to me whenever you need someone."

"Well, what's going to happen when I'm older? When I move out? Are you going to stay here, or will you come with me?"

"I don't know. I really don't know."

"You don't know because I don't know. Because I'm not certain if I'll ever leave home. You cling. You cling to what's comfortable. Home is comfortable. The outside world is not."

Larry raises his eyebrows, then softens them. "I'm sorry you feel that way."

"Don't worry about it. It's my burden, not yours. You just keep being you. And I'll keep being me. Okay?"

"Okay, Rae-Rae." He smiles with his eyes. "Sounds like you've got it all figured out."

"Not entirely, but it's a work in progress." I sit up and stretch, ready to get on with the day. But when I place my hand on top of Larry's, it phases through again. I try once more, but the third time isn't always the charm.

Arnold and I don't see each other on Sunday. He has to go with his parents to a Cherokee festival in DC, followed by dinner and who knows what else. I spend the day at home, working on my garden with Breezy or watching Netflix with Larry. Mom's sleep schedule is always a mess, so she doesn't get around to doing anything until late afternoon. We end up ordering that pizza.

"So, are you and Arnold a couple now?" she asks as we eat at the kitchen table.

There goes my appetite again. "Is that okay?"

"It's surprising."

"Why?"

"You've only known each other for a little over a week."

"So. We like each other. Why wait?"

"No, you're right. If you like someone and want to be with them, it'll happen if it's meant to happen, no matter the timing. I just want you to take things slow with him."

I rip the pepperoni off my slice of pizza. "Mom, you don't have any control over that."

She swallows hard and forces a smile, but the annoyance is visible behind her eyes. Mom never likes it when I use the word "control." Probably because it gives her flashbacks of my dad yelling at her. *You're a control freak!*

She calmly refutes, "I can control whether you see him or not."

I pull the cheese off my pizza. "You don't trust me?"

"I don't know if I trust him. He could be way more experienced than you, have different expectations, and make you do things you're not ready for."

"Not all guys are like that."

She sighs heavily. "How does he feel about you having schizophrenia? Did you even tell him yet?"

"Yes. He knows. And he's very accepting and understanding."

"I'm glad to hear that. But I hope he's encouraging of your recovery."

"My recovery?" I drop the pizza; it's a mutilated mess now. "I can't recover from this. I don't know why you can't get that. You're a freaking doctor! I'm sorry, Mom, but I'm not going to recover, get married, and pop out grandkids for you. I'm not. And I know that sucks for you. But it sucks even more for me. Because I don't get a choice. Even if I wanted to settle down with someone and have kids, every doctor would tell me no, you can't have kids when you're on antipsychotics. It's too dangerous. And no freaking adoption agency would allow a schizophrenic woman with an assault record to adopt a child, even if her husband is perfect."

"Rachel, you don't have an assault record. Irwin did not press—"

"It's just not going to happen!" I pound my fists against the table, knocking over the pepper shaker this time. "I can't get a new brain. They can't replace the wiring like they do with cars and computers. This is for life!"

"It doesn't have to be." She grabs the salt and pepper shakers, always the protector of those cheap commodities. "We caught it when you were a child. All your symptoms could go away. You just have to be consistent with your medication. And when you see the others, you have to block them out. You must, Rachel. They're not real. They're not going to hold you when you're scared or lonely. And they can't make you happy. They can't give you love."

I wipe the pizza grease off my fingers before rubbing my forehead. "Why does it always have to be about love? I don't see you actively looking for love."

"I have tried. I tried very hard, but it's difficult now."

"Because you're scared I might go crazy if you date anyone?"

"No, it's not that."

"Yes, it is. And I'm sorry. I'm sorry that your life sucks because of me!"

"My life does not suck."

"Yes, it does. You work long hours. You never get to do anything fun. Your idea of going away is visiting grandpa on the weekends. You never go on vacation. You never want to do anything anymore."

"I have to consider what's best for you."

"Not all the time. Don't you think you deserve some time off? A chance to relax or go on vacation?"

"You remember what happened the last time we went on vacation."

"That was a long time ago. What about *now?*"

"You haven't expressed any desire to go on vacation. Is there somewhere you want to go? If so, you have to tell me. I'm not a mind reader."

"I don't know where I want to go. Half the time, I'm not even sure where I am. If this life is even what I want."

Her eyes narrow. "What are you saying?"

I take a deep breath and think about my list of goals, how half of them Mom would disapprove of, especially the dog one. Then I remember what Arnold said about freedom…*we have to rebel sometimes if we want to experience anything.* But why does it have to be that extreme? Why do I need permission to dive off the deep end? Why is the deep end so taboo? I don't understand the concern as long as there's water to jump into and not an empty pool.

I clasp my hands together and lower my volume so I'm not yelling. "I'm saying that I need more in life than just comfort and safety. I need to experience things. I need a chance to figure out who I am. And you need that too."

"I had my chance."

"Mom, you can't just—"

"Have you talked about any of this with Melinda?"

"No."

"Arnold?"

"Yeah, we've been talking. A lot."

"Rachel, he's from California. They do things differently over there. He's not used to the culture here."

"Don't say it like that. You sound prejudiced now."

"I'm not being prejudiced. This is the first boy you've gotten to know. He doesn't have to be the last boy you get to know. You know, there are other people you can talk to."

"Why can't I just be happy with Arnold?"

"I'm not saying that you should break up with him. I just don't want you influenced to do something just because some boy has your heart now."

"My heart?" I laugh. "Definitely not."

"Well, maybe you should talk to Melinda about this when you see her tomorrow. And maybe I should go over and talk to Arnold's parents."

"What?" I nearly jump out of my seat. "Why do you need to talk to them?"

"To get to know them better. To get to know Arnold better."

Oh, hell no. Knowing my mother, she'll ask for Arnold's medical records. Why does she always have to pry? After everything we've been through, she still doesn't trust me? I've stayed in school. I've pushed through AP classes. Unless she's against interracial dating. But she marched in the DC Pride Parade last year. The woman worships the Obamas. If anything, she should be worried about me dating a white guy, a loser like her ex-husband.

"No," I say. "I don't want you going over there to collect data so you can cultivate a reason for why we shouldn't be dating."

"I never said that."

I throw my hands up. "You've been *begging* me to make friends."

"Yes, to make friends. I didn't think you would skip over making friends to having a boyfriend."

"Arnold is my friend, too. And he's a good person. And you should trust that I have good judgment about him. And that there's nothing to worry about."

"I didn't mean to—"

"You did. Admit it."

She puffs out a plethora of air. "Okay. Fine. I admit it. I jump to conclusions too quickly. You know that. And I can be judging. But I am also human, just like you, and I make mistakes. So just promise me, if you make a mistake with him, don't feel like you have to keep it a secret. I want you to be able to open up to me, to trust me. Like you used to when you were…"

"When I was normal?"

"When you were a little girl."

Now I understand. Mommy's little girl is all grown up, and Mommy can't handle it. Is that what this is all about? Why couldn't she just say that from the start? Instead, she puts me through an emotional roller coaster. And she wonders why I can't trust her completely?

Then again, trust is a two-way thing. If I don't trust her, how can I ever expect her to trust me? That's the static reality of our relationship. We won't change for each other. It sucks. It's stupid. And it saddens me. But do I dare tell my mother that?

I brush it off my shoulder and take the typical teen route instead. "Hate to break it to you, but I'm not a little girl anymore." I sigh and lean back into my chair. I pinch my eyes shut and focus on a brick wall, anything to get away from these negative thoughts.

"Rachel, honey?" Her voice cracks. "Rachel?"

I open my eyes and sit up straight. "I'm fine."

Even when my mother is on the verge of tears, she just lifts her head high and finds an excuse to go into the kitchen for more iced tea, even though her glass is nearly full.

"Are you done eating?" Mom asks.

"I'm fat." I toss her my crust.

"You're not fat."

"Yeah, right." I roll my eyes and lay my hands across the table. "Look, can we just agree to disagree that it's my decision to be with Arnold and mine alone? If I can't have this chance, if I can't have the freedom to experience a relationship on my own, then what shot do I have at a normal life?"

"I can't even ask questions?"

"Not like you just did."

"Alright. I'll tone it down and back off a bit. As long as he treats you right and you're happy, then I suppose I should keep my distance. A healthy one."

"Exactly."

"But if he ever hurts you, you can tell me. So I can go kick his little butt." Her lips veer to one side, suggesting a smile. I finally let go of my frown.

"Don't kick too hard."

And with that, we finish our meal together, splitting a slice of pizza, so we don't feel any guilt for overeating.

117

eleven

I DREADED last Monday so much, I avoided it altogether. This Monday, I'm thinking about skipping again. Because I'm not sure how Arnold will act toward me around other students. What if he ignores me? What if everything that happened over the weekend was just his way of reaching into my pants so he could brag about it to people like Tommy and Ale? Or what if...?

And there I go again, jumping to crazy conclusions. Always assuming the worst is going to happen. No amount of drugs or counseling can suppress the paranoia. It takes control when it wants to, and only I can calm myself down. Deep breaths and positive thinking. That's all I can do.

Larry assists with my makeup before I take my medication. I don't want to look like crap today. I want to look poised and presentable, just like Arnold's mom, so I choose to wear a knee-length skirt and a sleeveless green blouse. Then I realize how overdressed other students might find me, so I swap the skirt for jean shorts. My legs could use some toning, and with Arnold's help, I could lift weights and have an athletic body again.

Mom is working the noon to midnight shift, so she offers to drive me to school. I tell her no. I want to walk with Arnold. But from the kitchen window, I see Arnold getting a ride to school with his mom, so I change my mind and end up riding with my mom.

"You're quiet today," she says and notes my rigid pose. "You look nervous. Are you worried about something?"

"No."

"Is it Arnold?"

"Why do you…" I shake my head. "Okay, fine, I'm nervous about seeing him in school today. It could be awkward. People might talk."

"Some people might be happy for you. Did you ever think of that?"

She pulls her SUV directly behind Mrs. Begay's convertible. Oh great. We're all going to get out of the car at the same time. I take a deep breath and remind myself that I am safe with Arnold.

"There he is," Mom says. "Now, you go right up to him with your head held high. And don't forget to go to your therapy appointment this afternoon."

"Thanks, Mom."

Arnold gets out first. He's dressed in jeans and a black T-shirt. His hair is combed to one side to cover his scars, and the veins in his arms seem to bulge today as if he just did a thousand push-ups. He turns around and waves for me to get out. I bite my lip, tongue, and the inside of my mouth. It's eighty degrees with a breeze, but it feels like we're standing next to a volcano. My hands are so sweaty. What if he wants to hold my hand?

I take my time getting out of the car, grabbing my backpack, and making sure my shorts are pulled down low enough that nothing hangs out. Once I'm securely outside the vehicle, Mom drives away. Mrs. Begay drives away. It's just me and Arnold now.

As he walks toward me, the wind wafts the smell of his cologne right up my nose. It feels like a head rush. I sway forward, but Arnold thinks I'm coming in for a hug.

"Hey," he says, catching me. "Good morning."

We hug. Quickly. And then I pull back. "Hi. Good morning."

"How are you?"

"I'm fine. How are you? How was the festival?"

"Well, my parents loved it."

My eyes are glued to my shoelaces. One of them isn't tied completely. I could bend down and use that as an excuse to avoid eye contact, but then Arnold does something unexpected. He reaches down and ties them for me. When he looks up, we make eye contact, and I release my held breath. He smiles and reaches into his back pocket. As he stands, he pulls out a Moana keychain.

Instantly, all feelings of uncertainty disappear. My eyes are all over him, and I feel satisfaction, relief, and comfort knowing everything that happened over the weekend was real and that Arnold has no intention of ignoring me today.

"I got this at the festival yesterday. Moana is more of a Pacific Islander, but I guess some people don't know the difference."

"Thank you. I really like it."

He helps me to attach it to my house key since I'm too jittery to do it. Now comes the part where we should go inside, so we avoid being late. We don't have any classes together, but I could sit with him during lunch. But if he's made friends, I might be with other people too. Which is totally normal, but totally not what I'm used to.

"You look terrified," he says.

"Nervous."

"To be seen with me?"

"A little."

"I don't embarrass you, do I?"

"I'm worried I'll embarrass *you*."

"*Rachel.*"

"I'm sorry. Not just for that, but for Saturday too. If I hurt your feelings, if I wasn't sympathetic enough, I…"

"Rachel, it's okay. It was a lot of stuff for you to hear, and I think you did a kick ass job."

"Really?"

"Absolutely."

I smile. "I'm still nervous."

"It's okay. Just take my hand. And don't let go until I do."

The first walk always makes a statement. Everyone looks at you, immediately making the connection that you're either dating or on the verge of dating. Some will whisper, anxious to find out more, while some people don't care at all. I've always been a part of the "I don't care" group. It feels weird being on the other side now. Weird, but satisfying.

Arnold squeezes my hand as we walk up the stairs and into the building. It's a big deal, holding hands. But after it's all over and Arnold and I part ways to go to class, I don't feel stressed about it anymore. He didn't try to kiss or hug me in front of anyone, just held my hand because he knew that's all I would be able to handle today. I'm thankful for that. And thankful I stopped sweating.

———

School is a waste of time if you're in any AP classes. The seniors are gone, and exams are over, so we get to watch "educational" movies and play card games. Or if you're social, chat and sign yearbooks.

During fourth period, Tommy sits next to me while I'm playing Solitaire. Every part of my body tenses, so much that the card I'm holding starts to bend. Tommy hasn't talked to me in years. I think the last time we spoke was in Spanish class in seventh grade. And it wasn't even in English. I asked Tommy, "Where is the bathroom?" and Tommy answered, "*Al lado de tu mamá,*" which means "next to your mom."

"*Hola,*" he says as if he could read my memories.

I nod my head and continue to play, first unfolding the bent card.

"How are you?" he asks.

"Fine."

"Do you have any Memorial Day plans?"

I shrug my shoulders.

"Nothing planned with Arnold?"

Another card starts to bend.

"Arnold says you two are together now. And that you talk to him a lot. Which seems kind of hard to believe since you never say a word at school unless you're talking to a teacher. But Arnold seems like a cool guy, so I don't think he's lying."

"Yes." I restack the cards; I'm done playing. "Arnold and I talk a lot."

"Well, there she is." Tommy smiles and runs his hands through his curly blond hair. I don't think he ever combs his hair or washes it that often. "It's nice to hear your voice again."

"Is there something you want?"

"Just wanted to talk to you. You've been idle awhile."

"I wonder why."

"Me too." Not really, says his body language. "But I was thinking maybe we should all hang out together. You, me, Arnold, and my brother."

"Define 'hang out'."

"Uh, what normal people do? Eat food, listen to music. We have a pool at our house. Do you remember?"

"Yes."

"Maybe you should come over and swim."

"Only if Arnold comes too."

"Well, duh, of course."

The bell rings. For that, I am grateful. It's lunchtime, and I can sit next to Arnold, instead of mophead Tommy, who smells like Dr. Pepper and cheap deodorant. His proposal to hang out isn't entirely out of left field. He is friends with Arnold now, so naturally, he would want to become friends with Arnold's girlfriend, even though she's been on mute for three years.

It just seems odd that Arnold hasn't said anything about his new friends or mentioned the possibility of us all hanging out together. I thought Arnold wanted to let loose with me, and only me. Since I always have "friends" around at home, it would make sense for Arnold to have friends too. At least with Tommy and Ale, we can all see one another.

As I walk to the cafeteria, searching for Arnold, the fire alarm goes off. Despite numerous drills since kindergarten, it's complete chaos. Everyone is in the hallway all at once, so it's a push-and-shove battle to get outside. Some people are screaming, and some people are laughing. Just get outside and shut up. That's what you're supposed to do during a fire drill.

As I scuffle down the hall, I feel like someone is poking me in the back with their finger or the end of a pencil, just to be cruel. I wait until a few more people pass before turning around.

I face Mary.

I stop dead in my tracks while the rest of the student body pushes by without delay. The hall clears up around us. It's just me and her.

She looks like a ghost with her porcelain white skin and dark eyes. She covers her mouth with one hand and points to the ground several times. The second I look down, Mary is gone, and the hallway is billowing with smoke.

This isn't a drill. There's an actual fire somewhere in the building.

It smells sulfuric, like burning wires, so my immediate guess is something caught fire in the computer lab, which is only a few classrooms away.

I drop to my knees and start to crawl. I'm safer close to the ground, but I continue to panic. What if I don't make it out in time? Or what if none of this is real? I could be hallucinating that the building is on fire, and if anyone were to see me right now, they would think I had gone mad again.

But I took my pill today. I took my pill, and I *still* saw Mary. What the hell is going on?

I can't be hallucinating this much all at once. That burning metallic smell is toxic and real. There's also a tangible nearby. Another student, a girl, lying unconscious on the floor. Her forehead is bleeding. She must've slipped or gotten pushed over by the crowd. I hear sirens in the distance. The fire department is on their way, but I'm not positive they'll make it in time to save us both. The sprinklers will eventually kick on, right? Or wait, am I in the old part of the building where there are no sprinklers?

Stop overthinking and do something. The girl is wearing a scarf, so I wrap it around her head, grab her by both arms, and start to drag her. I can't see where I'm going, but I know this hallway leads to an exit. I just don't know how much further I have to walk.

I hear an awful blast from the computer lab, followed by a ringing sound in my eardrums. It feels like my skull is vibrating. Then comes a muted yell from a teacher outside. He sees us struggling down the hall and calls for help. Idiot, why don't you come inside and help us first? It's too late to wait for backup. I have to hold my breath now. I can't take the smoke. My throat and lungs are burning.

Someone sprints inside the building. It's not the scared teacher, but Arnold. He grabs the unconscious girl and hoists her over his shoulder. With one arm holding her up, he uses his other arm to guide me out the door. I close my eyes and lean into him. He has to drag me across the pavement. I pass out as soon as my feet touch the grass.

A white room. A bright, white room.

Propped up on a hard, uneven bed with a railing, I look for the restraints, but there are none. Not this time. My hands are twisted up with tubes, and there's a Darth Vader mask stuck to my face.

I didn't expect to end up in the hospital so soon, but at least I'm surrounded by balloons, flowers, and familiar faces. Mom is to my right, still in her scrubs, smiling and gently tapping my leg. Dr. Lewis is on the other side of the bed, checking my vitals.

A paralyzed fear takes over me. I'm convinced I am badly burned, and that explains why I'm incapable of moving. I try to speak, but nothing comes out. How bad am I? Somebody say something! All I can hear is that faint buzzing noise.

"It's alright, Rachel," Dr. Lewis says. "You're just being treated for smoke inhalation. Nothing else is wrong. You may feel some numbness because we gave you a sedative along with the antibiotics."

"Rachel, honey?" Mom touches my arm, but I barely feel her. "Rachel, can you hear me?"

Her voice sounds faint, as if it's trapped in another dimension. I close my eyes and wait for the buzzing to go away.

I'm not sure how much time has passed when I wake up next, but I'm much more aware of my surroundings. A teenage girl sits next to me, reading a magazine. She has muscular arms, short frizzy hair, and bright green eyes. She never wears a bra and prefers men's soccer shorts over anything remotely tight fitting. I know her, obviously, but it's been years since we've seen each other. She hasn't aged a day.

"Michelle?" I croak.

She closes her magazine. "Hey, you're awake."

"What are you doing here?"

"I'm just here to say hi and see how you're doing."

"I haven't seen you since eighth grade. You used to come to my basketball games. Sometimes you would try to play."

"Yeah, I miss those days. I got lost when they took you away."

"But you're here now? I'm so confused. I took my pill today. I'm..."

She taps my forearm with the magazine. "Don't overthink it, kid. You're always overthinking."

"Is this a dream?"

"Maybe. Or they drugged you too hard this time. Whatever. You'll be okay. But I can't stay for long." She lifts a knee to her chest and scratches the back of her calf. She doesn't shave; she's a naturalist. Pure to the extreme. "But I'd like to see you again if you don't mind me dropping in sometime. How are Larry and Breezy doing?"

"Always home, but fine otherwise."

"Yeah, they never like to get out much. But you know I do. So hopefully, I'll see you around."

"Yeah, same."

"Feel better, kid." She pats me on the shoulder and heads for the door. As she leaves, a glowing white light encompasses her body before radiating out across the entire room. My eyes roll back. I feel like I'm falling off a roller coaster.

When I open my eyes, everything is still. Michelle is gone. And now Arnold is beside me, smelling like smoke and a tad greasy in the face.

"Hey." He reaches for my hand. "How are you feeling?"

"Terrible." I try to remove the oxygen mask so it's easier to talk, but he won't let me.

"You have to keep that on."

"My throat hurts."

"That's normal."

"How long have I been out?"

"About eight hours. It's nighttime."

"Did I pass out?"

"Yes, but you weren't breathing either, so I gave you CPR until the medics arrived."

"Really?"

"Yeah. You inhaled a ton of smoke."

"Jesus. What happened? What started the fire?"

"A faulty wall wire in the computer lab overheated and blew through a ton of circuits. The whole school has to be shut down since they're being ordered to rewire the building and install updated sprinklers. You were in the hallway that didn't have any sprinklers. You could've died."

He squeezes my hand, but not too hard since I have tubes connected. His eyelids are so heavy, almost swollen.

"Are you okay?" I ask.

"I'm fine. Just dirty."

"You haven't been home yet?"

"No, of course not. I had to be here to make sure you're alright. I didn't want you to wake up panicked or confused. Your mom wouldn't let me in at first, but then she softened up and let me come sit so she could get coffee and talk to Alexia's parents."

"Alexia? Why would she be talking to Alexia's parents?"

"Alexia is the girl you saved."

The heart rate monitor picks up speed. "That was Alexia? Alexia Whelan?"

"Yeah, you didn't know that?"

"I didn't know who it was. I just saw someone in trouble and tried to save her."

"You did save her."

"I didn't save her. You did."

"Rachel, she would have been left inside to die if it wasn't for you. You're being called a hero right now. It's all over the news."

"It is? That sounds awful. I don't want people talking about me."

"They didn't disclose any personal information, just said that two brave students helped to rescue an unconscious student from the building. But everyone at school knows it was us."

"Well, it's a good thing we won't have to go back to school this week."

"We won't be going back until September. Summer break has started early. They may try to send everyone some homework to do, but I doubt it'll go through when they have bigger problems to deal with. Alexia's parents are threatening to sue the school system."

"Good. I need a break from school. It's too stressful. All of this is too stressful." Damn, my throat hurts. "When can I go home?"

"Soon, baby. Soon."

He presses his lips to my forehead, and I relax against the hard bed. I don't feel much like a prisoner when my inmate is so kind and caring.

twelve

JUST LIKE FASHION, one day you're in, the next day you're out. That's how it goes for heroism nowadays. While at the hospital, Alexia's parents thank me for saving their daughter and that Alexia, once she fully recovers, would be thanking me as well. I'll believe that when I see it. Alexia hasn't shown an ounce of kindness since eighth grade. And even then, she was always pretentious.

School officials keep my identity a secret from the press, but that doesn't stop my name from getting out. It only takes one student to post my name on social media, #schoolhero. Boom. I receive several requests from news stations to conduct an interview. Mom turns them all away and threatens to call the police should they come near me.

After a two-day stay at the hospital, I'm finally allowed to go home. I relax on the couch while the rest of the world finds someone else to talk about. Across town, a college professor is convicted of child pornography. And *boom*. I'm out of the spotlight and relieved. Just the idea of people talking about me raises my paranoia.

Mom stays home with me the rest of the week. She's frantic the first day, worried the antibiotics will affect my Seroquel, even though Dr. Lewis told her not to worry. *Calm down, Beth. You've got to let her lungs heal first before you worry about her head.* And really, the antibiotics shouldn't interfere. If anything, they should help. A study done a few years ago proved that antibiotics could treat mental illnesses, as it alleviates inflammation, even in the brain. Melinda and I had a long talk about this and all possible treatment plans, but only a small percentage of drugs are sanctioned. Which means there could be a cure for schizophrenia. It just hasn't been legalized yet.

Eventually, Mom calms down and allows Arnold to come over. She stays out of our way for the most part, but she snoops whenever she can. So our conversations are pretty basic and boring, but Arnold and I make the best of it. We watch an entire season of *Doctor Who*, about fifty YouTube videos, and some new cooking shows. We attempt to bake cookies but end up burning them. Arnold "accidentally" finds my baby album, and while he and Mom look through all the embarrassing photos, I hide out with a bag of Doritos in the kitchen. I know Arnold is not the kind of guy to sit inside all day, and I can't help but adore the simplicity of our relationship. It's comforting to know he's willing to lay low until I'm all better.

By Friday, my lungs are deemed pink and happy again, and I'm able to walk up and down the stairs without feeling like an emphysema patient. Saturday, Mom finally leaves the house to get a massage, pedicure, and manicure, something she should do more than twice a year. But all that could take hours, so Arnold and I head upstairs for some much-needed alone time.

As soon as we enter my room, Arnold puts his hands around my waist and kisses me hard. I instantly fall backward onto my bed, pulling him on top of me. I run my hands through his black hair and inhale his sweet aroma. My body and mind are worn-out from all the medications, but I want to be touched. I want to be awakened.

His hands are in my hair, and my hips are pushing against his. He smiles and pulls away for a second to ask me if I'm okay. Of course, I'm okay. I'm better than okay. Then he asks if Larry is around, and I say no, not at all.

"You have to let me know if it's too much," he says.

No, it's not too much. Keep going.

Arnold kisses the space between my eyebrows and then the space between my lips and chin. He reaches one hand behind my back, and with little effort, unsnaps my bra and slides it off. Then he removes my shirt. Instinctively, I want to shield my stomach from sight, but he pushes my arms aside and presses his forehead against my chest. I take a deep breath and close my eyes.

When he removes the last of my clothing, I stay calm and

collected, even though I'm shivering from the AC blowing through the vents.

Then he removes his clothing. Crap. I should've said something before it escalated to this. Skin to skin feels like heaven, but my thoughts are in purgatory.

"Arnold?"

"Yes?"

"Are we going to have sex?"

"It's up to you."

"Do you want to have sex?"

"I do. But I'd rather wait until you're ready."

I bite my lip and look down at him. He's obviously ready, but I don't think I am. Maybe physically, but not mentally.

Arnold covers our bodies with the comforter and relaxes beside me. "It's okay, Rachel. You don't have to say anything. There's no rush."

"I'm sorry. I just…"

"Shh. Don't be sorry. Do you want me to put my clothes back on?"

"No, it's okay. I like feeling you next to me."

And just like that, everything slows down. We spend the next several minutes lying next to one another. And little by little, we touch each other. Hold each other. Play each other like musical instruments. And while it all still seems so innocent and sweet, I can't stop looking forward to what is to come. Because I know we'll do more together. Have more experiences. More pleasure. And along the way, become the people we're meant to become without anyone else telling us what to do.

Naked on the floor, listening to The Beatles, Arnold and I make a vow to one another. As long as we're together, we won't take our medications.

"It bleaches our connection," Arnold says. "We could be so much more if we just took a chance."

"But I've never gone off Seroquel for more than two days in a row."

"I just skip the weekends. But my parents don't monitor me during the school week. They haven't since we moved here. It was part of the agreement we made."

"We could still have a relapse. Both of us. You could get depressed again. Mary could come back."

"We don't know unless we try." He sits up and runs the tip of his thumb down my spine, one vertebra at a time. "We'll do a trial week. Just to be safe." He massages my lower back, applying just the right pressure. "Come on. I know you're dying on those pills. You're not completely yourself. I've seen you off. You're so much more alive."

I roll away from his warm hands and sit up, reaching for the comforter to wrap myself in. "I'm still nervous."

"You won't go crazy. I'll be with you. I won't let you slip away. I promise."

There's no telling what could happen. I could ruin my life again. Or I could finally start to live my life. What's the bigger risk? A life behind bars or a life on the edge of a mountain?

Monday is Memorial Day, but Mom is scheduled to work. Arnold and I won't see much of her this week because she has a lot of shifts to make up. Combined with Arnold's parents working ten-hour days, there's no worry of anyone disrupting our plans. By plans, we mean skipping our pills and getting naked. That's what we enjoy the most. Followed by Arnold teaching me how to bench press and me teaching Arnold how to spin a basketball on one finger. And, of course, more gardening.

Larry and Breezy are present the whole week, not interfering too much, but I don't find myself wanting to reach out to them, even though I'm off my pill. The more real they become, the less I like them. Larry's bubblegum aroma is overwhelming at times, and Breezy's overbearing presence in the garden is enough for me to scream. I'm still polite and talk to them; I don't want to hurt their feelings, especially Larry's. I've always sought his advice for major decisions, especially when it comes to my medication, and this time I excluded him completely.

But I don't let Larry's melancholy keep me from enjoying the freedoms of being medicine-free with Arnold. The most noteworthy change is my desire to move, run, and exercise. My energy levels have skyrocketed. I find myself laughing more than usual. But I also cry, especially at night when Arnold isn't around. I tell him these things, though. He assures me the feelings I'm having are just symptoms of withdrawal, and as long as they don't intensify, I should be fine.

I should. Be. Fine.

Eventually, we branch out beyond the comforts of home. Friday, Arnold and I accept an invite from Tommy and Ale to swim at their pool, but not before Arnold reassures me they're "cool" people with a chill lifestyle. Still, I'm nervous about being around them again, especially in a bathing suit.

Tommy is the more talkative and outgoing of the twins. He greets us at the fence while Ale lies back in the shallow end of the pool, smoking what looks to be a cigarette. Ale has curly blond hair like his brother, but keeps it cut very short.

"How's it going?" Tommy asks, opening the gate for us.

"Pretty sweet. Can't complain," Arnold says, stepping back to allow me to enter first.

"And how are you, Rachel? Miss Hero!"

"Don't call her that." Arnold frowns and grabs my hand.

"I'm fine," I answer.

"Hey, no worries." Tommy shuts the gate behind us. "You guys want anything to drink? We got a cooler."

"Water?" Arnold asks Tommy and me.

"Yup," Tommy says. "Help yourself."

Arnold and I walk to the cooler while Tommy does a flip off the diving board. The pool is pretty big for such a small yard. There's enough walking space around the water, but not many places to lie out. The recliners look like they haven't been cleaned in years. But the pool looks clear and reeks of chlorine, so someone must take care of it.

Ale waves to us but doesn't say anything. His eyes look incredibly bloodshot. I hope he doesn't have pink eye. That stuff is very contagious.

Arnold opens the cooler. It's full of Bud Light but buried at the bottom is a single bottle of water, which he hands to me. He looks at the beer cautiously as though waiting for my approval.

"If you want to have one, I don't mind."

"Really?" He kisses me hard. "You're amazing."

Arnold and I hydrate, well, at least I do, before we take off our clothes to swim. Arnold removes his shirt in one swift movement while I inch away my summer dress like it's made of paper. The bathing suit fits me differently than it did a few weeks ago. My butt doesn't hang out nearly as much as it did in the dressing room. Maybe I've lost weight? Or maybe all the exercising with Arnold is starting to pay off? Or maybe this is what happens when you ditch your pills and give your metabolism a chance to restart?

Arnold studies my chest, as the suit does an excellent job of highlighting that area. "You look good in red."

He wraps his arms around my waist and squeezes my butt. I love it when he does that, but not with an audience. I clear my throat and gently remove his hands. He smiles sweetly and walks backward into the pool, making a ridiculous splash.

My eyes linger on the diving board. The deep end is my favorite place to be. As a kid, I would jump off the diving board and sink as low as possible before swimming up. It drove the lifeguards crazy, but I didn't care. All is still at the bottom of the pool, and you can open your eyes and see what you want to see. Mermaids, fish, sunken treasure, maybe even a submarine. The best part is the silence. Most people hate the pressure on their ears, but not me. Right then, that should have been a clue something was off about my brain. But kids do weird stuff all the time, so it's not always clear if it's a mental disorder or just their imaginations at work.

Arnold and Tommy talk about a concert coming up in a month. Ale still looks out of it. While no one is watching, I tiptoe to the diving board and prepare myself for a simple drop. I walk to the end of the board, squeeze my legs together, and hop off the edge.

I hold my core tight and sink low. The pool is only eight feet deep, but it's enough for me to find that special place down below. When my feet touch the bottom, I use my arms to keep my body from floating upward. I open my eyes and look around, noting Arnold's and Tommy's legs on the other side of the pool. I see a quarter near my foot. Hello, George Washington.

When I spin around, I see Michelle. I'm not startled since she often used to swim with me. She smiles and waves before going back to the surface. I follow her and gasp for air when I reach the top.

"You okay?" Arnold calls. "You were down there for pretty long."

I give him the thumbs-up before turning around to find Michelle. To my disappointment, she's gone. It's not unusual for her. She comes and goes as she pleases. Always the most adventurous of the intangibles. Distracting during basketball games, but kind at heart. I'm glad she's back. I just wish I could get her to stick around for longer.

I swim to Arnold, and he instinctively puts his arms around me and holds me in his lap while he continues his conversation with Tommy.

"So, it's the Fourth of July weekend?" Arnold asks. "Are there still tickets available?"

"It's sold out. But a buddy of mine bought a bunch, so I might be able to get some from him."

"Sweet. Rachel, do you want to go to a punk rock concert? The lineup is amazing, and the opening act is a Sex Pistols tribute band."

"I don't know any of their music, but okay."

"For real?" Tommy exclaims. He turns to his brother. "Hey, asshole, put on some Sex Pistols for Rachel. Put on 'God Save the Queen.'"

A waterproof Bluetooth speaker floats next to Ale. He turns up the volume and puts on the song for us. This kind of music isn't what I'm used to listening to. I prefer the quiet tracks of The Beatles and Simon and Garfunkel. But it has a decent beat. I smile and nod along with the tune.

"You like it?" Tommy asks.

"Yeah, it's cool. Where are they from? They sound English."

"London."

"We should go," Arnold says.

"Sweet." Tommy flips onto his backside, allowing the sun to penetrate his pale white chest. "I'll get four tickets. And some pregame stuff. We should meet up beforehand and all pitch in for an Uber since Metro sucks."

"Sounds good," Arnold says. "Rachel?"

"Sounds good to me. I just have to check with my mom to make sure it's alright."

"That sucks you have to check in like that," Tommy says. "My dad never asks us what we're doing. Except for that one time, Ale tried jumping off the roof into the pool. That was like the only time in the last decade." Tommy turns over and swims for the stairs. "Hey, you all want anything to smoke?"

"No, I'm good," Arnold says. "Only edibles for me."

"Oh, right, you said in Santa Cruz you and your friends did gummies?"

"Yeah, it was the only way to go unnoticed. No smell."

"Right. Well, you know I could get some here. They just cost more. But if you're willing to pay, I can talk to my guy."

"For real?" Arnold's eyes are beaming now. "Yeah, it'd be cool to get some. I wasn't sure who to go through or what's the norm around here."

Tommy grabs a beer from the cooler. "The norm is only to have one or two connections, and that's it, especially since you're under twenty-one. Don't ever give anyone your full name, your address, your email. Nothing. Have a regular meet-up spot in a normal place, not an alley or a playground set. The idiot druggies go there, and the cops are readily on them. Fortunately, the cops aren't as hard-pressed these days to find your average pothead since it's been decriminalized and a lot of people do medical marijuana, which by the way, when you're twenty-one, you should totally apply for a green card."

"I definitely will."

"Cool. So as long as you keep to those rules, you're in the clear and pretty much free to do whatever you want. Just be smart about it." He looks at me with a lopsided grin. "What about you, Rachel? You want in?"

"Well, I already hallucinate, so I don't think I need anything else to help with that."

Tommy bursts out laughing. Even Ale laughs, his hands smacking the water with every snort. And then Arnold joins in. Apparently, what I said was hilarious, or maybe it was just my nonchalant delivery.

"Rachel, weed doesn't make you hallucinate," Tommy says. "It just makes you feel good. Makes you feel relaxed and happy."

"That's it?"

"Yeah, it's not gonna make you hallucinate unless you were to take a shit ton of it. Or maybe have it laced with something else. Or just do something more hardcore."

"Oh, okay. But doesn't it make you dumb and stupid? Don't you forget things?"

"Uh, I still passed eleventh grade. Only got one C all year. But I don't do it when I go to school. I save it for the weekends and summer break."

I look up at Arnold and remember what he said before, about going to school every day high. I never got around to asking him about his grades. But it wouldn't matter now because it's summer and our grades are set. Our parents work a lot, so they're out of the way. And we're not taking our pills anymore, so we don't have to worry about drugs overlapping each other and causing health problems. Then again, the whole point of not taking our medications was not to let anything or anyone get in the way of our connection. To be totally ourselves. But Arnold has claimed numerous times before that the gummies are a stimulant and would bring us closer together.

"But do share with us some of your hallucinations," Tommy says, distracting me from my worried thoughts. "I'd be down for hearing."

"Yeah," Ale says, suddenly interested in the conversation. "Share."

"Are you actually interested or just want another laugh?"

"No, we're totally interested," Tommy says. "Tell us."

"Okay...well, another person was swimming in the pool with us just a minute ago."

"Whoa, really?"

Ale spins around, trying to find the imaginary person.

"Don't mind him. He's high right now," Tommy says. "Tell us more about this person."

"Uh, well, she has short curly brown hair, kind of frizzy when it's dry. She's tall and thin, and she likes to swim."

"Was she swimming naked?"

"No, she had a bathing suit on."

"Where is she now?"

"I don't know. She comes and goes."

"I want to meet her!" Ale exclaims. "Bring her back, Rachel."

We all laugh. "Sorry, can't," I say. "It doesn't work that way."

"Rachel, you don't need to tell them more," Arnold says, giving my thigh a good squeeze. "It's none of their business."

"We mean no harm," Tommy says. "We just want to get to know Rachel so we can all be friends. Right, Ale?"

"Yeah!"

"We're not gonna go around sharing your business with anyone, either. What happens here stays here. We appreciate you doing the same."

Arnold smirks, but nods his head. I'm not sure if he's pleased with Tommy's sudden interest in my imaginary friends. It could be a recipe for disaster, but I don't see the harm as long as everyone is chill and happy.

Arnold and I don't stay for much longer. I burn easily, even with suntan lotion on. Tommy offers up the inside of his house, but it smells like dirty socks and Chinese food. Tommy and Ale don't have a mother, and their dad is rarely home, so the house is always a mess. I remember that even when I was a little girl and got invited to their pool parties.

As we walk back to my house, Arnold asks, "So, are you down with everything we talked about over there?"

"You mean the concert?"

"The other stuff."

"Oh."

"It's important you tell me exactly how you're feeling."

"I feel…enlightened, I guess? I mean, if everything you said is true, then I don't see the harm. Especially since it's summer, and we agreed we were going to have fun. But we still have to be careful. It's only been a week since we've been off our meds. I'm seeing Michelle now."

"But Michelle is cool."

"She's also very distracting. She shows up whenever she wants, and she doesn't have a filter like Larry and Breezy. They know the rules. They know when to keep quiet."

"You just let me know if she becomes a problem. Right now, you seem perfectly normal. And cool with Tommy and Ale. You did great today with them."

I smile and grab hold of his hand. He kisses my palm.

"How are you feeling?" I ask.

"I'm great," he says.

"Are you sure?"

"Yeah, totally."

I want to believe him, but he was oddly overprotective at the pool. Unless that's a normal thing for boyfriends to do around other guys. Still, he seemed on edge, like at any moment he might snap.

"So, will you do it with me?" he asks.

"The…gummies?" I whisper, even though no one is nearby, minus the birds and the bees.

"Yeah?"

"Not today. And probably not tomorrow. But soon?"

He puts his arm around my shoulder and kisses my cheek. "I love how open-minded you've become."

Open-minded. That could be a dangerous word for someone like me.

thirteen

"SO, is there anything else you would like to talk about?" Melinda asks at my next therapy appointment. It's been a while since our last session, but I'm not complaining. Her office gets too warm in the summer because she insists on "natural" air flow instead of AC. Ceiling fans have nothing against Maryland humidity.

"I think we've covered everything," I say. "The fire, the hospital, and how nice it is to have a boyfriend now."

"Yes, but you haven't gone into much detail about Arnold beside his likes and interests. You mentioned you're starting to hang out with some old friends from childhood. What do you do together?"

"We chill at the pool and listen to music."

"Is that all you do?"

"When we get bored, we might go somewhere else, like the lake or a food place. We went to Chipotle yesterday."

"Do you like Tommy and Ale?"

"They're fun to be around. They seem genuinely interested in what I have to say, so that's always good."

"What made you want to become friends with them again?"

"Well, Arnold befriended them first. And I'm Arnold's girlfriend, so we hang out together. We're all friends now. Is that weird or something?"

"No, it's not weird. It's quite common for groups of people to mingle like that. I'm just curious if you ever hang out with Tommy and Ale without Arnold."

"Oh, no. I couldn't. That would be…awkward." I adjust my position on the couch, placing another pillow behind my head. I wonder how many people have sweated all over Melinda's furniture today.

"Why is it awkward?"

"I don't know. I just wouldn't know what to do without Arnold. He makes me feel at ease around other people."

"You've said similar things about Larry and Breezy. How they make you feel at ease around your mother and Mrs. Martin."

"That's true. But Larry and Breezy aren't real."

"Correct. But let's imagine if Arnold suddenly had to move far away, and you never got to see him again. Would you still want to hang out with Tommy and Ale?"

"Probably not."

"How would you feel if Arnold moved away right now?"

"I'd be upset. But I don't think he's going to be leaving anytime soon. He and his parents have only been living here a month."

"Yes, only a month now. And a lot has changed for you since. Are you not at all concerned that you may be rushing things a bit with Arnold?"

I pinch my lips together. "I wouldn't call it rushing."

"What would you call it?"

"It is what it is. It feels right to me. It's exciting. It's new and sometimes scary, but I haven't had these kinds of feelings before, and I don't want to lose them."

"Let's dive into these feelings a little more. What about Arnold? What specifically do you feel for him? Do you feel love?"

I sit up to stretch my back. It's becoming increasingly harder to find a comfortable position. I lifted with Arnold yesterday, but I feel sore in all the wrong places. It's like I worked out my brain more so than my legs.

"Rachel?"

"I don't know. I like him. I like him a lot. I have feelings for him, of affection and friendship, but I don't think I love him."

"Could you live without him?"

I bite my lip and lean my head back, so I'm looking straight at the ceiling fan. I don't like where this conversation is going today. I was having a perfect day with Larry, then Breezy, then Arnold, before having to sweat my way to Melinda's humid office. I should be at the pool, losing a shade of white.

"I don't think it's healthy to say you can't live without someone," I finally answer.

"Why is it not healthy?"

"When my dad left, my mom used to say that. She'd cry and cry and say, 'I can't live without him.' But she did live, she was just miserable for awhile, and then slowly, she picked herself up again. Finished medical school and now she's a surgeon, getting to cut people open and put them back together."

"Do you believe your mother is happy?"

"Some days. But mostly, no. She's not happy. She has to deal with me, my grandpa, the stress of work. I really think she needs a boyfriend. Or at least someone to…" I bite my tongue this time. "I really shouldn't say such things about my mother."

"You don't have to hold back. Please share."

"I think she needs to get…" I can't believe I'm saying this out loud to a tangible. "Laid."

But Melinda doesn't seem offended or offset by my remark. "When you say laid, are you referring to sexual intercourse?"

"Yes." It feels about ten degrees warmer now. The room is turning into a sauna.

"We haven't talked about this. I'm curious to know your thoughts about sex."

"I know what it is. I had health class, and my mom explained it to me. And I watch a lot of movies and read a lot of books, so…" I'm not an expert. "I know what it is."

Melinda smiles politely. "Going back to your mother. Do you think sexual intercourse is necessary for her to be happy? For anyone to be happy?"

"Not necessarily, but it helps."

"Do you say this based on something you've read or watched or by personal experience?"

"By personal experience, are you referring to Arnold?"

"Yes, or maybe something from the past you would like to share?"

"I don't think I should share that stuff with you."

"Rachel, you know everything we talk about is confidential.

Nothing you say is repeated to anyone else, not even your mother. It's only if I believe you are going to harm yourself or someone else that I am entitled to break our confidentiality."

"But your interpretation of harm could be different from my own. I mean, I believe drinking caffeine is harmful, but people drink caffeine all the time."

"Rachel, by harm, I mean the extreme of causing physical, tactile harm to yourself or someone else."

"Oh, you mean like throwing plates at people? Nope. Not doing any of that. I threw a Frisbee yesterday. Does that count?"

Melinda clears her throat and leans slightly forward. "Rachel, I do sense you are a bit annoyed with me today. I'm not sure why you feel that way."

"I'm sorry." I close my eyes for a second and remember that Melinda is a tangible I can trust. I also need to maintain my composure, or she might suspect I'm off my medicine. "I just wish I had more privacy, that's all."

"You don't have to share anything with me that you don't want to. This is your hour, not mine."

"I know. I'm just a little overheated, and we started to talk about something I'm not ready to talk about."

"I understand, Rachel. But think about what you just said. If you're not ready to talk about it, are you ready to experience it?"

I respond with silence because I don't know what to say. Sometimes I think about what I ought to say or what a normal person would say. Anything to avoid the truth because, quite frankly, I'm not sure what the truth is. I'm not sure how I feel about certain things, especially sex. But a part of feeling something is in the experience, right? Then again, I don't need to jump off a mountain to know what it's like to jump off a mountain.

Maybe Melinda is right. But Melinda is *paid* to be right. Melinda is *licensed* to be right. Just like those damn pills.

"Perhaps next time you'll share more with me?" She stands, signaling the end of our session.

"Yes, perhaps."

"And Rachel, if you want me to turn on the AC, I can. You just have to ask."

"I thought you said…" I shake my head, not bothering to revisit the past. "I'll ask next time."

I meet Arnold at his house. He's in the midst of programming something on his computer, but when I enter, huffing and puffing like I'm gonna burn the place, he stops and gives me his undivided attention.

"Are you okay?" he asks.

I make myself at home on top of his unmade bed. "Just stressed from therapy."

"Do you want to talk about it?"

"Not right now. I kind of want to forget all about it and pretend like it never happened. Is that childish?"

"Nope."

"I knew you'd say that."

"Well, you know how I feel about therapy." His grin stretches far. "I got something for us." He reaches into his back pocket and pulls out a small plastic bag full of square gummies. "You ready for one?"

"Are they from Tommy?"

"Yes."

"Where'd he get them from?"

"His source. Don't worry. It's legit. He doesn't buy from sketchy people."

Arnold lies next to me and hands me the bag. "They look so harmless," I say. "But I'm still nervous. What if I go crazy?"

"You won't. I'll be with you. Nothing bad will happen. I promise. You're going to love it."

"What time is it?"

"Four."

"My mom is on the noon to midnight shift. Will it wear off before she gets home?"

"You'll be asleep before she gets home. But yes, it'll wear off before then."

"What does it taste like?"

He opens the bag and pops one into his mouth. "It tastes like a sour gummy. It's good. Try." He takes another one out for me.

I let it sit on my tongue for a few seconds before biting into it. Sour, but good, just like Arnold said.

"Do we only take one?" I ask after swallowing.

"Definitely only one. Especially since this is your first time."

"I don't feel any different."

"It takes an hour or so to kick in."

"Okay, good. Because I need to water the garden and see if any grape tomatoes are ready to be picked."

"You could do all those things high. You'll still be functional."

"Not taking any chances." I jump off the bed, prepared to get as many tasks in as possible before the gummy kicks in.

Arnold enjoys watching me garden in my bare feet. He knows Breezy is with me because I'm talking to her openly in front of him. He doesn't mind. Sometimes he'll ask questions about what she's saying or what she's doing. Breezy seems to be a little more relaxed today, probably because the garden is growing beautifully.

Larry, on the other hand, isn't as fun to be around these days. He has an opinion about everything and isn't afraid to hold back, even in front of Arnold. Back in eighth grade, before the pills, Larry was never so bold. Then again, he had Michelle and Breezy around to do most of the talking. He also had Donovan, his boyfriend. And I was single.

Because of Larry's scrutiny, Arnold and I don't spend much time inside my house anymore. We hang at Arnold's, Tommy and Ale's, or Chipotle. I've seen Michelle a few times in passing, but she never stays for long.

We have enough tomatoes for salsa. There's leftover chicken from the night before, already cooked up, so chicken tacos it is. Since Arnold's parents are home this evening, it's best to make dinner at my house, even with Larry around.

As we're cutting up the tomatoes, I feel a strange tingly sensation in the back of my head. Everything feels like it's moving in slow-motion, even the knife. I stop what I'm doing and look at Arnold. The window light radiates a ball of red around his head. He looks like he's from another world, a god of some sort, a warrior. I feel like I'm shrinking.

143

"Hey, beautiful, how are you feeling?" Even his voice sounds heavenly, as if it's been amplified.

I cover my mouth to muffle my sudden outburst of giggles. "I'm good. But I don't think I can cut up any more tomatoes. My hands...well, look at them, Arnold! My hands are like, they're so...weird. Look at them!" I rub my hands together; the skin feels rubbery like it isn't my own.

Arnold laughs. "It's okay, baby. You're just high right now. Go sit down, and I'll finish everything in here."

"Go sit down? How can I possibly sit down?" I sit down on the couch. "Man! This couch is so comfortable. Oh, my Lord. If I had to choose one place to stay the rest of my life, it would definitely be right here on this couch. It should win an award for best couch in the world. Hell yeah! Oh...wow! That smells good, babe. Whatever you're doing in there, you keep it up."

"I'm just heating up the leftover chicken."

"Well, you're doing a great job!"

"Thanks, baby."

"You should win an award too. Best boyfriend in the world!"

"*Rae.*"

Larry is standing next to the window, drinking his latte. He looks so smug in his tucked-in collared shirt and dark blue jeans. I swear Larry drinks ten lattes a day. He must have to pee all the time. Then again, I've never seen him pee. He never has to use the restroom. He never has to shower. He never eats. He never changes his clothes.

He's like a cartoon character. All of them.

"Why are you rolling your eyes at us?" I ask.

Larry takes a large sip of his latte. He crosses one leg in front of the other as if he's posing for a photo or trying to act like he's better than us. He rolls his eyes again. "You idolize each other way too much. Do you even care how ridiculous you sound right now?"

"Larry, Larry, Larry." I laugh every time I say his name. "You need to eat a gummy with us."

"I am perfectly satisfied with my soy vanilla latte."

"Where does it even come from? I mean, don't you have to go to Starbucks to have a Starbucks latte? And if you never leave the house, then how do you always have a Starbucks latte? Do you just wish for one and boom, ya-da-ding, you have one? Is it like a magic trick? Or does Breezy go and get you one? Oh, no. That couldn't work because she doesn't leave the yard. Okay then, you must be talking to Michelle; that girl goes wherever she wants. But Michelle hates Starbucks. Hates anything commercial, so it can't be her. And we haven't seen Donovan in forever. So, am I the one getting you the Starbucks every day? I mean technically I must. My imagination, that is. My imagination must give you a latte. My imagination gives you everything, right?"

To avoid answering, Larry reapplies his bubblegum ChapStick. He takes his good, sweet time as though none of my questions matter.

"Do you ever think about Donovan?" I ask.

Larry raises an eyebrow. "I don't want to talk about him."

"Don't you miss him? I do. He was so quiet and sweet. I wish he would come back."

"No, you don't."

"You don't want Donovan back. Because he broke your heart. Aw, I remember you guys holding hands at my basketball games. You were so happy together. That's when you used to go out, Larry. You used to go out and have fun."

"I still have fun."

"No, you don't. You're just like my mom."

"If you mean sexually frustrated, then yes. But other than that, I don't hold any commonalities with your mother."

Arnold joins us in the living room with a bowl of salsa and a bag of tortilla chips. "Is everything okay? Is Larry okay?"

"Yeah, he's alright. But I think he's sad."

"Aw, how come?" Arnold asks as he sets the food on the coffee table.

"I think he wants a boyfriend, too. But he won't leave the house."

"Oh, that's too bad." Arnold looks around the room. "Hey, Larry, why don't you go out for the evening? I bet there's a nice art show you could go to or a poetry reading. Maybe you'll meet someone?"

Larry rolls his eyes yet again and takes large, calculated steps to the front door. He untucks his shirt and leaves his latte on the floor, next to the welcome mat.

"Are you going somewhere?" I ask.

"Out."

"For real?"

"Yeah, you two enjoy yourselves."

"Are you okay, Larry? I'm sorry if I made you mad."

"You're not sorry." His eyes widen for a second before narrowing in anger. I almost think he will snap and do something crazy, but Larry's words are his best weapon. "You just don't give a shit anymore. And the worst part about it all is you know you should give a shit. But you're taking the easy way out. The wrong way out and you know it."

"What? What are you talking about? What don't I give a shit about? Talk to me."

"Oh, now you're interested in talking to me again? Now you want my help? Figure it out yourself. Later."

"Larry! Come on, wait!" I charge after him, my legs like Jell-O, but he phases through the front door, and when I open it, he's gone. Vanished.

"Is he gone?" Arnold asks.

"Yeah. He's really gone." I let the door slam shut. "Wow. This is… weird." I rub my back against the door, noticing how cold it feels. "And sad."

"Don't let it get to you. Come sit back down. Relax."

It's easy to sit, hard to stand. So the couch becomes my haven yet again. I still can't believe Larry left the house. Was it building up? His desire to leave? Or did I push him out? Maybe I don't satisfy him anymore. Maybe he doesn't like Arnold after all. Or maybe he just wants to find Donovan. Maybe he just needs to feel like he belongs to someone again.

My mind is racing with ideas, and my body feels like it's in constant motion, even though I'm just lounging. Everything I touch feels more real and concrete than it usually does. My eyesight feels enhanced. The house smells better, fresher. And the salsa and chips? I moan with the utmost satisfaction when I take a whopping bite.

"I taste everything. I taste the cilantro, the onion, and the tomatoes. I can even taste the roots from the ground, the dirt it grew in. Wow. And you made it? How did you make it taste so good?"

"Anybody can make salsa."

"No, there has to be a special ingredient. Some Cherokee spice you're not telling me about."

"I'll show you some Cherokee spice."

Arnold folds himself over the back of the couch to kiss me. I feel the tiny bit of stubble on his face, something I'm not used to noticing so intensely. I taste the salsa on his lips and inhale the aroma of his sweet sweat. My senses have been fully activated. I feel so much, all at once, and I'm not overwhelmed. I'm alive.

"Are we really alone?" Arnold asks.

I nod with a roguish grin. "I don't think he's coming back tonight."

"That sounds perfect."

I'm anxious to take Arnold upstairs to my bedroom, but he insists we eat dinner first, and I'm glad we do. We wrap the leftover chicken in tortillas, smothered with salsa. I love the spicy tang of the chicken mixed with the tomatoes. We use the chips to scoop up the over-flowing pieces of salsa. I savor each bite as if the meal were sacred.

After dinner, we clean the dishes, so we don't forget later. I never like to leave messes for Mom to deal with when she comes home late. I lather my hands with soap and blow bubbles like I'm five again. Who knew chores could be so entertaining when you're high?

Rather than go straight to my bedroom, Arnold pulls me into the upstairs bathroom and turns on the shower. A small portion of my brain says no, what are you doing? But the rest of me screams *hell yeah! Go for it!*

We've been naked many times before, but it's different inside a shower. Washing can be difficult, depending on what areas you're trying to reach, but with Arnold there, he makes sure to bathe every part of my body. He takes his time as the hot water shoots down on us. I breathe deeply, feeling the heat buildup inside my chest. It makes me pant, makes me want Arnold so much more.

Arnold puts the soap down and massages my body with his robust hands, digging deep into every muscle, every opening. My legs tremble, and I start to lose my footing. Arnold wraps one arm around my waist to hold me up. He kisses the back of my neck so hard, I almost pull off the shower curtain.

That's the cue to end the shower, but not our attachment. Keeping one arm around my waist, he bends down to turn the water off. Then without a slip or fall, he hoists me out of the tub and carries me to my room, my legs wrapped around his, our pelvises pushing together. The bed squeaks when we fall into it, but there are no worries of anyone hearing. For the first time, I am certain we are alone in my house.

He's on top of me, and I'm not stopping him, but he pauses anyway. "Is this what you want?" he asks.

"Yes."

"I don't want to hurt you."

"You won't."

"I…"

I shut his lips with one finger. He doesn't say another word.

Arnold wakes me with a gentle tap across my face. I rub my eyes. He has the lights on, and it's incredibly blinding. I moan and try to pull him back into bed with me, but he's already into his shorts and seemingly in a hurry to leave.

"What's wrong?" I ask.

"It's almost midnight. I've got a strict curfew, and your mom will be home soon."

"It's that late?" I panic and throw my robe on. My body feels weird, like I'm walking on land after being on a boat for weeks. "How long have we been asleep?"

"I don't know. I lost track of time earlier. But I have to go now. I'll see you in the morning."

"Okay." I try not to show my dismay, but Arnold leaving me like this makes everything we did earlier feel insignificant and *rushed*. And while that instantly makes me think of what Melinda said, I can't allow myself to feel any ounce of regret. It was my choice. It's not like I was going to wake up to flowers in a hotel room.

Arnold grabs both of my hands and kisses them. "Are you alright? Tell me how you feel."

"I feel good. Tired, but good."

"Are you okay with what happened?"

"Yeah. I mean…I didn't think it would happen like that. But I'm glad it happened."

"I'm glad too." He glances at his phone. "Crap. I really have to go, but we should talk about this more tomorrow. I just want to make sure you're always okay, you know? I care about you so much."

I smile and kiss him once on the cheek. "I'll see you in the morning."

He kisses me back and slips out of my room. For a moment, I lay there, drifting from cloud to cloud until I root myself to the ground. I look across the room, wondering if Larry came back while we were sleeping, but I no longer feel his presence. I wonder if Larry will ever come home. I mean, what reason does he have to be here anymore when I have Arnold? Still, I feel lonely right now. I feel lonely, and I shouldn't. But I do.

The thought of losing Larry would have destroyed me a month ago. The idea of losing Larry now doesn't sound as bad. But the thought of losing Arnold?

I can't even think about that.

fourteen

EVERY DAY IS PERFECT. We wake up, wait for our parents to go to work, and then we have sex. Sometimes we take a gummy first. Sometimes we wait until after. It's different when you're high. You feel more friction, but it's more intimate and lasting when we're completely just ourselves. We take turns with whose house we go to, dependent on our parents' work schedules, but I prefer Arnold's therapeutic bed.

In the afternoons, we work out or hang with Tommy and Ale at their pool, but as the days get hotter, we visit more frequently, so much that we don't even need an invitation to show up. Arnold always has one or two beers while I drink my water. Then at night, if we're tired, we watch a movie or lie out under the stars. If we're up for an adventure, we go to Chipotle or Dairy Queen. Or we get high one more time. We never have a plan; we live spontaneously. Arnold seems happy. I haven't gone crazy. What more could we ask for?

I occasionally see Michelle when we're out, but she still doesn't say much. I haven't seen Larry since the night he walked out. And Breezy has been pretty apathetic as well. And this is me, off my medication. Maybe I am capable of being cured. Maybe I can have a normal life. So long as I have Arnold. So long as we can enjoy these highs together.

"Medical marijuana has been proven to help with so many disorders and diseases," Arnold tells me one afternoon, taking a break from his computer. I'm listening to Sex Pistols while trying on all of Arnold's concert shirts. "My ancestors used it to recover from illnesses. They even used it to make rope."

"Does it cure schizophrenia?" I ask.

"Don't know. But a lot of people with ADHD benefit from it."

"How so?"

"It helps me to focus, more so than my Adderall, without the nasty side effects."

"Even at school? It didn't affect your grades?"

"There wasn't much of a difference in my grades, except for the classes I hated. Then you saw some slippage, but not much. When I'm on Adderall, I'm focused, but I'm so depressed I don't care about school. Or anything really. So there's the Lexapro to help with that, but then I lose motivation. So it's like, what's the point? But if you take both away, I'm a wild turkey. When you add the marijuana, I can be a little spacey at first, but I'm happy, and if something interests me, I'm compelled and motivated to work on it. Like computers. I can program for hours high. But on Adderall, no way. I'd rather just go watch a movie."

"So, you're saying the drugs your doctors prescribe don't help you? Not at all?"

"If we're talking about my overall happiness, no. They don't help at all. It's different for everyone. I'm sure many people benefit from all those pills. But not me."

"You don't seem depressed. Not ever. And I've never really noticed how you have ADHD, minus the leg tremors. I never would have guessed that when we first met."

"Well, I was on my medication when we first met. And I've only been off it a few weeks now, and we've been getting high almost every day, so you wouldn't notice it unless I just stopped doing everything for a long time. Then I'd be out of control, unable to concentrate on anything, even you. I'd be running ten miles a day just to keep sane."

"And would you get sad again?"

"I don't know. My sadness…I don't want to talk about that." He plays with his bag of gummies as though tempted to take one, but we've already had our morning high.

"Does it embarrass you?"

"No."

"You know you can tell me anything. I may not always say the right things, but I'm always listening. I'm always here for you."

"I know, but this." He points to the center of his chest. "It's not something I can articulate with words. It's just something that's there. Like an extra bone in your body you have no use for, but sometimes you use it anyway."

"That's a good way to put it. That's using words."

"A metaphor."

"A *simile.*"

He smiles.

"You know it's alright if you ever feel sad, even for no reason," I say. "Sometimes, we just need to feel down."

"Not me. If I go down, I go very down. It's best just to stay high. Honestly, I never would have suggested we tank our meds if I wasn't planning to find a drug dealer."

"Wait. What?" I specifically remember the first time he suggested getting high with me. *It was just an idea,* he said after I freaked out about it. Definitely not a plan.

"I'm saying I wouldn't have been able to handle being off my meds without something else to fill the gap."

"No, the other part." I can't let him get away with this. Honesty and trust go hand in hand. "You said you planned it?"

"Not really planned it. More like, thought about it. Considered it."

"Okay…" Fair enough. "But what if I hadn't been onboard? Like what if I had never agreed to get high with you? Like wasn't the whole point of going off our meds to challenge ourselves? To see if we could survive?"

"The point was to stop feeling so numb all the time and to experience life the way we're meant to. To connect. To be present. And I have felt way more with you in just these past few weeks than in my whole life. You're my favorite high. You're my favorite everything."

When he says it like that, it makes sense. But still, I worry for his health. His happiness. More so than my sanity.

Arnold sighs and leans back in his computer chair. He motions for me to sit on his lap. I've got his favorite Sex Pistols T-shirt on. He was planning on wearing it to the concert, but I'm kind of hoping he'll just let me wear it instead.

"You're amazing," he says, running his hands across my waist. "Your body is changing. You're healthier. You have life behind your eyes. You've got muscle in your legs from all the workouts we've been doing. When I met you the very first time, I thought you looked so sad and miserable. I thought someone had been abusing you."

"Really? Wow. That sounds awful. No one has ever abused me. No one tangible, that is."

"Your intangibles aren't around as much."

"No. And the weird part is I don't even notice it half the time. I'm not even worried about Mary anymore. I think it's because I'm with real people now, and maybe that's what I needed all along. I just needed to be social again."

"You see? You're not on your medication, and you're doing better."

"Yes, but things could always change. What goes up must come down, right?"

"It doesn't have to be that way. We don't have to come down just because everyone says we do. We play by our own rules."

That's the last serious conversation Arnold and I have about our medications. The rest of the week is dedicated to pleasure and fun. Tuesday, Arnold and I go to Mattress Warehouse to figure out what bed would be perfect for my room by jumping on all the mattresses. We run out of the store when the manager threatens to call the police. Wednesday, we climb the biggest tree in the park, and Arnold hangs upside down from the highest branch while I take dozens of pictures to post all over my new Instagram account. Thursday, while Tommy and Ale are at the dentist, we sneak into their pool and have sex on the stairs. I will never do anything like that during the daylight hours again. It hurts to sit down because of the sunburn. I'm high every morning with Arnold, but he's high in the afternoon as well, claiming he burns so much energy from working out that he needs more stimulation than I do.

And then Friday rolls around, and it's the most exciting day ever. It's the punk rock concert.

Mom has to work the graveyard shift and always dreads the Fourth of July weekend because she has to deal with countless accidents. It's illegal to set off fireworks in Maryland unless you're licensed to do so. Pretty lame. All the rules and regulations we have. Just let us have fun, and if we blow ourselves up, that's our fault and no one else's.

I spend the afternoon helping her sort through old clothing to donate to Goodwill. Really, she doesn't need my help; she just needs an excuse to lecture me about the concert.

"Even though I'm working all night, you still need to be home before midnight."

"The concert only goes until eleven."

"Yes, but I'm sure there'll be all kinds of activities going on afterward, mostly illegal ones, so I would like it if you just came directly home. You all are taking an Uber still?"

"That's the plan."

"And it's just you, Arnold, and the twins?"

"Yup."

"No other girls?"

"Nope. Just us."

"It'd be nice if another girl was going."

I drop the shirt I'm folding. "Seriously?"

"What? What did I say?"

"Why can't you just be satisfied?"

"I am satisfied. I—"

"I have friends again. I have a social life again. I'm getting my life back."

She stares at my arms, still glistening with sweat from my workout with Arnold. We ran three miles today in the heat. Arnold likes to exercise immediately after our morning high. The endorphins make him happy.

"Am I ever going to be enough?" I ask.

"Sweetheart." She takes a step toward me and then immediately back, always aware of the wall I keep between us. She folds the shirt I gave up on. "I worry about you. I worry about how your mind is handling all these changes. Two months ago, you barely made eye contact with other students. And now you're going to concerts? You're not concerned about all the people, the noise, the craziness? I know it's a tribute band, but if it's anything like a real Sex Pistols show, it will be wild."

"How would you know? Did you see them when you were younger?"

"Your father took me to see them during one of their reunion tours. It was before you were born. I hated it."

"Dad liked Sex Pistols? I didn't know that."

"He got out of punk rock after you were born. He needed to grow up."

"He needed to? Or did you make him?"

She drops the shirt on the floor; it must not want to be donated. I reach down to look at the shirt. It's just a plain blue T-shirt with a sun in the middle. There's a hole in one of the armpits. Could be sewn and wearable again. Could be fixed, but she just wants to toss it.

"Anyway," she says, tying up the trash bag of clothing, minus the sun shirt. "Just be safe. That's all."

The conversation dies right there. Mom never wants to take any blame for why her husband literally ran away from her. She always plays the victim role.

But it was never fair that he ran away from me. That part I'll never understand. And I've been thinking about it more lately.

Why was I not enough for him to stay?

We meet at Tommy and Ale's house around 6:00. We hang in the basement to "pregame." New word to add to my dictionary. Their dad is upstairs, drinking away his sorrows, so we're pretty much free to do whatever we want. He doesn't care what his boys do so long as they graduate from high school, not get anyone pregnant, and stay out of jail (according to Tommy). Even though his standards are low and neglecting, at least he's around and goes to work each day to support his kids.

Tommy and Ale cleaned up the basement, meaning they put away all their laundry and lit a few candles to mask all the funky smells.

The boys sit on the couch to enjoy a few beers while I linger near the sliding doors, smiling at the stairs, wishing Arnold and I had a private pool. I imagine owning a house with Arnold, somewhere remote. Arnold programs video games, making a fortune, while I am a pro-basketball player. We're both healthy, athletic, happy, and sane.

People look up to us and think, wow, what a great couple! Look how far they've come!

Arnold comes up from behind and gives me a gentle tap on the shoulder. He smiles and guides me back to the couch.

"What's your poison tonight, Rachel?" Tommy asks, reaching into the cooler.

"H2O."

"You don't want anything else? I can get some liquor from upstairs if you don't like beer."

"No, thanks."

"What about some weed?"

"No, I already got high this morning. I'm only good for one high a day. Two makes me too tired."

"Are you tired right now?"

"No, I'm…" Sunburned on my ass and it's starting to itch. "I'm good."

"She needs something," Ale says, nudging his eyes to the back corner of the room where their beds are. "Something to keep her going."

Tommy's grin stretches from ear to ear. Ale, already too high or drunk to move, motions for Tommy to get whatever it is they're referring to. Tommy reaches into his nightstand and pulls out a small white container full of round pills.

My stomach drops. "No prescription drugs for me."

"It's not what you think," Tommy says, returning to the couch. "I didn't get this from a pharmacist."

"Is that E?" Arnold asks, his eyes like little fireworks.

"Yeah, man," Tommy says, handing Arnold the container. "This is pure sweetness right here. I did it a few times last summer. It was ridiculous. The energy level you get to. I danced for five hours straight at a party. Even when they turned the music off, I kept going."

"How long have you had these?"

"I just got them a few days ago. I was going to save them for Matt Dwayne's party next weekend, but I'd be up for doing them tonight instead. I just didn't know if you two would be down."

"Is E some kind of dancing drug?" I ask, hoping I don't sound too naive.

"It's ecstasy. The happy drug," Tommy says.

I vaguely remember ecstasy from health class. But the description the teacher gave was somewhat different.

"It makes you happy?" I ask.

"Yes, it makes you the happiest you will ever feel in your life. You will love everything and everyone around you."

"Is that true?" I ask Arnold. "Have you done E before?"

"Once. It didn't do as much for me. Just made me want to hug people. I ended up cuddling with a cat for most of the night."

"This was at a party?"

"Yeah, like two years ago."

"So, would E be good to do right before a concert?"

"Oh my God! This is the best night to do it!" Tommy exclaims. "It'll make the whole experience better. We'll feel unstoppable."

I look at Arnold, who's on his third beer. He knows more about this stuff than I do. The gummies have been harmless so far. Would stepping things up for one night be a big deal? Would it enhance the experience? How far could we go? Is there a limit? Should there be a limit?

"If we do this," Arnold says. "We stick together. The whole night. Nobody go solo."

"Alright, alright," Tommy says, taking out four pills. "Rachel, are you in?"

fifteen

EVERYTHING IS NORMAL. We all pile into a nice Hyundai. The Uber driver is chill and nonchalant, keeping the music low so we can talk amongst ourselves. It's mainly just Arnold and Tommy, conversing back and forth about what songs will be played and if they'll get a chance to go backstage. I have no desire to meet any of the bands or to meet anyone new. I just want to dance next to Arnold. It's an outdoor event, so hopefully, I won't feel too overwhelmed. Arnold has promised to stay near me the entire night. He knows if anything bad happens, he's to take me home right away.

That was the plan before we all decided to take E.

I don't know what to expect from this drug. I didn't bother to do a Google search; I just said yes. When I take a gummy, I'm usually silly and hyper for about fifteen minutes. I feel tingly and warm. And then, I gradually settle down and take notice of my surroundings. I'm way more focused, I love to move, and three-pointers are a breeze. Sometimes I get hungry, very hungry, and want to eat a whole bag of hot tamale chips or drink chocolate syrup straight from the bottle. Sometimes I just want Arnold to touch me for hours. It's not always the same, and I like the variety. It's like a bag of Skittles. I taste the rainbow but get a different hue each time.

Back at the house, Tommy explained that E is different for everyone. The reactions. But it's nothing to worry about. "We're all going to have a good time," he promised as we each took our pills simultaneously, like a pack.

While we wait in line for the security checks, I notice how incredibly hot it is. The humidity is insane. I lean my head back and inhale slowly. The air tastes clean and lubricated; I want more of it. Lots and lots of it. I open my mouth as if I'm catching raindrops on my tongue.

"Rachel?" Arnold squeezes my hand. "You okay?"

"I'm thirsty," I say, smacking my tongue against the roof of my mouth. "I'm so thirsty."

"We'll get you water once we get inside. How are you feeling?"

"Thirsty!"

Arnold rubs the back of my neck, radiating heat down my spine until I feel it bursting out of my tailbone. I'm a candle, but the wax is moving up and down my body like a fountain. With such fluidity, I bet I am capable of moving in any way possible. I wonder if I could do a backbend right now. Or the splits. As Arnold and I near the security checkpoint, I imagine myself phasing through unnoticed. I imagine myself invisible.

Girls always get through security checks way faster than guys, even though we're usually the ones with heavily loaded purses. Guys are patted down like they're all sneaking cocaine up their buttholes. I'm not carrying a purse, just ID, ticket, cash, and phone, all stuffed in my back pockets. I pass through practically unnoticed. While I wait for Arnold to be overly searched, I notice how far my feet are from my head. I reach down to touch my toes. The stretch in the back of my hamstrings feels phenomenal. I love the pull, releasing such warmth and tenderness, up into my glutes, hitting my hip flexors. I can't believe how many muscles I have and how wonderfully strong they all feel.

"Rachel, what are you doing?" Tommy asks, squatting down in front of me. He's gone through security with Ale. We're still waiting for Arnold.

"I'm stretching," I answer. "It feels so good. You should do it too."

"I think I'm good. But you go ahead and keep on stretching. We like the view you're giving us."

I stand up quickly, the blood rushing to my head like a kick. "Whoa." I stumble into Tommy's arms. "Sorry."

"All good. You okay?" He steadies me, his hands on my waist.

"Yeah, I'm good." I back away. "Why do they need two people now to check Arnold's pockets?"

"Because they're racist fucks," Tommy says.

"That's not fair," I say. "Not fair at all. I'm more likely to bring a weapon to a concert than Arnold is."

"Shhh, don't say things like that. You don't want to get kicked out right before the show."

Arnold is finally released from his temporary prison. He immediately comes to my side, his face fuming, and takes my hand.

"Jeez, that was some bull," Arnold says. "Is it always like that around here? I never had to go through anything like that back in Santa Cruz."

"Afraid so, my friend," Tommy says. "Welcome to the East Coast where we've got every kind of asshole you can imagine. Woohoo!"

"Why would you be happy about that?" I ask.

"I was being sarcastic," Tommy laughs.

"Oh. I just thought…you were just so passionate. Your words were like Shakespeare. It was really moving."

The boys all look at one another and nod their heads simultaneously. They know the drug has hit me. Because everything makes me happy now. The humidity makes me happy. Even the pebbles getting stuck between my toes makes me happy because it gives me an excuse to stretch again.

Arnold buys me a large bottle of water which I consume like an elephant. It tastes so clean and pure as if poured from the Garden of Eden. I'm getting younger with every gulp.

"She's gonna be fun tonight," Tommy says.

"She's always fun," Arnold says. "Hey, Rach, you gonna save some of that for me?"

I hand him the empty bottle, and everyone laughs.

I haven't been to an outdoor concert since I was a kid, and it was with Mom to see Taylor Swift. It was a very calm show with a mostly female audience. This place is swarming with such a mix of people, from middle-aged men dressed like they're twenty to teenagers who hate today's music and live for the past. Some people have leather jackets on, even though it's eighty degrees. A few women are hardly dressed at all. Their bottoms barely fit, and their crop tops are cropped to the extreme. I'm glad I'm wearing Arnold's T-shirt and simple jean shorts. Comfort is a must when you're outside in the heat.

"It's about to start," Tommy says. "Let's get up to the front!"

No chairs either. It's a standing free-for-all. Arnold holds my hand as we squeeze through the crowd. Every time I touch someone, a blast of energy shoots through my body. I feel like Sonic the Hedgehog, flying through gold rings, gaining power despite all the impact.

People scream as the opening band introduces themselves as The Sexy Pistols. Wow, how *original*. They briefly explain who they are, that they mainly cover Sex Pistols tracks but have a few originals. The lead singer is shirtless, with a red tie around his neck. He looks just like the original singer of Sex Pistols, complete with the adorable accent. I reach a hand forward as if I could touch him.

"Rachel! Are you okay?" Arnold yells over the start of the music.

"Yeah! I'm great!"

"Are you…?"

Can't hear anything else. The music is in high effect as they open with "Anarchy in the UK." I pay close attention to the bass player, watching his fingers go to town on his red instrument. Every note strikes me to my very core, lifting me out of my shell, into new places all at once, and I'm so excited, I scream at the top of my lungs and start to jump up and down with Arnold. He screams too. Everyone is screaming.

Tommy and Ale bounce together but join us midway through the song. It's all four of us huddled together, our arms around each other, jumping continuously while shaking our heads up and down. I feel so many hands touching me all at once, and I like it so much, I grab whosever hands are around my waist and thrust my hips back and forth. I'm still connected to Arnold, his eyes on me, but Tommy is right behind me, and Ale is to my side. I feel like the center of a sandwich, and everyone wants a piece of me. All those hands, and then Arnold's lips on mine.

We stay like that, conjoined in a jumping touch-fest, for the next three songs, but then there's this sudden shift in tempo when the band plays an original. The music is so fast and hardcore, I can't keep up, and I find myself bouncing off strangers, being shoved and jostled around like I'm in a mosh pit. I'm not scared, not yet at least, because I still have someone's hand to hold onto. But I'm no longer enjoying the music. It's too fast. Too loud. My energy starts to deflate like a balloon. What happened to the bass line? Where is the ground, and where is the sky? Where am I?

I can't do this anymore.

I let go of his hand.

I turn around, duck low, and move away as quickly as I can from all the sweaty tangibles, pushing so closely together you would think no one needed any air. When I find a spot to move without friction, I lean my head back and take slow, deep breaths. The sky is so beautiful. Not a cloud in sight. My feet rock back and forth to a calmer beat. I feel the ground through my sandals. The pebbles between my toes. I would like to stretch again, but I'm afraid I might tip over.

"Rachel?"

A soft hand touches my shoulder. I stare into Michelle's green eyes. Please stay this time. I need someone to talk to.

"You're here," I say, my insides and outsides beaming. Every bit of me smiles at her.

"I am! And so are you! Where's your boyfriend?"

"I don't know. He's probably still up front. I can't go back there."

"Yeah, I know. It can be rough. And this is just the first band. But I'll hang out with you back here where it's safe."

Michelle reaches for my hand. I feel her. I feel her alive with me. Michelle is someone I always looked up to. Not afraid to be herself. Not afraid to take risks. No wonder she hasn't been around in years. I've been cooped up in my boring world, talking to my boring home buddies, not experiencing anything outside my comfort zone. I was safe. I was comfortable. But I was never alive. And never happy.

"Michelle?"

"Yeah, kid?"

"I'm happy. I'm so happy."

Michelle smiles and looks at me as though she wants to kiss me. She is beautiful, even with frizzy hair and those baggy clothes of hers. She has the strength of a thousand women. She's my Jo March and my Lucy Pevensie. Characters who weren't afraid to speak up. To make change. To be something else. How I wish I could dive into a book with Michelle and go on an adventure back in time, or to Narnia, or even just to a different town.

But I'll settle for a kiss. I lean my head forward, hungry to taste her lips. Right before we make contact, Michelle jerks her head back and releases my hand.

"What's wrong?" I ask.

"Ah, it's just not right." Her smile vanishes along with mine. "Not anymore."

"What are you talking about?"

"What are you doing here, Rachel?"

"What do you mean, what am I doing here? I'm at a concert with my boyfriend and my friends. We're having fun."

"You're on drugs."

"I've been on drugs for three years. I'm just trying something new."

Michelle rolls her eyes, just like Larry. "You need to grow up. Like seriously, grow up. This is all just another masking. Another way for you to hide."

"What?"

She was going to kiss me, and now she's mad at me? I don't understand. Before I have the chance to say anything else, she turns around and disappears into the mosh pit. I debate whether to chase after her, but I know I won't find her. Like Larry, she just doesn't want to be friends with me anymore. I have to accept that, but it saddens me that my intangibles don't like me anymore now that I'm with Arnold.

Now that I've changed. And not like Jo March, who became a great writer, or Lucy, a child with more courage than most adults. I'm the character who's forgotten at the end of the book. I'm the one who loses everything.

I stare at the stage, full of excitement and life. And then I find myself walking backward, trying to get away from that world, that shining place of hopes and dreams. I end up falling into the arms of another person.

I look up and see a face, but it's upside down and swirling like a funhouse mirror. I can't speak. Can't move out of this person's arms. Is it Arnold? Please be Arnold. I know I'm safe with him.

He turns me around and presses his lips against my open mouth. I close my eyes and taste the heat. His tourniquet of energy is invigorating. We kiss for what feels like hours and hours, our tongues reaching to all the dark places. We are timeless. A clock running backward and forward all at once.

I open my eyes, and his face comes into plain sight.

"You're not Arnold."

"I could be." Tommy kisses me again. It feels so good. His mouth, his body, just dying to consume me. He's not as tall or robust as Arnold, but his body calls to me like a siren. Our white skins blend, but underneath, we are entirely different colors. It feels right and wrong. Terribly, terribly wrong.

I stumble away from Tommy and turn around several times. No sign of Michelle. No sign of Arnold. The concert goes on, with or without the stragglers.

"I need to go home," I say.

"Are you sick?"

"No, I just can't be here anymore. Where's Arnold?"

"I don't know. We all got separated."

"Crap."

"Do you want me to take you home?"

"We should find Arnold."

"We're not going to find him. There's over a thousand people here. All bunched up together. If you're freaking out, this is not the place to do it. Let's go somewhere else."

"Yes. But first..." I attempt to call Arnold, but it goes straight to voicemail. Odd. Why would he have it turned off? Unless his battery died. "Damn."

"Come on, Rachel."

"One second." I try texting him; it takes about six years to type one sentence.

R: **Tommy is taking me home. Too much noise.**

"Everything good?" Tommy asks, taking my hand. "You're shaking."

"I am?"

"Yeah. We need to get you out of here."

Tommy buys me a bottle of water before we leave. I drink it slowly this time. My head is spinning like I'm coming off a merry-go-round, and my mind hasn't caught up with my body. Tommy holds my arms to keep me from falling over. Every time something explodes in the sky, I scream. No matter how many times Tommy tells me it's just fireworks, I'm still convinced someone is shooting at us.

"I don't know if we should take an Uber," Tommy says while we wait in the parking lot. "You're really messed up right now. And I don't know how you're going to act when you start to come down."

"Down? What does that mean?"

"It's when the drug starts to wear off. Some people get sick or sad. Or just pass out."

"Are you down?"

"No, I'm still feeling it. But it didn't hit me nearly as hard as it hit you."

I cover my ears when the fireworks go off again. "I just want to go home. What time is it?"

"It's still early. Why don't I take you to my house? We can just chill out for a bit before you go home. I bet all you need is some quiet time by the pool."

"Okay."

"But you have to act normal for the car ride, okay? Don't say anything crazy or start talking to your imaginary friends. If you get scared, just close your eyes."

I close my eyes as soon as we get inside the car.

sixteen

"RACHEL? Rachel, wake up. We're here."

I lift my head off Tommy's shoulder and blink several times. We're in Tommy's driveway, and the driver is mumbling something about Tommy being such a good guy for taking care of his drunk girlfriend. I don't remember Tommy telling the driver that. Then again, I don't remember anything about the Uber ride, minus getting in and out of the car.

I'm able to walk to the basement, but as soon as I reach the bottom of the stairs, I fall forward and bang my knees against the ground. The pain is dull, not throbbing. I feel it, but it doesn't seem to matter right now. Nothing seems to matter. I'm here with Tommy. I'm away from the noise. What next? What am I supposed to do now?

"I don't like this anymore," I say, curling into the fetal position. The carpet smells like dirty socks and catnip. Tommy doesn't even have a cat.

"I'm sorry, Rachel. Sometimes we don't get to ride the high like we want to. Sometimes we just hit low, all of a sudden."

He's on the floor with me, rubbing my back, but that doesn't comfort me. I should be yearning for Arnold's touch, but the thought doesn't fill me with much hope. It leaves me with doubt and confusion.

"Have you heard anything from Arnold?" I ask. "Has he texted or tried to call you?"

"No, nothing."

"What about Ale?"

"Ale doesn't know how to work a phone when he's high. He's not entirely the brightest person in the world."

"Do you think they're alright? Do you think they're still at the concert?"

"Probably. I don't know."

"I can't believe Arnold didn't text me back."

"I'm sorry. That sucks, Rachel. That's a dick move on his part."

"Yeah, I know. He promised not to leave my side. He promised…"

My phone buzzes. I have a tingle of hope, but it's just Mom.

Mom: **How's the concert?**
R: **Too noisy. Coming home.**
Mom: **Aw. I'm sorry! At least you tried.**

"I should go home," I say, crawling onto my feet. "I can walk. It's not far."

"Rachel, you're sad right now. You shouldn't be alone."

"I'm not sad. I'm just confused."

"You should stay and talk to me for a little bit. It'll make you feel better. You want something to drink? Some water?"

"I really need to pee."

By the time I finish in the bathroom, Tommy is no longer in the house but swimming. It feels good to go back outside. The temperature has dropped a few degrees, and I no longer have that pressing desire to consume a million bottles of water.

I walk to the edge of the pool, halting when I realize Tommy is naked. His shorts and T-shirt have been thrown on top of a chair. He swims on his backside, giving me and the angels above us, a direct view of his man parts. I can't help but stare, and it's not because I want to do anything sexual with Tommy. It's just out of pure curiosity, since Arnold is the only guy I've ever been with. Tommy isn't as big, isn't as dark, but he's still a guy. Same basic anatomy. Same basic wants and needs.

"Do you want to swim?" he asks.

"Uh, no, I'm good."

I sit down and soak my feet in the water. Tommy swims over and grabs hold of my leg. I gasp, thinking he will pull me into the pool, but he just removes my sandals for me. At last, no more pebbles.

"So, what made you and Arnold a thing?" he asks, folding his arms across the ledge.

"He didn't tell you?"

"Not really. He's a pretty private guy when it comes to things like that."

"Oh, that's good then."

"Why? Do you guys do a lot of private things together?"

"Don't all couples?"

"No. I dated a girl last year who was pretty prude. I'm pretty sure that's why we broke up."

"Maybe she just wanted to take things slow."

"No, she was just a prude. Are you a prude?"

"Um, no."

"Hmmm, interesting." He rubs his knuckles against my knee so tenderly it almost tickles. "You never talked to anybody before meeting him. It was like he woke you up or something."

"I did talk. Just to nobody you'd know."

"Ha. You mean your imaginary friends?"

"Yeah. Them."

"But now you've got real friends. Me and Ale."

"Yeah. I guess I do."

"Do you like us?"

"Yeah. You guys are cool."

"What about me in particular? Do you think I'm attractive?"

"Uh. You're nice. But…"

"I'm not your type, is that it?" He's rubbing my calves now. "You like the exotic type, like Arnold?" He shakes his head, giving my leg a good squeeze. "I don't get it. Every white girl I go for, she ends up with a black guy, an Asian guy, and now an Indian."

"Arnold is Native American. He's Cherokee."

"Whatever. Same thing." Tommy flips onto his backside again and sort of floats beside me, not at all attempting to shield himself. My eyes are getting heavy again. I want to go to sleep now. And in my own bed.

"I should go."

He grabs my leg hard this time. "Just take a quick swim with me. Then I'll walk you home. You shouldn't walk home by yourself."

"Fine. A quick swim. But only if you put your shorts back on."

Tommy doesn't hesitate with my demands. Within seconds, he's out of the pool and back in, covered and ready for me to join him. Me, I'm still trying to empty my pockets so I don't get my phone wet.

"Are you going to swim in all of those clothes?" Tommy asks.

"Yeah. All of them."

I don't jump in where Tommy is. I go for the diving board, fully prepared to do my usual drop to the bottom of the pool. Everything starts normal, but the minute my feet hit the water, the world closes in on me like quicksand. I sink and sink. And that's all I do.

I don't know if I'm dead. If I've been revived. Or if I'm floating somewhere in between. I see light and darkness all at once, but no color. Just harsh streaks of white and black. If I focus hard enough, I can blend them.

Someone whacks my back, and I cough up a fountain of water. The rest of me feels weak and heavy, like I've been dragged to hell and back.

Finally, my eyes open, and I see Tommy hovering on top of me, his mouth reaching down for mine. "Rachel, there you are." He kisses me hard. I try with all my might to move him away, but he's too heavy. After all the bench pressing, I still don't have the strength to push someone off me.

No. Stop it. Stop it, you perv.

"It's okay. You're alright. I pulled you out in time. No worries. Don't cry."

He runs his fingers through my hair and kisses my forehead. I don't want him to touch me anymore. I can feel too much of him growing, and it drives my thoughts to dark places.

I try to grab an empty bottle of beer, but it's just inches out of reach. Tommy runs his hands down my body to the zipper of my wet shorts.

This can't be happening. *Get off me. Get off me!*

Wham! Tommy collapses to my right, giving me just enough space to wiggle free. His eyes roll back into his head. He mumbles and moans, rubbing his forehead. There's no blood, but surely he'll have a nasty bump by tomorrow morning. From the bottle. The bottle? How did it get into my hands?

I toss it into the pool, like it's a murder weapon, and look around, just in time to see Mary before she disappears.

I'm horrified and grateful all at once. Mary saved me?

But that doesn't entice me enough to stick around to ask why. I scamper away from Tommy before he has any chance to revive, grab my stuff, and make a barefoot run for it. I leave the sandals behind.

It's less than a quarter-mile to my house, but I sprint like I'm trying to outrun a leopard. The sidewalk digs at my feet, scraping at will, but once I pass Arnold's house, I switch to grass and head straight for my front porch.

"Rachel!"

I scream and throw my phone at the intruder before spinning around, set for another retreat. But he's faster and jumps in front of me.

"Rachel, it's me! It's Arnold."

I halt mid-swing. I was about to punch Arnold, my boyfriend.

"Ar…nold?" I'm so out of breath from running, my heart is in my throat. Or that could just be the onset of vomit. My stomach isn't feeling too good either.

"What happened to you?" Arnold asks. "You and Tommy both disappeared."

"I called you and texted you."

"I dropped my phone during the concert. I've been looking everywhere for you. I even tried to get them to pause the concert to call your name on the loudspeaker. How did you get home?"

"I…Tommy…" It's all coming back to me. Everything. Losing Arnold in the crowd. Running into Michelle. Kissing Tommy. Falling into the pool. Waking up with Tommy on top of me. Mary saving me.

But that's not all I see.

"Rachel?"

I gasp and look over Arnold's shoulder. Everyone is there. All my intangibles. Larry, Breezy, Michelle, Mary, even Donovan. All five of them, looking at me with harsh eyes and empty souls. Like zombies who bite at your insides from a distance. I feel pain everywhere and nowhere all at once. I'm only half-connected to my body, and the other half of me is lost.

"Rae-Rae, I feel sorry for you," Larry says, holding hands with Donovan.

"You should have listened to me," Breezy says, her eyes unmoving.

"You need to grow up," Michelle says with the force of a cyclone.

Donovan mumbles something in Spanish, criticism, I'm sure.

Mary opens her mouth, but the others step in front of her. She doesn't belong, but they allow her to stand with them. Why? Are they teaming up? If so, what are they trying to prove? That I'm incapable of defending myself? That I'm worthless without them? Or are they trying to take control of me? Please, God, no. Don't let them in.

I strain my vocal cords, trying to scream, but nothing comes out. A choked cry forces its way up my throat, a teardrop runs down my cheek, and I stop breathing. I can't see Arnold anymore. My house. My yard. Only the intangibles, closing in on me. The rest of the world could be on fire, and I wouldn't feel a thing.

"What the fuck do you want from me?" I look straight at Larry, his eyes unblinking, his gangly arms like a scarecrow's. When Larry speaks, I can't hear anything but TV static. My brain is going to explode, literally, figuratively, and every way in between. I have to get out of this nightmare. Get back to reality, where it's safer.

I smack the sides of my head, trying to push them out, but someone pins my arms down. I can't tell who. My vision is skewed now.

"Get off of me!" I scream, twisting side to side. "All of you, just stay away from me!"

"Rachel, there's no one else here. It's just me. It's Arnold. I've got you. No one's going to hurt you."

I look up, and Arnold is there, holding me like a straitjacket. I can see him now. My house. My yard. But the intangibles are still there, ready to feed.

"No one's going to hurt you," he says again, wiping the tears from my face. "You're safe with me."

"Let me go. Please. I have to go inside. Now, before they get me."

"Baby, let's go inside together."

"No! No! Get away!" With every ounce of strength I have left, I shove Arnold away and race to my front door, but it's locked, and the key is in my back pocket. I can't get it out because Arnold is all over me, trying to hold me, kiss me; I don't know what he's trying to do. He's still high. And I'm so low right now, I want nothing more than for him to go home and stay home for a very long time. I want to curl up in my bed, my stupid squeaky bed, and be totally alone.

"Let go of me, Arnold. I don't want you to touch me right now. I don't want anyone to touch me!"

He doesn't listen, so I bite his arm.

This time he releases me because I'm pretty sure I drew blood. I can taste it in my mouth. He stumbles away from me, looking so pathetic alongside the intangibles. It disgusts me. Him. Everyone. The world. It's so ugly. So very ugly. I want to get as far away from it as possible.

"Rachel, baby…" He falls to his knees.

I leave him out there, all alone, to cry, to weep. I don't care if he's hurting. I don't care about anything. I shut the front door, lock it, kick it, yell when I realize I'm still barefoot, then kick it again. I run straight to my bedroom, remove my shirt, and hurl it at my record player. I want to break things, but I don't have enough energy, so I throw myself on my bed and cover my head with two pillows. I can still hear the intangibles; their voices are stuck inside my head. *Rae-Rae, I feel sorry for you. You should have listened to me. You need to grow up.* Silence from Mary. And so, for the first time, I concentrate on her. Her empty soul lulls me to sleep.

seventeen

IT IS VERY strange waking up this time. At first, I can't tell where I am because my head is covered in pillows, and I'm lying sideways on my bed. My hair is plastered in sweat, and my throat burns when I swallow. I sit up and blink at my books, scattered all around the room. Why is it such a mess in here? And where's Larry? Then I wonder if I have to go to school today and if I have any quizzes or assignments due.

Snap out of it. Get your days straight. It's freaking July. You don't have school, and Larry's been gone for weeks.

My body hurts like I ran a marathon, and my brain is on fire. I can't go back to sleep. And I can't relax. So I have no choice but to lie awake and revisit everything that happened last night. The memories play out like a movie trailer. I have an idea of the plot and characters but not the resolution. So I go back to the beginning and force myself to play it all out, but it's mostly just fragments again. I remember being confused, going from place to place with Arnold, then Tommy. I remember seeing the intangibles. I remember what they said to me. And how terrified I was.

"Michelle?"

She's never been inside my house, but I don't feel anything from her when I say her name. I can't remember if her eyes are blue or green. Or what her voice sounds like. The memory of Michelle feels washed over, like a water painting left in the rain.

"Larry?"

Nothing. I can't smell the bubblegum ChapStick or his everlasting Starbucks latte. My room looks like a bomb went off. And all the books appear foreign and strange, as if I had never read them. Or that Larry was never here at all.

"Breezy?"

I feel something from her. And I am desperate to hold onto her, even if it turns out bad. I stand up and look down at my body. My legs are covered in bruises. I have blisters and tiny scrapes all over my feet from running barefoot. Everything hurts, even my teeth. How could one night do so much damage?

I spend an hour in the bathroom. First to throw up, then to take a long, hot shower. I scrub everywhere, even against the bruises. After the wash, I tie my uncombed, wet hair into a messy ponytail and wrap up my battered toes with Band-Aids. I throw on a tank top, shorts, socks, and a pair of slippers. Then I brush my teeth for several minutes, in an attempt to get rid of the vomit taste, but it lingers on the back of my swollen throat. Every time I swallow, I taste it again.

As I walk down the hallway, I hear Mom snoring away. Most likely, she'll be asleep the rest of the day. I notice the pictures on the wall, mostly from my childhood. I remember when there used to be pictures of all three of us. Before Mom swapped them out for pictures without my dad. It's like she tried to erase him after he left. She even changed both our last names to her maiden name. I went from Rachel Hansen to Rachel Andrews as soon as the divorce was finalized. I couldn't keep anything of his, not even his Father's Day gifts. I painted him a flowerpot when I was four, and every year we would plant new flowers and watch them grow by the kitchen window. A few weeks after he left, the flowerpot was gone.

In its place is a generic flowerpot, with generic fake flowers in it. It doesn't even need sunlight, but it's by the window. This flowerpot holds no character or purpose. No sentimental value. If I were to toss it in the trash can, it shouldn't upset anyone. It shouldn't matter.

But the flowerpot I made for my dad did matter. And I'm only realizing now how much it hurts that my mother threw it away.

After a glass of water, I head for the front yard. My phone is on top of one of the porch chairs. I have several text messages from

Tommy, three from last night, right after I left, and two sent just a few minutes ago.

T: **Why the fuck did you hit me?**
T: **Are you crazy?**
T: **I'm throwing your shoes away!**
T: **I didn't throw your shoes away.**
T: **I'm not sure what happened last night. If I did anything wrong, I'm sorry.**

I can't text him back. What would I say? *Oh, it's fine. Attempted rape is no big deal.* Or how about: *It's good you don't remember.* Or maybe: *Stay the hell away from me!* I have no idea how to process anything that happened between Tommy and me. In a way, it's probably better if I try not to remember.

I walk around the house, noting how overly dry the ground is. I hear whimpering from the backyard. Breezy is curled up next to the garden, sobbing a canvas of tears. I stop in my tracks, unsure how to approach her. I've never seen Breezy cry like this before, like a little girl. But I always forget that she is a little girl. A little girl that will never grow up.

"Breezy? Are you okay?"

She doesn't move from her spot or bother to look at me. "It's dying."

"What is?"

"The garden."

"What?"

We just picked tomatoes a few days ago, or maybe it was last week? Everything was growing perfectly, no weeds, the soil moist, and all the leaves green. Now I'm looking at dead plants. A graveyard of dying vegetables.

"What happened?" I pick up a string of chewed-up tomatoes. "How did everything die so fast?"

"You haven't been doing anything right. You left the gate open, so the groundhog got in. And it's been almost a week since you watered anything. It hasn't rained all week. Everything is dead."

"Breezy…"

"I warned you not to venture off with anyone else. I knew bad things would happen if you started hanging out with those stone-heads down the street."

"Breezy, we can fix this."

I run to the side of the house to grab the hose, but when I return, Breezy is gone, and it's just me, my dying garden, and my upset stomach.

"Breezy?"

I feel nothing from her. I might as well call for Donovan, but I have no luck with him either, even when I speak Spanish. Am I truly alone now? Will any of them come back? Was last night their way of saying goodbye together?

The only way to test the theory would be to call *her* name. But that invitation could prove to be deadly. She could have killed Tommy last night if she wanted to. She could have made me hit him more than once.

Arnold is outside now. He's just in his boxers, but he doesn't seem to notice or care. I walk over to his side of the yard very slowly, my head down low. I don't know why I feel such shame. I didn't do anything wrong, or did I? Then I notice the Band-Aid on his arm, covering up my bite marks.

"Hey," he says softly.

"Hey," I whisper, my throat roasting.

"How are you feeling?"

"Nauseous."

"Did you throw up?"

"Yeah."

"I'm sorry."

"It's fine."

"You're covered in bruises."

"Yeah, I know. I fell a lot last night. I'm sorry about your arm."

"It's not your fault. You weren't yourself last night."

"Maybe I was."

"Rachel, you—"

I shake my head to stop him from trying to reason with me. He always wins. Because he's always right, and I'm always wrong. Or misinformed. Or just too damn naive. And I already feel foolish enough as is.

We wait several seconds before speaking to one another. A few birds seem to be having a tweeting contest nearby.

"I lost my phone at the concert," he says. "I wanted to call you."

"I know. I'm sorry."

"Why did you leave?"

"We got separated, and I got confused and started seeing things. Michelle and I got into a weird fight. And then Tommy found me."

"You're shaking."

Arnold takes a step toward me. I take two steps back. I never retreat from Arnold like this, not since the night in the kitchen, when I questioned his motives.

"What's wrong?" he asks.

"Nothing. Tommy found me and got me home."

Arnold pinches his lips together and shakes his head several times. "You're not telling me everything."

"Uh, well, I was kind of messed up last night, so I'm not entirely sure of anything. Only that we lost each other, and now we're together again, and I'm not feeling this huge desire to be near you right now."

"That's okay. It can take a few days to feel normal after you trip like that."

"That would have been something good to know beforehand."

"I know. I wasn't thinking how it might affect you in the long run."

I roll my eyes. "You were drinking. Of course, you weren't thinking."

"Babe, I'm sorry. Really, I am. But don't worry. You'll be back to normal soon enough."

"Normal? What is normal for someone like me? Is getting high *and* crazy normal? No, Arnold. It's not. It's not who I am. It's not who I want to be."

"It was a one-time thing. It'll never happen again."

"Nothing like that will ever happen again. And I mean nothing."

His eyes narrow. "What do you mean by that? Are you saying you want it all to stop? You want to go back to your pills?"

"I'm not saying that."

"You want to go back to talking on and off with your make-believe friends?"

"They're not around anymore."

"Then who were you screaming at last night? You were totally freaking out."

I close my eyes, remembering what it was like having all five of them gang up on me. I'm surprised I didn't wake the neighbors with my yelling. All my hysteria. It was complete chaos, one of the most terrifying moments of my life. Having no control over my own perception, and then Arnold there, trying to calm me down, like he can fix everything with the press of a button? Yeah, Arnold, let's just give Rachel a drug that will probably make her hallucinate even worse and hope it all turns out like a Disney World mirage. What the hell did you think was going to happen? I'd magically stop seeing the intangibles and let you save me?

I rub the bags under my eyes. I can think all that, but to explain it to Arnold right now? I don't have the energy, and I don't think he'd get it.

"It doesn't matter," I finally say. "They're gone now, and I think it's because they don't like me anymore. Because I've stopped caring about them, about myself."

"You care about yourself."

"I let my garden die. My garden, Arnold. The one thing I care more about than anything else. I let it die!"

I'm still in disbelief over its decay. The one responsibility I have all summer and I completely blow it.

"What are you talking about?" Arnold asks. "How is it *dead*?"

Is he blind? You can see the desiccation from here.

"I've been forgetting to water it," I say, pointing at the hose. "It's been so hot this week, and it hasn't rained. And we've been getting high every day."

Every *single* day. No breaks. No time to consider the consequences. Just sex and drugs. The life of a rock star. Exciting, but short-lived. I don't have the stamina for that kind of life. I'm not like Arnold, with excess amounts of energy to burn.

"Okay, I understand," Arnold says. "We've been a little neglectful."

A little? I cover my face with both hands and suffocate for a few seconds. "It wasn't supposed to get like this." I drag my fingers down the sides of my face and wag my head side to side. "I lost control. I let myself slip."

"I'm sorry. It's my fault. I shouldn't have let you take any drugs last night. I knew the concert would be crazy enough as is. It was stupid. I didn't know Tommy was into that kind of stuff."

"Tommy isn't who you think he is."

Arnold takes another step toward me. This time I stay in place. He kneels and runs his fingers across my bruised calves. He's gentle, but I feel the burning urge to kick him. To knock him over. To make him bleed again. I clench my hands into fists and hide them behind my back. Where are these violent thoughts coming from? Am I that angry with Arnold that I can't forgive him? Is it the E still? Or is Mary fueling this somehow?

"Some of these are fingerprint bruises," Arnold says. "Did Tommy do this?"

My knees press together, shooing Arnold's hands away. "He wasn't himself last night. Or maybe he was. I don't know."

"What did he do to you?" Arnold jumps to his feet, his eyes livid. "I'll fucking kill him."

"Nothing!" I know touching him would help thaw his anger, but words are my only defense. "He didn't do anything because Mary came and saved me."

"Mary came and saved you?"

I nod my head. I can't repeat her name. I feel her presence, even though I can't see her. The others left because they don't like me anymore. Mary lingers because she clings to darkness, pain, and destruction. And that's all I feel right now. It's all I'm able to let in. Unless I choose numbness. My pill.

"I need to take my Seroquel today." I turn around several times, checking to see if she's hiding anywhere. Behind a bush. High up in a tree. My skin prickles with goose bumps. I don't have the energy to fight back this time. I just want it to stop.

"Why?" Arnold asks, grabbing my hand to keep me from spinning. "Why do you need your pill now?"

"If she comes back, I'm done for."

"But you just said she saved you? Jesus, Rachel, what the fuck happened?" Arnold is about to lose it. The veins in his neck protrude like tree roots. For a second, I imagine his scars breaking apart and all that blood flowing out. Like a river. Covering me. Infecting me with his rage.

My head shakes violently. "It doesn't matter. I can't trust her. I can't let her in again. I know my limits now, and I'm sorry, but I can't push it anymore."

"We made a promise."

"And we agreed we would stop if things got bad. I'm not going to feel *safe* otherwise." I pull away from him; he holds on for a second before releasing me.

"You're safe with me. You're always safe with me."

"I wasn't last night. And neither were you. You're lucky I only got your arm."

Arnold presses a fist against his mouth to keep from exploding. "What did Tommy do? I want to know everything. I'll kick his ass if he—"

"No, no, I don't want you to kick anyone's ass. Let's just stay away from them, from Tommy and Ale. Let's just go back to the way things were at the beginning, when you just wanted to hang out with me and get to know me. When things were nice and slow. This go-go and get-high life, I just can't do it anymore."

The rage in his eyes fades with disappointment. "No more gummies?"

"No. No more gummies."

"Well, Tommy is my source for that, so I guess without a source now, I don't have a choice."

"It doesn't have to be permanent. I just…we both need a break from it. It's not healthy."

Arnold's face reeks of misery, like a child who just had all their Christmas presents returned to the stores. He runs his teeth across his bottom lip and rubs the back of his neck. Am I asking for too much? After all, he's not the one who tripped last night. But he is the one with bite marks, a clear hangover, and a traumatized girlfriend.

"Okay," he finally says, though his eyes aren't glowing with approval. "You do understand that I'll have to go back on my medicine now, too? Because I can't live on air. I have to have something, or I go nuts."

"You have me. I thought I was your favorite high?"

"You are." He reaches for my hands, glued to my sides. "Didn't you like it? Not last night. Last night was bad. But every other day. Didn't you like it? Didn't it make you feel good? Make you feel happy?"

"Yes, but it's not…real."

"Real?" Arnold laughs. "Rachel, you've been talking to imaginary people for years. You're with me now. I'm real." He beats his hands against his chest. "You can look into my eyes anytime you want, I'm always real."

"But I don't feel real." I feel hollow. Drained by sadness and guilt. The urge to cry comes and goes; it sits heavy on my heart, and I have no idea how to make it go away.

"Rachel, baby." He grabs me by the arms, forcing my hands to unknot, and bends down, so we're both at eye level. "You're just sad right now. You're feeling down. It's okay. It'll pass, baby. Just give it a day or two."

I nod my head slowly. "Okay." I almost rest my head on his shoulder but pause and pull back. "I should sleep."

"Okay, babe. That's a good idea. Will you call me later when you wake up?"

"You don't have a phone, remember?"

"I'll get a new one today."

"Then I'll call you later."

When he tries to kiss me, my head falls, and he kisses my forehead instead. He doesn't try to do anything else. He knows, or at least I hope he knows, I'm in a different place right now, and I need space. Lots and lots of space.

Every time I wake, I feel too depressed to get up, so I roll over and go back to sleep. I don't know how long I've slept, whether it's morning, afternoon, or evening. I don't care. I don't feel happy about anything. What bothers me the most is the guilty feeling I have about Tommy. I have to take some responsibility. I let Tommy kiss me at the concert. A lot.

And from what I can remember, I enjoyed it. Even when I realized it was him that I was kissing. Do I blame the E? Or do I blame myself? I wish so badly I could hit the rewind button and erase everything from last night, even the happy moments I had jumping up and down with Arnold. Because even in those happy moments, I wasn't truly myself. I wasn't truly free. For every high, there is a low. And in my case, the low lasts longer.

Despite working the graveyard shift, Mom is pretty lively and anxious to talk to me about the concert. She orders Chinese food for dinner and offers me a cup of coffee, saying one cup won't hurt, and I keep thinking how one small pill wouldn't hurt, and it did. I reject the coffee and settle for water, the only liquid I trust. I wear leggings to cover up the bruises and an oversized T-shirt. I still haven't combed my hair. And now that I'm on the couch, I probably won't move again until I have to pee.

"You look exhausted," Mom says. She is sitting next to me with her gigantic mug of coffee, overloaded with vanilla cream, and it makes me think of Larry's immortal latte. "I thought you came home early."

"I did. But I didn't go to sleep right away. I had a headache from all the noise."

"Was it crowded?"

"Yes, very."

"But you stayed with Arnold the whole time?"

"For the most part."

"Did you drink?"

"I drank water. Are you asking if I drank alcohol?"

"It wouldn't shock me if you did. That's what teenagers do at concerts. Or right beforehand. I was guilty of it too when I was your age. But with your mental condition, I would be extra concerned if you did."

"I didn't drink any alcohol."

"That's good. Did Arnold?"

I release a heavy sigh. "Why does it matter?"

"I just want to know."

"If I say no, you're going to think I'm lying. And if I say yes, you're going to assume that Arnold is this awful person, and I shouldn't be with him anymore."

"I don't think he's an awful person. Not at all. I just...well, you spend an awful lot of time with him. I don't think you've spent one day apart since school let out."

"We're not seeing each other today."

"Are you two fighting?"

"No. We're just both tired from the concert and need some space. Is there something wrong with that?"

"Nothing is wrong with that, I just—"

"Stop prying. Jesus. Like seriously, you're always telling me to go and make friends. Why don't you do the same?"

"I don't have time for friends, Rachel. I work long hours to afford this house, to pay off debt caused by your father's reckless spending habits, to pay back student loans, and to save enough money so that you can go to college without having to endure any debt. I make sacrifices for that. I would love to go out to a bar with a bunch of middle-aged single women and drink and lament about my life, but I would rather come home to you and make sure you're okay. To talk to you. That's what it means to be a mother. But you'll never understand that because you never, ever want to open your heart to anyone, not even me."

"That's because you ruin everything."

Her eyes widen, and the air gets stuck in her throat. She wheezes and coughs before firing back, "What are you talking about? I've done everything for you."

"You threw away my flowerpot. I worked hard on that flowerpot. And you just threw it away because it made you too upset to look at it. You could've just put it in my room, so you wouldn't have to see it every day. But instead, you threw it out. You didn't even tell me. Didn't even ask me if it was okay. Just like when you changed my last name. You just went ahead and did it. You didn't care about my feelings then, so why should I care about yours?"

"Are you talking about that flowerpot you made for your father when you were in preschool?"

"Yes, that flowerpot. The one you threw away."

"I didn't want to throw it away. Mrs. Martin accidentally knocked it over when she was dusting one day, and it broke. I didn't want to upset you, so I thought maybe if we just got rid of it without telling you, you wouldn't even notice."

"I did notice."

"Then why didn't you say anything?"

"Because you're the mom!" I bang my fists against the coffee table, rattling the glass centerpiece. "*You're* supposed to say something. Not me."

"In certain situations, it's best not to say anything at all."

"Like when your husband is walking out on you? Right after you cook him fucking breakfast?"

I never swear like that in front of my mother. But she doesn't appear shocked by my word choice. She's more hurt than anything.

"There's nothing I could have said to keep him from leaving."

"You could have tried. You gave up too easily."

Mom bites her lip. Her knees squeeze together. There are so many things she could say, but it's easier just to be silent. She presses her mug against her mouth. Sip your coffee, sip it nice and slow. That's it, Mom. Just keep pretending it was all his fault. And that my feelings never mattered.

I take a difficult, deep breath and look my mother dead in the eyes, noting the extra wrinkles today. There's no reason for me to be so hard on her. If anything, I should feel remorse. I should apologize. But I don't. Because right now, I just don't care enough to do anything but walk away.

Later that night, Arnold attempts to reach out to me by calling and then texting. I was supposed to call him earlier, but I didn't feel like it. I haven't eaten all day, and even though there's orange chicken and fried rice in the refrigerator, I feel like I would puke it all up. My stomach still hasn't settled and the lump in my throat seems to be growing, like a tumor. I wish it would just kill me already.

A: **What's up? There's fireworks tonight.**
R: **Good.**
A: **Do you want to see them with me?**
R: **No. Too tired.**
A: **I'm sorry. I wish you would talk to me. Can I come over?**
R: **Not tonight.**
A: **What about tomorrow?**

I can't think about tomorrow. What if I feel worse? Or what if I feel nothing at all? What if I can't be saved? What if I just curl into a ball and never wake up? I have no intangibles to talk to, and I can't confide in Arnold now, so I am alone. Truly and utterly alone.

I finally take my pill and wait for sleep to do its job yet again.

eighteen

THE REST of the weekend drags by like one big funeral. I have no one to talk to except for Mom, and she's not in the best of moods either, no thanks to me. Now would be an excellent time for Larry to return, hear all about the weekend, and offer me advice and cheer without expecting anything in return. The weather is gorgeous, so going outside to save the garden would be productive, but it's just not the same without Breezy.

I want them to return, but it's not like I can go back to the way things were when I skipped in moderation. I have to be consistent now and take my Seroquel as prescribed to keep my emotions from spiraling out of control. And to keep Mary away.

With all this time to myself, I revisit the list I made in May. My teenage bucket list, I should call it. *Play basketball. Get driver's license. See ocean. Climb a mountain. Get a dog. People like me for who I am. Speak to anyone. Confidence. Maturity. Be in control.*

I can't cross anything off the list. Shooting hoops with Arnold doesn't count for the first one. I haven't even gotten my learner's permit. There's been no attempt to see the ocean or climb anything taller than a tree. A dog? Yeah, right. Mom would never agree to that. And people liking me for who I am? Do I even like myself? I'm not confident. I'm not mature. And I don't feel in control. Maybe when I'm high with Arnold. But it's only temporary. And I need something more stable. Something more reliable.

I'm not sure what I need. Pills, people, or silence?

Monday morning, I actually look forward to reading the text messages from Arnold, but to my dismay, there are none. I press the cold screen of my phone against my chest and take a deep breath before typing.

R: **Are you home?**
A: **Out for a bit. What's up?**
R: **I want to see you. My mom's leaving for work soon.**
A: **Okay. I'll be over in a few hours.**

A few hours? It might as well be another day. I make good use of the time, trying to work on my garden, relieved to find that only half the plants died, and the other half can revive thanks to a YouTube video on how to save your neglected garden. After I finish outside, I take a shower and put on a bright orange summer dress. I braid my hair and lather myself in lotion. I don't want to look or smell like I've been lolling all weekend.

Right around noon, the doorbell rings. I open the door to a very smiley-faced Arnold. He looks overjoyed to see me, but his eyes are dilated and red. He doesn't say a word, just grabs my chin with one hand and kisses me three times on the lips. I pull him inside and close the door behind him. He saunters into the living room and stretches out across the couch.

"Are you high?" I ask immediately.

"Yes." He won't stop smiling. "Is that a problem?"

"I thought…" I cross my arms and lean one foot against the coffee table. "We were going to take a break from that."

"I did. For the weekend. It's Monday now. Did you go back on your pill?"

"Yes."

"Have you taken it today?"

"Yes."

"That's too bad." He reaches into his back pocket and pulls out a new bag of gummies. I thought for sure he was almost out the last time we got high. He tosses the bag on top of the coffee table. "How long ago did you take it?"

"Arnold, I'm not getting high with you."

187

"Why not?"

"You think I want to after what happened this weekend?"

"That was a one-time thing. Not to be repeated. We're not going to hang with Tommy and Ale anymore. I talked to Tommy about what happened between you two."

"You did?" My teeth clench together. "What did he say?"

Arnold stands, and I shrink. "He thinks he may have tried to kiss you, several times. And you hit him on the head with a beer bottle. Is that true?"

"Yes." Minus a few other parts. "Are you mad?"

"I'm mad you didn't tell me. Were you afraid or something?"

"I was worried you'd…"

"Go over and beat the shit out of him?"

"Did you?"

"I wanted to." He cracks his knuckles against his chest several times. That seems to relax him because he's back to smiling. "But his wimpy brother was there, and his dad was home, too. So we just had a very intense conversation. Which ended with him swearing on his life to stay away from you. If he tries to call or text, you let me know immediately."

"Alright." I guess I better delete all of Tommy's messages. "But without Tommy, how are you going to get your gummies?"

"Don't worry about that. To avoid any further damage to his head, he loaded me up, free of charge."

"Arnold, that's…"

"A fair deal, considering he tried to take what was mine."

"I'm not…" Ownable. "I'm still not sure. I'm not sure about anything right now."

"What are you confused about? Is it me? Are you still upset with me? Look, I've tried to do everything to make things right. I've reached out. I've given you space. I've dealt with the asshole who tried to take advantage of you. What more do I need to do?"

I pinch my lips together and wander toward the window. My arms won't uncross, and that bag of green hasn't moved from its spot on the table. I'm tempted to take a gummy just to let go of this doubtful feeling. But that would be stupid.

"Did you even miss me?" Arnold asks. "Cause I missed the hell out of you." He reaches his arms out.

"Yes, I missed you."

I release the tension in my arms and return to the coffee table. I pick up the plastic bag and tuck it back inside his pocket. Then I take his hands and put them around my waist. For a few moments, we rock side to side as though dancing, slowly annihilating the gap between our bodies. I don't need drugs. I just need him.

We retire to my bedroom to enjoy ourselves. It's different this time, with him high and me on my pill. He breathes so much more than I do. He's slow and deliberate with every movement. I like watching his face, how his lips quiver ever so slightly. When he reaches down to kiss me, I feel his exhale through my throat. I like having him here, connected to me, but it's like a scene from a movie. It almost feels like I'm acting. Like I'm pretending. And I can't figure out why. Could I still be having withdrawal from the Ecstasy? Is it the pill? Or is this something deeper?

When it's over, and Arnold is resting his head against my bare stomach, I look across my room where Larry normally sits. My record player looks lonely, even dusty, because I haven't played any of my albums in weeks.

I detach myself from Arnold to play "The Long and Winding Road." I smile back at him, remembering what it was like the first time. How a simple tune could bring two people together. That was a defining moment for us.

But he groans and rubs his forehead. "Ugh, could you please turn that shit off?"

"What?" I'm shocked. "But you love this song."

"It's overrated. All their music is."

I don't respond. He's high right now, so maybe his taste in music differs. It bothers me to turn the music off. I suppose if I put on some punk rock, he'd be happy, but I wouldn't. Because deep down, I'm not in love with punk rock. And I didn't actually want to go to that concert. I just wanted to be with Arnold.

My afternoon appointment with Melinda starts pretty quietly. Me, just watching the ceiling fan while Melinda observes from her rocking chair. I don't mind her staring. Ninety percent of communication is nonverbal, and I'm sure my don't-care appearance says quite a lot. After being with Arnold, I didn't bother to brush my hair, so it's all tied back in a sloppy ponytail. I'm not wearing a bra. I probably still smell like Arnold. Didn't bother to spray myself with perfume or put on deodorant. If Larry were still around, he'd remind me to do those things. Now I have to remember all on my own. But do I care enough to remember? Not really.

"How are you feeling today?" Melinda asks after a few minutes of silence.

"Okay." Miserable. I'm already lying down, more inclined to take a nap than open up to Melinda.

"How was your weekend? Did you do anything fun?"

"Friday night I went to a concert. Then I pretty much chilled the rest of the weekend."

"Yes, you mentioned going to a concert during our last session. How was it?"

"Loud. Lots of people. I didn't stay for very long."

"How did you get home?"

"Uber."

"Did you ride alone, or was someone with you?"

"Someone was with me."

"I see. And what made you decide to leave the concert?"

My mood ricochets between low and lower, and while this may take a mountain of work, I need to accomplish something today with Melinda. Because I'm not getting anywhere with Arnold. The last few days have felt like an endless loop. And without Larry or Breezy to turn to, Melinda may be the only person in the entire universe able to help. But I have to be honest with her and myself.

"It just wasn't for me. I guess that's really what it comes down to. I don't like punk rock music. I like calm, pretty music. I like The Beatles, Simon and Garfunkel, and Taylor Swift before she turned pop. That's what I like."

Melinda's lips twist to one side. "Hmmm. Last week, you seemed very excited about the concert. What changed?"

"I did. I'm different now."

"You are different. A lot has happened since you met Arnold. You have a new group of friends. You're working out, almost every day it seems, and spending a lot of time outdoors. But I'm not hearing as much about all the things you used to do. Like reading. Have you read anything new recently?"

"No."

"Anything old?"

"Don't have time." That's not entirely true. I don't have the motivation to read without Larry.

"What about your garden?"

"It's just a garden." I swallow hard. It wasn't *just* a garden.

"Two months ago, we had an entire session solely about your garden. How's everything growing this year? I remember last year you had so many zucchinis you brought me in a bag."

"I'm not having as much luck with my garden this year."

"Oh? Why is that?"

I sigh and rub my forehead. "It's just not the same anymore."

"Why is it different?"

I close my eyes and take a deep breath. I wanted to talk to Arnold about my intangibles, how their departure is affecting me, almost to the point of depression. It eats at me from the inside. And the only way to heal is to act like I'm healing, but I can't fool Melinda. Eventually, she'll see right through me, if not already.

I feel myself breaking down inside, and for once, I wish I could cry like everybody else does at therapy, but I'm on my pill today.

"They're all gone," I say.

"Who?"

"My intangibles. I don't see them anymore."

"When did this happen?" Melinda sits forward in her rocking chair. "I know they weren't present when we had you on higher doses. But since reducing you to 400 milligrams, you've always been able to see Larry and Breezy, or at least their shadows."

"Not anymore. Larry left a couple of weeks ago, and Breezy left on Saturday. I don't feel their presence at all anymore. Not even their shadows."

"Perhaps your medication has finally—"

"No," I cut in. "It's not that. They left on their own. They wanted to leave."

"Why?"

"Well, Arnold is almost always around, so I guess they don't feel like I need them anymore."

"Do you need them?"

I look up at Melinda, the one person I trusted more than anyone until Arnold came into my life. I've known Melinda for over three years. It hasn't even been three months with Arnold, and yet here I am, wishing I had just listened to Melinda back in June. *Are you not at all concerned that you may be rushing things a bit with Arnold?* I'm concerned now, that's for sure. I've lost Larry and Breezy because of him. But is that necessarily a bad thing? Do I really need them?

"Well, Larry keeps my hygiene in line, and Breezy is my reminder to water the garden. But those are lame reasons to need someone. It's just…" I bite my lip and look away for a second, in case I do cry, but nothing comes out. "It's not the same without them. But in a way, I guess it's better. It's what everyone wants for me. To stop seeing make-believe people and to engage in the real world. But the real world isn't all that great, not always."

"That is true. The real world can be a dark and terrifying place. But you have Arnold in your life now. And you've said several times that he makes you feel safe and comfortable. Confident even."

"Yes. He does. For the most part. Sometimes. But I'm not sure, that is to say, I'm not sure he's always going to be able to protect me. And I don't think I should have to rely on him to do that because that's a huge task for one person to take on. I think I should take some responsibility and be able to take care of myself. I'll be eighteen soon. I should act like an adult, not a child."

"This is a new you." Melinda smiles, seemingly pleased with my response. "That's a very mature outlook. You must take responsibility for your own health, for your own well-being. It puts you in charge of your life. And essentially, that's what we're all trying to achieve."

"But isn't too much control a bad thing? Doesn't it make you uptight and anxious?"

"Not necessarily. Because when you're able to run your own life, you can differentiate when something is outside your range of control. Other people's actions, for example, you have little control over. But how well you respond and relate to those actions, keeps you in charge of your life, your goals, and your future."

"So what happens if someone I'm close to is doing something bad, and it has a negative effect on how we relate to each other? Am I supposed to accept their fault and live with it? Or am I supposed to help them?"

"It depends on what exactly it is they're doing. For example, if they're causing harm to themselves or you, then you have every right to tell them to stop, and if they don't, then you have every right to tell someone capable of helping them."

"I can't help them myself?"

"Rachel, is there something Arnold is doing? Something bad that you don't want to talk about?"

I don't know if it's bad, only that it makes me feel bad. Or it could just be the awful weekend I had, throwing everything out of proportion. Maybe it's post-traumatic stress? Or I'm getting sick? Or I just need a reason why I'm wrong and Arnold is right, so I can go back to him without fear and doubt.

"I can't tell you." But I should. "It may not even be that bad. It may just be me overthinking things, worrying too much."

"I see." Melinda stands and moves her rocking chair right next to the couch. She's never this intimate, but I'm not running for the door. Just a tad surprised.

Seeing her up close, I notice the gray hairs sneaking through her strawberry-blonde hair, neatly braided around her head. Her neck, while slightly wrinkled from age, is long and graceful. But she smells like suntan lotion, and it makes me think of my peeling skin and how neglectful I've been. Arnold doesn't have to worry about sunburn or imaginary friends, but I sure as hell do.

"Let me tell you a story," Melinda says at last. "I once treated a patient, a young woman who had been dating a man for almost a decade. She came to me initially due to anxiety, which she blamed on her stressful job, back pain, asthma, and so forth. But over time, it became clear that her biggest anxiety was her boyfriend. Because he was a crack addict. And she was embarrassed to tell me about it for years. She had kept his nasty habit a secret and worked double to take care of herself and him. When it came time to figure out exactly what to do, it was too late. He'd been an addict for years, and even when we had an intervention, he refused treatment. And so, my patient, after years of dealing with this, decided to leave him. She was heartbroken. But not defeated. She picked up the pieces and started over again. She eventually found and fell in love with a stable man and married him.

But she wasted ten years of her life. Ten years trying to save someone she could not save on her own."

"I'm confused. How does this relate to Arnold? He's stable. He's fine. He doesn't cause me anxiety." Or does he? I bite the tip of my tongue. I wouldn't be sitting here, cultivating such negative thoughts about him otherwise. "He just…" Air catches in my throat; I'm panicking now.

"Take a deep breath." Melinda's hands hover over my torso. "You know I'm not going to pick up the phone and call the police if you tell me Arnold is stealing or selling drugs or whatever he's doing."

I don't take a deep breath. I just go for it. "He likes to get high. All the time. He doesn't like to be on his medication. He doesn't want me to be on my medication, like ever. He wants me to get high with him. But I don't want to anymore. I just want to go back to what it was like at the beginning."

I cover my face with both hands, humiliated by my confession.

But Melinda has no reason to jump the gun like my mother would in this situation. She remains calm. Professional to the end.

"Rachel, have you been getting high with Arnold?"

"I…"

"Look at me, Rachel. Take your hands off your face."

I drag one hand away, then the other. "I did marijuana with him, the gummy kind. For weeks straight. And…" I swallow hard. "I've been skipping my Seroquel. A lot."

"Define a lot."

"Well, for the last year or so, I've been skipping just a few times a week. Larry and Breezy become more alive and speak to me, but only at home. Nothing crazy happened. I didn't have any withdrawal symptoms or complications. My mom didn't even notice. But then I met Arnold, and things just happened way too fast. We started having all these ideas."

"We or him?"

"Mostly him. But I…I contributed. And I agreed to everything, so long as we were safe and looked after each other." I gasp for air, realizing I've been holding my breath. I wait a few seconds to recharge before speaking again. "About a week after the fire, we stopped taking our pills so we wouldn't have to feel so numb all the time. But then we started getting high. Every single day. And then this weekend, I crashed. I just couldn't take it anymore. All the feelings, the emotions. All the doubt. And then…" I almost let it slip what happened with Tommy and the intangibles, but I move past all that. "I just needed it to stop. So I went back on my pill because I need to be numb again."

"Rachel, you don't need to be *numb*. You need to talk about your feelings. Talk about what happened. Does your mother know anything about what you just told me?"

"She'd freak if I told her."

"Are Arnold's parents aware of this?"

"Who knows? They're not around much. I hardly see them. But there's a history. A big history. They moved across the country to start over. To have a second chance. But every so often, Arnold says something or does something that makes me feel like that second chance is going to slip away. Like I'm going to lose him. I want to help him before it's too late, but I feel so helpless right now."

Melinda pats the side of the couch, rather than my hand, though I wouldn't object to physical comfort at this point. "It's good that you're telling me this," she says, her voice so warm it could thaw a frozen heart. "I can help you. I can help you both. Is Arnold seeing a therapist at all?"

"He saw someone once in May, right after they moved here, but it didn't work out. I guess maybe they're still searching for one? I don't know. His parents work long hours, and I guess they just assume everything is fine because he's with me all the time. And happy. He's so happy when he sees me."

"But you're not always happy to see him?"

I used to be. Before that concert, I woke up every morning with a big smile on my face, overjoyed with the thought of seeing Arnold. It never really mattered what we did because the minute we took a gummy, I had no apprehensions. I just went with the flow. Whatever idea Arnold had, I said yes, no questions asked. We lived in the moment. We lived for the now. I gambled and won so much, just to lose it all in one night.

"Let me ask another question," Melinda says when it becomes apparent I'm lost for words. "What do you think would happen if you no longer spent time with Arnold?"

"It would be bad for him."

"Bad for him. Bad for you?"

I cringe and pull my knees into my chest like a freaking toddler. "I don't know. I don't know anymore."

"Rachel, it sounds like Arnold needs you more than you need him. Sometimes marijuana users need another person to get high with to achieve validation. To make what they're doing seem okay, seem harmless."

"Arnold believes it helps me. And it helps him. When we're high, we're better."

"Getting high may give you temporary happiness and bliss, but it doesn't cure the underlying cause of one's pain or illness."

"But there's no reason for him to feel any pain."

"No reason? I would think about what you just said. You're far too intelligent to be saying such things."

"I just..." I pause and consider my words before speaking again. "Nothing bad happened to him as a kid." Except for the wolf.

"Rachel, we've discussed this before. One doesn't need to have a tragic childhood to develop a mental disorder. It's a combination of genetics, brain chemistry, and environment that contributes to the development of one's illness. ADHD is complex. And many people who have ADHD also have depression and lean toward drug use to justify their self-worth."

I squeeze my legs extra hard, trying to deflate the uncertainty crawling through my body like a storm of ants. "I just wish I knew what I could do to make him feel better, without the drugs." With a puff of air, I straighten my legs. I don't feel any less anxious, but at least I'm moving in the right direction.

"Something is lacking in Arnold's life. It's just not out in the open. It's something buried deep within him, and it sounds like he hasn't had proper counseling or treatment to let it out."

"He's just been fed pills."

"Medication can help, but whatever's in here"—she points to her head—"and especially here"—she rubs her hand across her heart. "If that's not at peace, then compensations will be made. Something has to fill the gap."

"I thought I was enough." I lower my head, feeling like I've made Arnold worse by compensating with him. "I told Arnold we should stop doing drugs."

"And did he?"

"No, he was high today."

"You need to tell him again to stop. You need to tell him how it makes you feel and how concerned you are for his well-being."

"He wouldn't understand. He's more concerned about my well-being."

"Well, from the sound of things, it seems like you're doing better than he is. Not only are you talking about your feelings, but you have a desire to improve and make things better, without the help of drugs."

"But what about my medication?"

"Prescription medication is vastly different from nonprescription drug addiction."

I sit up, my upper body rigid. "You're saying Arnold is a drug addict?"

"Do you think he's a drug addict?"

"He can't be. A drug addict doesn't care about others. Arnold cares about me. I know he does."

"Arnold depends on you."

I pounce off the couch and storm to the other side of the room. I grab one of Melinda's many pillows, and while I want to throw it or maybe beat the life out of it, I squeeze it with all my might and yell, "I'm not a drug!"

But I am Arnold's favorite high. So what does that make me? What does that make him? Us? Our relationship? Is it all just an escape from reality? Just a temporary fix? At the end of it all, if we were to separate, would we survive? Or would we both fall apart?

I feel the tears prickling. At last, they break through, hot and heavy, moving like lava down my face. I waver in the corner to sniffle against the pillow, embarrassed to cry in front of Melinda. In front of anyone. How did everything get so messed up? How could I let this happen?

"Rachel, are you alright?" Melinda asks, coming up from behind. She doesn't touch me but offers a tissue.

"I'm fine. I'm…" I nod my head several times and crumble the tissue into a ball. "I just need a chance to fix this. To make things right."

She guides me back to the couch. "You will have your chance to talk to Arnold. But you need to be ready for the outcome. It may not be in your favor."

Knowing Arnold, he could react in one of two ways. One, he could be sweet about it and thank me for opening up to him, for being so brave. And then turn it all around, making me out to be the one in trouble again. The one who needs saving. The one who is falling apart. At the beginning of our relationship, I played that part, and it's not something I want to go back to.

Two, he could get angry. But then feel like a jackass, calm down, and go the sweet route.

And knowing me, I'd fall right back to him. Or run.

What would Melinda do? What would any of my favorite heroines do? They would fight until the world ends.

But this is reality. Fights don't always end with a winner. And not everyone gets a happy ending.

"I could lose him."

"Yes," Melinda says. "But you can't lose yourself trying to save him."

I nod and finally pat my eyes dry with the tissue. I take several deep breaths, guided by Melinda, and then close my eyes for nearly a minute to steady my heart and thoughts. I remind myself that it's alright to feel low, and that there is always a reason for pain, even if I'm trying to hide from it.

"How are you feeling right now?" Melinda asks.

"Scared."

"Are you prepared to talk to Arnold?"

I nod. "You can't tell my mom about any of this. Or Arnold's parents."

"I won't, for now. But you need to keep opening up to me, Rachel. And you need to keep opening up to Arnold. To your mother. To those who love you. Don't ever be afraid to tell people what you truly think, what you truly feel. Nine times out of ten, relationships fail due to a lack of communication and honesty. You can say it's fine. Or you can say no, it's not fine. It's up to you. It's always up to you."

"And what about my pill? Is that up to me?"

"Rachel, it concerns me that you withdrew from your medication without my consent, but at the end of the day, I can't force you to take that pill. And neither can your mother, as much as she believes she can. There are laws that protect you from that. Unless, of course, you were deemed insane, but you're not insane. You're just a young woman going through a tough time right now. And like all young women, you have the opportunity to rise or fall. So I encourage you to make the best decision for yourself. One that will give you the best opportunity to rise."

nineteen

THE FOLLOWING MORNING, I shower, dress, and fix myself a well-balanced breakfast of scrambled eggs, whole wheat toast, and orange juice. I prolong eating because I know what I'm supposed to do right afterward. I'm supposed to take my pill. I consider what Melinda said about making choices that will give me the best opportunity to rise. Today I'm supposed to confront Arnold. And I want the outcome in my favor.

Arnold arrives around 10:00, completely sober, with a bundle of purple lilies. Am I dreaming, hallucinating, or is this really him? His hair is combed back. He smells extra amazing, like he just soaked in a bubble bath, and his mouth tastes like peppermint.

"Wow," I say in between kisses. "Where did you come from?"

"Safeway. And where have you been?" he asks, looking down at my bare feet, stained with soil. "In your garden?"

"Yes, I was trying to reinforce the lock on the gate."

"Do you need any help?"

"No, I figured it out, but thanks."

"Is everything growing again?"

"It's starting to pick up."

"Great."

After thanking him with another kiss, I take the flowers and search the kitchen for a vase. Arnold follows and helps himself to a glass of water.

"Is your mom home?" he asks, sitting down at the kitchen table.

"She's dead asleep. Won't be up until afternoon."

"Do you want to go back to my place?"

"What's wrong with here?"

"Nothing. I just thought we could do a workout together and then maybe go to the lake. Catch a movie later? Maybe even some Chipotle?"

"Is that it?"

"Yeah, unless there's something else you want to do."

"There is." I pour water into the vase. "I'd like to talk."

"Isn't that what we're doing right now?"

I look around, debating where to put the lilies. The best sunlight comes right through the kitchen window, but Mom's fake flowers are in the way. When I move them, the pot slips out of my hands and lands smack on the floor. I gasp, scared of it being broken, but it's just plastic.

"You okay?" Arnold asks, coming to the rescue again.

"Yes, fine." I quickly pick up the fake pot and toss it on the counter. Then I move Arnold's flowers to the window. "There, perfect."

"Is there something specific you wanted to talk about?" He puts his hands around my waist and kisses my neck.

"I…" That feels so good. That little nibbling he does on my earlobe. Always puts me in the mood.

"Yes?" He kisses me smack in the middle of my throat. It causes me to smile, then cough, just enough of a distraction to pull me out of his trance.

"You're normal today." I look into his eyes, no dilation and no redness. "I mean, you're not high today."

"You said we needed to take a break."

"Yes, but yesterday…"

"I was very stressed after I saw Tommy. I didn't want to see you all loud and angry. Not after what you went through on Friday."

"Oh."

"I also need to stay sober for a while. Not just because we're taking a break, but because I'm going to the doctor on Friday, and I'm ninety-nine percent sure there'll be a drug test."

"Arnold, you're not going to pass. Even I know that stuff can stay in your system for weeks."

"That's if they collect urine. But I cheated my way through several urine tests in Santa Cruz, so my mom will request a saliva test. And while it can pick up THC pretty easily, it's only accurate for recent usage. If I go four days sober, it won't pick up anything."

"Just four days?"

"Yeah. I'll detox the whole week, work out extra hard, drink lots of water. It's no big deal. It only becomes a big deal if my parents decide to do weekly home-tests again."

"Why would they do that?"

"They would only do that if they were suspicious of me using again."

"You don't think they'll ever find out?"

"It's not going to happen. I'm older now. Smarter about it."

"But what if they did find out? Like, what if someone told them?"

"I would never tell them. And you would never tell them. The only other people that know are Tommy and Ale, and I doubt they're interested in pissing me off again."

"Okay. I just thought…"

"You thought what?" His eyes harden then soften in all of five seconds. "It's okay to tell me, even if you think it will make me upset. You should always be honest with me."

"Well." I turn away from him and look directly at the lilies. "I'm not taking a break from it. I'm not going back at all. I don't ever want to do those drugs again."

He releases a held breath. "So, that's it? You're going to stick to your pill?"

"Not doing that either. I want to go clean. I want to see if I can handle being me, all on my own. I think I'll know myself better if I just allow myself to feel things again, even if it hurts. Even if it doesn't always make me happy. I have to give myself this chance. And if I fail, I fail, but I have to try."

"Okay." He folds his arms across his chest and nods his head. "Well, what do you think of me doing it? Would it bother you?"

"If it was once a week or so, then it would be okay. In moderation. But you seem to want to get high every day. After a while, it's not that special anymore. Just like you and me, having sex all the time, it's eventually going to get old. And we're going to want more. Feel like we need more. And then we'll start to fight. Get disconnected. Stop communicating. Stop wanting to see each other."

"Whoa. Whoa." He throws his hands up. "Are you talking about us breaking up?"

"No. I'm just saying that's what happens in relationships when you're constantly wanting more and not compromising."

"Are you saying I don't compromise?"

"You make decisions for both of us. You do it all the time without realizing it. Because you want me to go along with you. You want me by your side, always."

"What's wrong with that?"

"I just want to make sure you want me by your side for all the right reasons. Not because you just need someone to ride with."

"Just someone? You think you're just *someone*? You're everything to me, Rachel. If anything ever happened to you, I wouldn't be able to live. I'd die."

"No, don't say that." I slink away from him, the back door looking mighty safe. "Don't put it all on me."

"I'm not. I want to be with you forever. I want to get out of this place and take you with me. When we're both eighteen, that's what we'll do. We'll get out of here and make a life that fits us both. If you need your intangibles to come along, that's fine. I'm down for that. But if I need my drugs, then they need to come too. That's our compromise. Don't you see how perfect it is?"

"Arnold, I don't need my intangibles anymore."

"Okay, they don't come. Then it's you and me."

"And your marijuana? No." I start walking toward the door. It's not safe in here. I need air. I need my garden, something organic.

Arnold steps in front of me, blocking my exit. "What are you saying?"

"I can't do this." I turn around and head for the front door. Arnold nearly leaps over the coffee table to get there first.

"Where is all this coming from? Are you still down from Friday? If you're still sad, you need to tell me."

"I'm not sad. I'm just finally opening my eyes. I see who you really are, and it worries me. It scares me."

"I scare you? What the fuck?"

"You need help! *Professional* help!"

"I already got professional help. Remember? It didn't help. None of it helped. Just made me feel dead inside. Is that what you want? You want me to be medicated all the time? Well, you can forget ever having fun again. No more concerts. No more adventures. We'll just be two studs, sitting on a couch, watching Disney movies all day."

"What's wrong with that? I could be happy with that. I could be happy with just you and a Disney movie."

"That life sucks!"

"Then I must suck!"

"That's not what I said."

"But that's what you meant!" I'm hysterical now, pacing back and forth. Arnold tries to reach out to me, but I can't stand him right now. I can't stand who he is anymore. I can't even stand myself.

"Rachel, please."

When he tries to grab my arm, I twist side to side and scream, "I can't do this, Arnold! I can't go down this road with you. I'm not going to become a *drug addict* like you!"

Arnold's eyes bulge. But he's not looking at me. He's looking at my mother, standing at the top of the stairs in her nightgown. She covers her mouth with both hands, cemented in shock. Did she hear everything? Part of it? Or just what I screamed?

"Nice job, Rachel," Arnold says. "You just ruined everything."

Before I can say another word, Arnold opens the front door and runs to his house. I could chase after him, but I just stand there in the doorway, watching what could have been the best thing in my life, or the worst, disappear.

When I go back inside, Mom is standing at the kitchen counter with my medicine pack. Her skin is a shade paler, almost like chalk, and her eyes water. Rather than cry, she looks up at the ceiling to compose herself. She smiles and releases a strange laugh that half-sounds like a child screaming. I can't tell if she's lost her mind, still in shock, or actually humored by the situation.

Finally, she looks at me, and I know the answer. She's totally aware of what's going on, and I'm in big trouble.

"Rachel, what is this?" she asks in a near whisper.

"What is what?"

"This is your pack for July."

"Yeah?"

She tosses the pack onto the counter. "You've missed several pills." I forgot to flush some. "Why?"

"I choose when I want to take my pill. And I choose not to take them anymore."

"That is not a decision you are capable of making yourself."

"Melinda and I talked about it yesterday."

"She knows? She knows, and she didn't tell me?"

"Confidentiality agreement. It applies to minors too."

"And does she know about your drug addict boyfriend?"

"Mom, please. Before you get angry—"

"Rachel." She bites down on her bottom lip very hard. "You're not to see him anymore. And tomorrow morning, we're going straight to the doctor's office to get you on the shot."

"But Melinda—"

"Say one more word." She points a finger at me before curling it into a tight fist. "And that'll be the last time you ever see Melinda again."

"Mom, you don't understand. I skipped my medicine so I could—"

"I need to call the Begays." She rips the cordless phone off the wall. "They need to know what their son has been doing."

"Mom, don't!"

"Or maybe I should call the police instead."

"*Mom!*"

"Go to your room, Rachel!" She slams the phone on the counter so hard I'm surprised it doesn't break. "Go to your room now!"

She won't budge. No amount of begging, pleading, or crying will make her change her mind when she's so distraught.

I sprint upstairs, leaping over steps to my bedroom. My whole body starts to shake. I turn around several times, convinced the walls are closing in on me. I stop moving and shut my eyes; it's only my head that's caving in with horrible thoughts. I'm losing everyone. My intangibles, Arnold, and possibly Melinda too. And if I go on the shot, I lose myself. It'll feel like double doses every day. I'll be completely numb. And just like Arnold, I'll be dead inside. What's the point in that? What's the point in living? Doesn't my mom get it? I'm not alive on those pills. I'm not alive if I can't say what I'm feeling. I'm not alive if I hide any longer.

I rub my neck and think of Arnold's scars. If he had short hair, his scars would be in plain sight all the time. He chooses to have long hair to cover it up. To hide from the pain.

Melinda was wrong. So wrong. No matter how hard I try, I'll never be in control of my life. There will always be someone telling me what to do. Keeping me locked up. Confined to the gray. But I've tasted so many colors since knowing Arnold, and I want more. I want another chance at life.

I take out my phone and consider my options. Melinda or Arnold?

"So I encourage you to make the best decision for yourself. One that will give you the best opportunity to rise."

I can't rise at home with my hysterical mother. I can't rise in Melinda's humid blue office. I can't rise with Arnold when he's high. But today, he is sober. So maybe there is still a chance to make things right.

R: **If you want to run away, I'll go with you.**
A: **Grab some cash and meet me in my garage right now.**

twenty

I PACK a few belongings in addition to cash. Arnold can't expect me to run away without my phone charger and a change of clothes. When I creep down the stairs, Mom is on the phone with the Begays, talking a mile a minute about me skipping my medication and Arnold being a raging drug addict. She hasn't heard our side of the story, and she's already making awful conclusions, putting all the blame on Arnold.

"If he's into marijuana, he probably drinks as well!" Mom exclaims as she storms downstairs to check the basement liquor cabinet, where she stores her vodka. As soon as she's out of sight, I slip out the front door and run to Arnold's house. Arnold is in the garage, waiting in the driver's seat of his parents' SUV. They own two cars, but they ride the convertible to work. I jump into the passenger side and shut the door. Before either of us can say a word, Arnold puts the car in reverse and drives away.

At the first stop sign, he reaches over to put my seat belt on. "Don't panic," he says. "It'll be okay."

"I'm not panicking." I swallow the egg in my throat. "But you don't have your license."

"Doesn't mean I can't drive a car."

He's not a bad driver. He knows what to do. Drives the speed limit and uses his turn signal. Still, I'm a nervous wreck, thinking we'll drive off a bridge or have the entire police department on our heels.

"Do we have a plan?" I ask, my hands clenching my bag like a lifesaver.

"It depends. How mad was your mom?"

"On a scale of one to ten? Eleven-hundred. When I left, she was on the phone with your parents. She says I can't see you anymore because you've corrupted me. And she wants to put me on the shot to make sure I'm always medicated."

"That means she overheard a lot. And told my parents a lot."

I bite my lip and look down. "I'm sorry for yelling."

At the next stop sign, Arnold puts a hand on my shoulder. "I'm sorry too."

"For what?"

"For everything."

That's a lot to be sorry for. As much as I want to believe him, I'm not sure Arnold has the capacity to feel such remorse. And as much as I want to let go and care for him, I'm still not able to forget what he said in the living room.

"What's your biggest fear right now?" Arnold asks.

"Everything."

"Well, we should be okay, as long as they don't call the police. But it's best just to get as far away from here as possible. We'll drive west toward the mountains."

"My grandpa lives west. Hagerstown. It's about an hour from here."

"Do you want to go see him?"

"Not really. But it's the last place my mom would suspect I would go."

"He won't freak out when he sees us? Or call your mom?"

"I don't know. Just drive. We'll make the decision later."

Arnold turns onto the highway. He seems a bit tense, taking the car up in speed, but he relaxes his breath once he merges into the middle lane and switches to cruise control. He's persistent with keeping both hands on the wheel, but I'm more concerned about his leg tremors.

I check my phone, overflowing with missed calls from my mother and several all-caps text messages, asking me where I am and how I better get back home right this second. Arnold encourages me to turn my phone off as he did already, but I can't.

I lean my head against the window and exhale until the glass fogs. I'm exhausted, and the back of my head is especially tingly, as if I did something to my neck. Maybe it's just all the stress weighing down. Or maybe it's my mind drifting. Past, present, future. It all looks the same. Me, longing for something I can't quite reach. There's one particular memory begging to be replayed, so I close my eyes and recall every moment.

Our last "family" vacation was to Ocean City. It was the summer before eighth grade. It was right around the time I started to drift away from reality. I remember swimming into the ocean until I could no longer feel the bottom with my feet. Unafraid, I turned onto my back, closed my eyes, and let myself float along with the waves. I heard the most beautiful music, someone singing "Rainy Days and Mondays," a song my dad liked to play whenever it rained. Didn't have to be a Monday. I hummed along with the strange voice until a wave crashed over me. I realized how far I was out, and there was no way I'd get back to shore on my own. The lifeguard blew his whistle and waved for me to return. But there was a boat nearby I could swim to. A fisherman with blond hair and blue eyes humming that tune. He had a little girl with him. And she hummed too. So serene, so happy. Just the two of them. I wanted so badly to reach that boat, to get on board with them, to get away from my angry mother, crying at shore. But the lifeguard made it out to me and lugged me back to the beach. I screamed and cried like a preschooler being pulled out of a candy store. I tried to tell Mom about the boat, but she just blinked at the ocean and said, "What boat? What are you talking about?" I was too upset to talk about it anymore. She would never understand. So I stayed under the umbrella and never went back into the water again. The following summer the only swimming I did was at my grandpa's lake house. No waves. No boats. No nothing. Because I was on my medication by then.

I blink several times, making sure I'm awake and clear about what's happening. I look around the car, then at the highway signs. I cross my legs and try to relax. But I never had time to use the bathroom before we left.

"How long can you hold it?" Arnold asks after I express my discomfort.

"Uh, maybe twenty minutes?"

"Alright. We'll stop in ten. We just can't stop at any place for too long."

Because we're basically fugitives now, running away from our angry parents. This is how it would have been had Romeo and Juliet escaped together. But Shakespeare opted to kill them to teach the parents a lesson. I think of the tragic romance novels scattered about my bedroom, how most ended in death or despair.

Arnold stops at a gas station to fill the tank and grab some snacks for the ride. Get in and out as quickly as possible. Sure, no problem. I just have to pee, but as I wash my hands, an all-too-familiar face creeps up from behind.

I stop breathing, scared that a single exhale might make her do something crazy. But I can't hold my breath forever, just like I couldn't swim forever. Someone will pull me back, and this time it's me. I slowly blow out the air, release the tension in my shoulders, and speak to her.

"Mary."

"Rachel." She hasn't spoken to me in years. It's odd that her voice sounds so familiar, almost like I'm hearing a recording of myself. She is more real than anyone; even Arnold feels like a silhouette in comparison. I swear I can hear her heartbeat in sync with my own. I can smell her breath. She had eggs and toast for breakfast. And something citrusy to drink. A glass of orange juice, perhaps.

"What do you want?" I ask, quickly drying my hands against my shirt.

"What do you think?"

"Are you here to cause trouble again?"

"Trouble?"

"You're always out to get me. Why can't you just leave me alone?"

"I'm not out to get you. I'm here to help you."

"Help me?"

"I've been trying."

"How? When?"

"I saved you from Tommy. I helped you to grab that bottle."

"That was just the one time. What about the other times? Like when you slapped me."

"I didn't slap you. You slapped yourself."

"No, I saw you reach a hand toward me."

"To try to stop you from hurting yourself. And when I stopped you in the school hallway, it wasn't to keep you from getting out of the building. It was to get you to notice Alexia, to save her."

"Why would you want me to save Alexia?"

"Because she didn't deserve to be left behind. No one deserves that."

"Okay. So you've been looking out for me *recently*. But what about before? All those years ago when you messed up my basketball games?"

"I wasn't trying to get in the way. You asked me for help."

"What are you talking about? Why would I ask you for help?"

"Before the games, when you had your panic attacks, you'd ask me for help. You'd ask all of us. So I did my best, but it was hard with everyone else around. Everyone had their own way of helping you. Michelle would want to play with you, which was dumb of her. Larry and Donovan would try to coach you from the bleachers, causing you to ignore your own coach. And then Breezy would browse in, wearing that stupid sombrero hat, and prattle about gardening, a huge distraction."

I try to remember, but it's a jumbled mess. I definitely remember the noise; no one would shut up. My coach would yell one thing, the intangibles would yell something else. My heart would pound extra loud to mask the voices, and I'd spend too much time holding onto the ball, not passing, and then finally everyone would scream, *Pass the ball!* And I'd hurl it away, like a grenade. Sometimes I would pass to a teammate, sometimes to the other team, and the one time, I hit that kid in the bleachers. And that's when I got benched, permanently. Rather than sit, I walked out of the gymnasium, with all my intangibles following me, all trying to help, and when they wouldn't leave me alone, I turned around and told them to go away. But it was only my mother chasing after me. She couldn't understand why I was yelling at her. No one could understand. It wasn't until the episode with Irwin that my mother finally realized what was happening to me.

"Why did you attack Irwin?" I ask. "I know the guy was a creep, but why did you have to attack him and get me locked up?"

"I didn't attack Irwin or make you attack him. I tried to stop you from attacking him."

"That's not true."

"Rachel, you attacked him."

"Why? Why would I do that?"

"Because he reminded you of your father, and you turned him into a monster, so it would justify your emotions. But not your actions. You blamed me for that. Which is why I left for so many years, even when you started to skip your medicine, I stayed away. Because frankly, you made me pretty upset, putting all the blame on me. The others blamed me too, especially Larry, even though they all knew it wasn't my fault."

"Why would they do that?"

"It was easier to blame me than to blame you. You're our tangible. We feed off you, not each other. When there's nothing left to feed on, we go away."

"So taking my medicine doesn't make one bit of difference? You guys just come and go as you please?"

"Of course your medicine makes a difference. It puts up the wall, or the 'pole' as you like to call it. It makes it harder for us to break through when you're numb and tired. And the more you take it, the higher the wall grows. But even without the pill, you still have ways of blocking us. Every time you have sex or take a gummy, you block. You mask. You hide. You do exactly what Arnold does to hide from his problems."

"Arnold's problems aren't like mine."

"Oh, but he sure likes to think they are. It makes it a lot easier for him to cope. To hide from the truth. Just like you."

"Shut up."

"Do you want to know what I'm still feeding on?"

"No."

"I'm feeding on the truth."

"What truth? I've faced every truth. I've been through therapy. I've talked everything out."

"No, you haven't."

I rub the back of my neck. The pain from my head is spreading into my shoulders, making it extremely difficult to stand straight.

"Why you?" I shake my head. "Why you?"

"The others gave up on you. They couldn't handle all the changes, and they especially couldn't handle someone like Arnold. I'm the only one left because I'm the most like you. You didn't need a doll or story-book to make me up."

"You're not like me."

"I am, Rachel. And you need me."

"I don't need you! I don't need any of you! I just…want my…" I'm shaking now. Every bit of me is shaking. I want so badly to push her away, but I would only be pushing myself.

"What do you want, Rachel?"

My phone buzzes. I look up at Mary, wondering if she'll disappear if I read the text, but she nods her head as though encouraging me to do so.

Mom: **Please come home. I'm sorry.**

"It's a trap."

"No, it's not," Mary says. "Your mom loves you."

"She wants to take me away from Arnold forever. And I can't…"

"You can't live without him?"

Someone knocks on the door, causing me to jump backward. I nearly slip into the sink but catch myself last minute. I turn around several times and check the mirror. Mary is gone, but the terror she's left in me is apparent.

"Babe, is everything okay in there?" Arnold calls.

"I'm fine! I'm coming!"

I splash cold water on my face and rush out the door without drying my hands. I collide with Arnold, knocking over the brown paper bag he's carrying. A water bottle rolls out, along with several bags of beef jerky and pretzels and a few condoms. Seriously? Arnold has sex on his mind when we're on the run?

I should question his motives, but I bite my tongue. Why am I holding back? What am I so afraid of?

When we bend down to pick up the items, Arnold pauses to look at me, and I look, too. Our eyes seem to be screaming, *I'm so scared. This isn't a good idea.* But when we blink, Arnold grabs my wet hand and leads me out the door.

Mom continues to text and call for the next fifteen minutes, and I treat her with silence. I can only imagine how upset she is right now. How upset Arnold's parents are. I am filled with guilt. And the more

Arnold doesn't care, the more I care. It's like I have to fill the gap for him.

"Maybe we should at least tell them we're okay," I suggest.

"No. They don't deserve that."

"My mom does."

"Mine don't."

"Do you hate them?"

"No. I don't hate them. Even though I want to, I can't."

"Why?"

"If I hate them, then it's because they don't love me."

"You doubt that they love you?"

Arnold takes a deep breath, signals, turns his head several times to check for oncoming cars, then merges to the far-right lane. The exit to my grandfather's house is coming up, but I keep silent.

"It's the way they handle things," Arnold says, slowing the car to 50 mph, twenty miles below the speed limit. "They want a quick fix for everything. When I had problems growing up, whether big or small, they just turned to tutors, community events, or counselors. They never tried to solve any problem with me because God forbid it distracts them too much from their careers. They thought buying me nice things and sending me to nice places would make me happy. It didn't."

"You just wanted *them*?"

"I just wanted them to notice me. To teach me things. To love me. Care about me."

"I'm sure they still do."

Arnold sighs, obviously disagreeing. "They couldn't handle me once I became a teenager. Couldn't handle the teachers calling about my behavior and lack of focus. They send me to one doctor, and boom, I'm ADHD and medicated. That's what they did to solve the problem. They let someone else take care of it."

"And it never really got better?"

"No, it didn't. And I was all alone in my thoughts, in my world. I lost a lot of friends because I was so angry all the time. I had no one. No purpose in life. I had no desire to do anything but get high, and when they took that away and kept me home, it was the ultimate betrayal. The ultimate, 'we don't give a shit about you anymore.' So what if I was depressed so long as I stayed out of trouble? You know what they were doing the night I tried to kill myself? They were planning a vacation to Hawaii for just the two of them. My mom was lamenting about needing to 'get away from it all.' Meaning, get away from me. Her only son. Sometimes I think I did it to get back at them. To make them suffer for what they did to me. Because they still don't think they did anything wrong. And they're so picture-perfect, no one would ever blame them. It'll always be my fault."

"I don't blame you, Arnold. I understand."

"How though? Your mom has done everything to be a part of your life. Even when you don't want her there, she's there. My parents are only there when they have to be there, never because they want to."

"My mom is the reason my dad left. And why he never came back. I never forgave her for that. I never let go of it."

I see Mary through the rearview window. Her presence is like a cold day in July but encouraging. We've had a rough past, but this time I see through those dark eyes of hers. I see beyond the creepy clothes and pale skin. I see a person, waking up to the truth. And if the truth isn't enough to save us, then at least it's enough to save me.

"Tell him," Mary says. "Tell him the truth about your dad."

"From what you've told me, your dad was reckless and gambled a lot," Arnold says. "He couldn't hold a job. And he took your dog away. Sounds like it was more his fault things ended. Not your mom's."

"But he was never reckless with me. He was always there for me. I could talk to him about anything. I trusted him completely. Then one day, he just got up and left, right after breakfast. I chased after him, begging, screaming for him to come back, but he didn't do or say anything. And neither did my mom. She just watched him drive away. Watched me cry and cry until I could no longer cry."

"But you both moved on."

"No. Not really. Because deep down, I still wish he would come back. It's been almost ten years, and I still want to see him again."

"Why?"

"Because I wanted him to take me with him. When I begged him to come back, it wasn't to come back and live with my mom. It was to come back to get me. To take me away. Rescue me. I needed him. I've always needed him."

"But you know he's never coming back." Arnold and Mary say those words simultaneously. And suddenly, everything makes perfect sense.

I never accepted my father's abandonment. I still believed, after all these years, that he would come back. It was my first delusion, which led to several others. The intangibles came into my life to save me from my own despair, but they were nothing more than a distraction —all but Mary in the end.

I take the deepest breath of my life.

"He can't help me," I say at last. "He's never coming back. And that will never change. He will never change."

Mary smiles. I've seen that gummy smile before. I realize who she is now. She isn't some creepy girl from a horror movie. She's everything I couldn't come to terms with. A little girl that just needed to face reality. To face it and move on.

I close my eyes, and Mary disappears forever. They're all gone now. Every last one. Because I finally let go, and I'm ready to move on. If I don't, they'll come back, one way or the other, pills or no pills. And maybe that's what a child would want. But I want to rise on my own. I want to be free of delusions and fear. I want to grow up.

"Arnold, stop the car."

"I can't. We're on the highway."

"Just pull over."

"There's a rest stop one mile ahead."

I'm patient enough to wait, but the minute he stops, I unbuckle my seat belt and get out of the car, dragging my duffel bag behind me.

"Are you sick?" he asks, running to my side.

"No. I'm not sick."

"Then what's wrong?"

"I don't want to go to my grandpa's house."

"Okay, we don't have to go there. We can find a campground somewhere else. Or maybe a motel."

"No, Arnold, I want to go home."

"Home? You just got done saying all this stuff about wanting to get away from your mom. And now you want to go home? You know what will happen. They'll separate us. And feed us pills until we're dead."

"Not if we talk it over with them. I know my mom can jump to conclusions way too quickly, and she's a stubborn control freak, but she's still my mother. I can't abandon her like my father did. I can't run away just because it's hard to live with her. I don't want to be like that. I don't want to be a coward."

"You wouldn't be. You'd be brave for finally getting away."

"What? Like my dad?"

"No, I didn't mean it like that. I meant…" Arnold groans and pulls on the back of his hair. It's not like him to struggle for words.

"Well, wherever my dad is, I hope he's happy. But he isn't brave."

"Rachel, please, don't go home." Arnold clasps his hands together. "Just stay with me. Talk to me. Tell me more about your dad, your life. I want to know more."

"I need to tell my mom these things."

"Do you really trust her with the truth?"

"Yes."

"More than me?"

"Yes."

Arnold's arms go limp. He takes a deep breath and stares at the ground, his mouth twisting ever so slightly. He could be trying to laugh, to mask his pain, or he could be trying to cry, to let some of the pain out. He stays like that for almost a minute, blinking only once. And then he lifts his head slowly to look at me. No smile. No tears. Just emptiness.

"I'm sorry if that hurts you," I finally say. "But I can't lie to you. I can't pretend everything between us is alright. I wanted it to be. I wanted it so bad. So bad that I was almost willing to leave everything behind. But I can't leave my mother. I just can't."

Arnold steps away from me, bobbing his head like a dying puppet. He finally releases that laugh, and he's gritting his teeth so hard, I know he's doing whatever he can to keep from crying. My instinct tells me to hug him. Kiss him. Make him feel better. Tell him how wonderful he is. And he is wonderful, despite all his darkness. But his darkness has hit me too hard this time. I have to step back.

"I'll take an Uber home," I say. "Or we can drive back together. It's your choice."

"I can't go back."

"Arnold, if you come back with me, there's always a chance we—"

"I'm not going back! So fuck off!"

"Fine. I'll fuck off." My body goes stiff, but my fingers work vigorously to put the Uber request in. The nearest driver is only a few miles away. When I look at Arnold, he's back to staring at the ground. Every exhale makes him seem smaller and smaller. "I know you're mad, but please say something. Let me know you're going to be okay."

"I think I've said enough." He laughs again and leans on the hood of his car. He reaches into his pocket and pulls out his bag of gummies, right in the middle of the parking lot. I gasp, thinking he's going to eat one or possibly the whole bag, but he merely holds it out and says, "Take this."

"I don't want any."

"Just, please take it. Throw it away. Do what you want with it."

I take the bag and shove it inside my duffel bag before someone sees it. "Where will you go?" I ask.

"I'm a wild turkey," he says. "I'll go where I please."

I don't like the sound of that. "Please come back with me." I reach for his arm, but he shrugs me off. "I don't want to leave you like this."

"You already did." He looks at me with this hard, awful smile. And then he's gone. It takes several seconds for me to make the realization that he is walking away with no intention of turning back. He crosses the parking lot and heads toward the woods, hands in his pockets, head down low. There's a mountain in the distance. I wonder if he plans to climb it. Or fall from it.

My heart stops at the thought. Is it wrong to let him go like this? Will I regret my decision? I keep thinking of when Melinda asked, *What do you think would happen if you no longer spent time with Arnold?* And my immediate response was, "It would be bad for him."

I look inside my duffel bag. My key chain is at the bottom. Disney movies are so far from the truth. Moana had her fair share of challenges, but you knew she would eventually save her island. You knew she wouldn't give up.

twenty-one

I SEND Mom one text message: **I'm coming home.** I send Arnold a similar text. And then I set my phone to vibrate and try not to think too hard about anything for the rest of the ride. Which proves to be impossible. My Uber driver is a middle-aged man, balding badly, with long, gangly arms. His car smells like evergreen, which instantly makes me think of Arnold, trekking through the forest all alone. I imagine him coming face to face with that wolf again. Would the wolf attack Arnold? Or would they make peace and go their separate ways?

I try calling him. It goes straight to voicemail, which means his phone is still off. I don't bother leaving a message. I can't think of anything else to do. Anything that could make him change his mind. All Arnold ever wanted was for his parents to love him. To care about him. To be present. How do I give him that?

The drive home seems shorter than the ride I took with Arnold. Mom is waiting for me outside on the front porch, still in her night-gown and robe. The Begays are sitting with her, still in their work clothes. Everyone has coffee. Why caffeine is always a necessity to solving problems is beyond me. Why not a cup of water?

I take my time getting out of the car, making sure to take my bag and thank the driver. I have no idea what kind of reaction I'll get from these three seemingly calm parents. Mom only shows her emotions in front of me, and even then, she wears a barrier.

I wait by the mailbox. The sun is still high, peeking between the tall maple trees in our backyard. I raise a hand to shield my eyes. I feel the prickling of a memory, causing pain to radiate into my neck and shoulders again.

It plays out in crystal clear images. My dad walking out the front door with a suitcase and Rosie, our basset hound, on a leash. He throws the suitcase into the back of his Honda Civic and puts Rosie in the front seat. Then I come out, asking him where he's going, but deep down, I already know. He doesn't answer, doesn't turn to look at me, just gets into the car and drives away. I run to the end of the driveway, screaming for him to stop. *"Come back. Please, come back."* But he's gone. He's not coming back for me. Mom eventually comes outside to get me. She tries to hold me, but I push her away and run straight to my room. I pack a suitcase. I'm going to follow him. I'm going to find him. And the first thing I'll ask is, "Why did you leave me?"

But I don't. Because I'm just a little girl. And I would only be chasing a memory.

When I look back at the front porch, Mom is no longer there but instead moving toward me. She pauses on the other side of the mailbox, not sure if she should touch me since we all know what happened the last time she tried to do that. I pushed her away. And I continued to push her away to make room for my delusions. My intangibles.

But no one will ever hold me like my mother does. Not even Arnold.

I step forward and put my arms around her waist. I don't squeeze, don't try to force anything, I just hold her. And eventually, she puts her arms around me and does the same. I feel a piece of me finally die, like an old candle that has burned for too long.

"I'm sorry," I finally say. "I made a mistake."

"I know," she says. "I'm sorry too. I made one too. Several."

"Please don't put me on the shot. Please just let me talk. Let me tell you everything."

"We'll talk it over with Melinda tomorrow. But right now, we need you to help us find Arnold. We haven't called the police yet, but…"

Another car pulls up in front of our house. It's the SUV. It's Arnold.

I can't believe it, but somehow I do.

Arnold stumbles out of the car and crashes to his knees. He covers his face with both hands and sobs uncontrollably, like a little boy. He even bites his own hand to stop himself from screaming. I find my place in the grass with him. And I hold him. Cradle him in my arms. Keep him from hurting himself. A dam has broken inside of him, and the pain is bursting out. But I will hold him until the water is still again. However long it takes.

He rubs a finger against his neck, and I notice that one of his scars is bleeding, ever so slightly, as if he scratched it open with his own fingernails. "I couldn't do it," he says. "I couldn't leave."

I fear there's a double meaning in his words. And it hurts twice as much. My tears fall and mix with the tiny streaks of red, creating a trail of pink down his neck. I will never know sadness like this. Even in all my days of despair, I always stood up. I always kept going.

I could tell Arnold to stand, to face his parents and tell them the truth. But the truth can't always be said with words. And right now, this is what Arnold's parents need to see. And this is what my mother needs to see. That I'm not going to give up on Arnold, despite his darkness. He is worth more than saving. He is worth compassion. He is worth forgiveness. And he is worth love.

Eventually, the Begays come toward us. They're not crying, sobbing, or looking to hug or hold anyone. And that's fine. That's how they handle themselves. That's their reality. But they do say something, something important that Arnold needs to hear and hear more often.

"Son, we're glad you're home."

"I don't understand why they hurried to get him back inside. Do you think they were embarrassed?"

Mom sits next to me on the couch with two glasses of water and a plate of sandwiches. "I think they just wanted to get him somewhere safe."

"He's safe with me."

"Rachel, after everything that happened today, don't you think it's best if Arnold has some time alone with his parents? Just like you and I are doing right now?"

I take one of the sandwiches. "Yes." I bite, but the bread gets stuck to the roof of my mouth. "But I can't help but worry. He's—"

"Someone special?"

"Yes." I take a sip of water. I'm not that hungry. "I know you guys are really mad at us for what we did, but I still care about him. I want him to be happy."

She smiles and runs her fingers through my tangled hair. I need a shower, food, water, and rest, but above all, I need reconciliation.

"I was worried about you today," she says. "So worried I didn't know what to do. I couldn't imagine you never coming back."

"Like Dad?"

"Yes." She nods and looks at the floor. "That was hard for us, wasn't it?"

"Yeah."

"I'd like us to talk about what happened today." She coughs to clear her throat. "If you're ready to share with me, I believe I have some things to tell you as well."

"About what?"

"About your father. The divorce."

"What else is there to know? You guys fought. He left. He never came back."

"All true, but there's more to it than that." She takes a deep breath and exhales slowly through her mouth. "When you were six, your father had an affair with one of his coworkers. There wasn't much I thought I could do at the time, with our financial situation and the fact that I was three months pregnant with what would have been your younger sibling. But I was heartbroken and miscarried as a result. Your father felt guilty, as he should have, and ended the affair. But about a year later, after he got laid off, he started cheating again with the same woman. Only this time, the woman had accepted a new job in Seattle. And she told him if he wanted to be with her, he would have to go with her and leave his family behind. When he told me this, I told him to go and never come back. And that's what he did. He packed a suitcase, took Rosie, and left without another word."

"Did you want him to leave?"

"I wanted him to choose us, but he chose her. And even if I hadn't told him to go, he still would have. Maybe not then. Maybe he would have waited another year or just wasted more of our money, traveling back and forth to see her. It didn't matter to him when he left because he was already gone. Inside. He felt nothing for me."

"What about me?"

"Oh, Rachel." Her eyes are watering. "He did love you. Very much."

"But not enough to stay?"

She doesn't answer, and I don't blame her. Sometimes you just have to accept things for what they are. Like my schizophrenia. It could have been triggered by my dad, or it could have been inside me all along, or a combination of both. I'll never really know.

"Why didn't you ever tell me any of this?" I ask.

"You were so little when it happened. I wanted to wait until you were older, but then you got ill…" Beads of water spill from her eyes without a sign of stopping. The floodgates may never close again. "Telling you the truth would have driven you further from reality. But not telling you the truth has caused a lot of strain in our relationship. And made you question your self-worth. And for that, I am sorry. I am truly, deeply sorry for what your father did and for what I did."

"It's okay, Mom. You just tried to do what was best for me. You've always put me first. You're my…" She's everything and so much more. "I love you, Mom."

Mom squeezes my hand and smiles through her tears. "I love you too, Rachel."

The next morning, I wake to the smell of bacon, eggs, and blueberry waffles. Mrs. Martin is in our kitchen, which scares me, considering she's a hound about my medication. But Mom is downstairs with her, and neither says a word about me taking my pill. Merely a good morning and how did you sleep?

Me, I have an overwrought feeling that two guys are going to jump out of the ceiling and hold me down so Mom can shove a needle in my butt.

"Melinda can see us at 10:00 today. Do you think you'll be ready by then?" Mom asks as she pours me a glass of orange juice.

"I think so."

"Best get a comb to that hair, love," Mrs. Martin says as she fills my plate with food. "And let's get you eating again. You look a stone lighter than last week."

I smile and pick at my food. I need to eat this morning, after only nibbles of bread yesterday. I haven't heard a word from Arnold, whether he's been talking to his parents or welled up in his bedroom, alone with his thoughts. I could just go over and knock on the door, but I have to meet with Melinda first.

Group therapy was an absolute failure in the past. I would never open up in front of my mother, and my mother was quick to react, which made me all the more reclusive. But today, she seems reasonably composed, sitting next to me in Melinda's blue haven. She knows as much as Melinda in regard to all the mishaps with Arnold. But does she know what's best for me?

"Legally, the choice is Rachel's," Melinda says. "And should she decide to discontinue her Seroquel, I encourage regular therapy sessions, as we've been doing, but also monthly behavior checks and psychoanalysis to monitor her mental health. Rachel's intangibles may be gone at present, but that's not to say they won't come back at some point. She must be able to cope with the changes and be willing to resume her medication should she ever become a danger to herself or others. Rachel will have to work hard to make sure she is taking proper care of herself, hygiene and all, and refrain from all recreational drugs as they could cause further damage. She should continue to work out, as exercise has numerous health benefits, and socialize regularly."

"But what about Arnold?" I ask. "Am I allowed to see him again?" I look back and forth between the two women, but neither seems to have a clear expression on their face that would hint one way or the other. I'm chewing the skin off my lip, just dying to have an answer. They both know how much Arnold means to me. But they also know how much damage he's caused.

"That's up to his parents," Mom says. "And whatever recommendations their health care provider has."

"But we don't even know if they're getting him any help," I say.

"They are. They said they would try at least. But Arnold isn't very receptive."

"Because they don't ever talk to him or listen to him. He only opens up to me. I should be over there. I should be with him right now."

"Rachel, we understand your compassion for Arnold," Melinda says. "But remember what we discussed before. You can't save Arnold on your own."

"He shouldn't be alone though."

"No, he shouldn't. I'll reach out to his family today. I cannot provide services as I already treat you, but I have several colleagues who would be most appropriate."

I sigh and lean my head against the open window. Arnold doesn't need to be sent to a shrink and prescribed another pill. He needs his parents to be parents. What if they're already medicating him? And planning to take him out of school again? Once was enough. Would they do it again?

Mom and Melinda talk at length about Arnold while I disengage and reflect on the last moment Arnold and I shared, outside on the grass, in front of everyone. We held each other and cried. And he said he couldn't do it. He couldn't leave. Yet I have this awful feeling inside that I'm losing him, right now, that he's slipping from existence into a black hole that no one can reach. And even if he survives to the end of the hole, how will he find his way back when he's so far from my arms?

"Are you alright?" Mom asks. It's raining, and she's driving exceptionally slow, probably to get a few more words out of me before we get home.

"You both don't want me to see Arnold, and it's driving me nuts."

"Rachel, we just gave you our blessing to stop taking your medication. Would it kill you to spend a few more days away from Arnold? Just while he's mending things with his folks?"

"I don't think there's any *mending* going on over there."

"Joslyn and Crew are good people."

"But are they good parents?"

"I can't be too harsh to judge. You know I've made mistakes, and I've reconciled for them to the best of my ability. Everyone deserves a second chance, right?"

I sigh and rub the corners of my eyes. "I just hope they're not making things worse for him. I can't stand to think of him in pain."

"Well, you can always call or text, but nothing else. Not yet," Mom says as she turns into our driveway.

Once we get inside, Mom goes upstairs to change for work. She offers to call out, but I know how important her job is, and I need some time alone to call and text Arnold, just as she said. From the kitchen window, I have a clear view of Arnold's house. Both cars are still in the driveway, which means both parents took off work to be home with Arnold. I text him once. Wait five minutes. No reply. Then I call. Goes straight to voicemail. So I call the landline.

His mother answers.

"Hi, Mrs. Begay, it's Rachel. I was wondering if I could talk to Arnold."

"Oh, Rachel, how kind of you to call. Arnold is sleeping right now, but I'll let him know you called. Alright?"

"Okay, sure. How's he—"

She hangs up before I can ask. My heart drops into my stomach. Am I really supposed to just sit here and wait?

Suddenly, there's a knock at the door. I leap to answer, hoping to see Arnold, but it's his towering father instead. I freeze in the doorway like a deer in headlights. I've seen Mr. Begay many times before in passing, but it's always his wife saying the hellos and how are yous, while he is more silent and reserved. He must save his voice for the courthouse or for pressing matters such as this is feeling to be.

"Hello, Rachel," he says. "Is your mother home?"

"She…she just left for work."

"That's fine. I came to speak with you. I know you just called, and my wife was quick to hang up on you."

"Oh." I swallow hard. "I just wanted to talk to Arnold."

"Yes, well." Mr. Begay smiles to one side. "It would be best if you talked to me first. Would you like to sit down? We can sit outside if that would make you more comfortable. It stopped raining, and it looks like your seats are still dry."

Following what Mom always does for guests, I offer to make

coffee, but he asks for water instead. After which, we sit outside on the front porch, Mr. Begay slowly drinking his water, me staring at my feet. He doesn't say anything for a few minutes. I'm bursting to ask questions, but I know this is one of those times when you just have to sit back and let someone else lead the conversation, even if they're going at a sloth's speed.

"Well," he finally says. "I'm not much for words when it comes to matters of the home, but I mainly wanted to come over to thank you."

"Thank me? For what?"

"For saving my son."

"I didn't save him."

"He wouldn't have come back had it not been for you. You know that, right?"

I nod. "I care about him. A lot."

"And he cares very deeply for you." Mr. Begay sets his glass down and clears his throat with a loud a-hem. "I never had a father growing up. And my mother wasn't around much because she worked three jobs. I basically raised myself and my two younger sisters. I put myself through law school, married well, and had a child. Did everything right according to the books. But I failed miserably at being a father. I suppose I could blame my own father for never being there. But at the end of the day, I have to take responsibility. I almost lost my son. Twice now. I'm not going to lose him again. I can't control him like I think I can. And he can't control himself like he thinks he can. But you…I believe you can help. You *have* helped."

"I don't want to control him. I want Arnold to be free to make his own decisions."

"I don't want you to control him, either. Last night, he said some things to me, things I never knew or realized because I wasn't paying enough attention. I wasn't listening. I caused him a lot of pain, and I have a lot of making up to do. I'm not sure how to do it. And I don't expect you to have the answers. A lot of this will require professional help, which has been our primary battle for the last twenty-four hours."

"He doesn't want to take those pills."

"I don't blame him. But for a while, it seemed to be working. He seemed happy." Mr. Begay looks over at his house and pinches his lips together. "I want him to be happy again."

"Me too."

He looks back at me. "Arnold needs you in his life."

I take a deep breath, allowing the truth to come out, even if it hurts us both. "He needs you more."

twenty-two

I DON'T SEE Arnold that day. Or the next. I'm confused because his dad seemed so pressed to keep me in the picture, but I'm still not receiving any text messages or phone calls, and Arnold hasn't left the house, not once. That's how much I've been lingering by the kitchen window, just waiting for him to come outside. It seems like the weather is linked to my torment, as it's been raining on and off, and the sun has yet to show itself.

My patience spent, I muster up the courage to go over to his house. At least one parent has been home all week, and this time, it's his mother.

"Rachel, how are you?" Mrs. Begay asks, opening the door half-way. Even when she's home, having no one around to impress, she still looks amazing.

"I'm fine. How's Arnold doing?"

"He's…" She forces a smile. "Well, he's not his best right now."

"Could I see him? Please?"

"Let me see if he's awake. Would you like to come in for a minute?"

She hurries upstairs while I linger in the foyer, unsure of my place anymore. Their house smells like chicken. I notice a pie in the kitchen, several actually, and assume she must be making chicken pot pies. But why so many? I also note that all the decorations and photos have finally been hung. I've never seen a picture of Arnold as a baby before. He was extremely chubby.

"Sorry," Mrs. Begay says as she comes down the stairs. "He's still sleeping. He sleeps most of the day and then spends the rest of his time playing video games."

"Oh."

"I've been cooking nonstop, as you can see. It's what I do to pass the time. Would you like to take a pie home?"

"No, thank you. I really would like to see Arnold."

"He's sleeping. But I'll tell him you stopped by and that he should give you a call."

I swallow hard. "Do you not want me to see him?"

"Of course I want you to see him. It's just…he's not much for conversation right now, and he needs to rest until we can get him to talk to a doctor."

"I could help."

"You already have. And we appreciate it, more than we show, but Arnold needs to rest some more."

I lower my eyes to the ground. I could just run upstairs and force Arnold to get up. But Mrs. Begay seems in no hurry to get him out of bed. Or maybe she just doesn't want me around right now. Still, I don't understand why she needs to make half a dozen chicken pot pies to "pass the time" when her only son is clearly not well.

"I'll take a pie," I finally say.

The pie smells like it came straight from Chef Gordon's oven. I take it home and cut myself a substantial piece. When I bite into it, I immediately spit it out. She used entirely too much salt. The pie is ruined. Even the crust is too salty. Rather than get upset, I laugh. Because Mrs. Begay wasted hours cooking just to have a bunch of salty pies. I could go back and tell her about the salt, but what if she likes her pies extra salty? Does that make her a bad cook? Or just a different kind of cook?

Is she a bad mother?

Maybe she isn't trying to keep me from Arnold. Maybe it's Arnold that doesn't want to see me. The thought of that makes me want to throw the pie right at his bedroom window.

It stops raining. I head outside to shoot some hoops. The driveway is full of puddles, but I don't care. I'm angry. So angry that I can't make any of my shots. Eventually, I stop trying and bang the ball several times into the ground until I'm punching the ball, causing all the puddles to break. Then with all my strength, I give the ball a good, hard kick, and it flies across the neighborhood, landing three houses down.

"Nice kick."

I turn around, startled by the sudden voice but even more startled by the person speaking.

"Alexia?"

The last time I saw Alexia she was unconscious and bleeding from her forehead. I never saw her in the hospital, even though her parents begged me to see her, insisting I would be the one to wake her. She eventually woke on her own. And now she's back to her normal, perfect self, minus the three-inch scar on her forehead. She's wearing pink workout clothes and sweating as though she just went for a run. I'm not sure why she's in my neighborhood. I doubt she's interested in Tommy or Ale. Her standards are way higher.

"What…what are you doing here?" I ask after several seconds of shock.

"I wanted to see you," she says.

"You wanted to see me? What for?"

"To thank you for saving my life. I know it's long overdue, but life has been one big migraine the last month. I'm just starting to feel like my normal self again."

"Yeah, head trauma will do that to you."

"I also wanted to apologize to you for how nasty I've been these past few years. I was a real jerk, and I have no excuse for my behavior."

I pinch my lips together and exhale noisily through my nose. I'm not sure what to say. I'm supposed to be working on my social skills daily, but with someone like Alexia? Where do I even begin?

"Well, anyway, I'm sorry," she says. "And I think you should try out for basketball next year. It's senior year, and you should play again. You were the best player on our team."

"For a time."

"Things are different now. You could be better."

My lips curve to one side. "Maybe."

"Think about it."

I spend the next hour in the backyard, cutting down the ugly red bush. I use an electric blade this time, hoping the loud noise will wake Arnold. After the bush is terminated and all the branches and leaves are swept away, I dig out the roots. It proves to be a very difficult task, one that requires a lot of strength. And stamina.

I lie down in the wet yard, too exhausted to continue. For a moment, the sun comes out and shines on me. I close my eyes and bathe in the heat, but it disappears all too soon. I think about that black hole again and wonder what would happen if I got sucked inside it too. Would Arnold and I be stuck inside forever? Would we be outside of time? If we crossed to the other side and returned to life, how much time would have passed? Would he still want to hold me in his arms?

My phone buzzes inside my pocket.

A: **Are you okay?**

Am I okay? He's asking me if *I'm* okay. I glance up at his window. The curtains are finally open, and Arnold is standing there, looking down at me.

My phone rings. He's calling. I don't answer. Something keeps me from moving. I don't know whether it's fear or anger. Or maybe I am just too exhausted to do anything. Maybe this is me finally giving up.

I close my eyes and wait.

I don't know how long I've been waiting. Seconds. Minutes. Hours. But my eyes finally open. The sun is out and more powerful than ever. I roll onto my side. My arms and legs are covered in mud. My chest hurts like I've been running through smoke. But I am capable of standing. I need to move. I can't just lay on the ground, expecting things to go my way.

Even though I look like a character from *The Walking Dead*, I go straight to Arnold's house, prepared to make an intense entrance, but just as I reach the door it opens from the other side and there he is. Arnold.

He leans against the doorway like he's out of breath from walking down the stairs. His hair is long and greasy and smells unwashed. He wears old gym shorts and a black T-shirt. There's a small Band-Aid across the scar that bled before. But no new wounds. None that I can see at least.

His mom calls something to him, and he says he needs fresh air. He shuts the door behind him and plops into one of the porch chairs.

"Would you like to sit down?" he asks in a monotone voice.

"I'm too dirty."

"I see that. What were you doing?"

"Waiting."

"For me?"

I nod. "Did your mom tell you I came over?"

"Yeah, she did."

"I wanted to see you. I wanted to see how you're doing."

"I'm…here."

"Are you on your medications?"

"No. I asked my parents not to force it, and they listened this time. But I'm going to see a doctor tomorrow, and depending on how that goes, things could change."

"How do you feel about that?'

"I don't feel much of anything right now." He sits up and forces a smile. "How might you be? How's your week been?"

"Well." Miserable. "I saw Melinda."

"And?"

"I'm officially off my Seroquel. For now."

"Are you happy about that?"

"A little nervous. They'll all be watching me more carefully now. But I'm glad to be given this chance."

"That's good." Arnold scratches the back of his neck and glances at the trees, at the ground, anywhere but my face.

"Are you glad to see me?" I ask.

"No."

My eyes lower to the ground, and two big tears crash on top of the Begays' welcome mat. I feel everything inside start to break, like a virus-infected computer. Nothing will work right. Nothing will load. I'm incapable of functioning. I would like to go home now, so I can cry in my room, but I can't even move my feet.

"It's not you," he says. "It's me."

I shake my head, confused. People use those words when they

want to break up with someone without hurting their feelings. But because it's so obvious, it hurts even more.

"Well." I wipe my face and quickly muster up some verbosity. "If you don't want to be with me anymore, then just please say it. So I can…" Figure out the next step. Like literally, figure out how to get off this porch without falling over.

"Not me. You. You won't."

"How do you know what I want?"

"You won't want *this*." He points at himself like he's some kind of bacterial disease. "Because this side of me isn't pretty. Isn't fun at all. And it can last days, weeks, months. You don't deserve to have to deal with that. To deal with any of this."

"Please don't say that. That hurts, Arnold. You may not feel anything right now, but I do. And I still care about you."

"I'm sorry." He forces himself to stand. His odor is enough to make me drop, but I manage to take a few steps in the right direction. I'm now on the grass. "Please don't go. Let me explain." He reaches out and grabs my arm. It feels like a jolt of electricity. "Look at me, Rachel."

"Please let go of me."

"I am sorry. Really, I am. I know I hurt you. I had a chance to start over when I met you. And I ruined everything because I thought I needed more. But you were enough. You were more than enough."

"But I'm not enough anymore?"

He releases his hold on my arm but still keeps his hand at my side. "I don't know if I'm enough. If I'm a person worth forgiveness. Worth anything."

"You are worth everything." I grab his hands. "And you are not alone. You have me. And your parents."

"They don't—"

"They do."

Arnold raises my hands and presses his forehead against them. The muscles in his face quiver. "Everything is so messed up. I don't know what to do to make things better."

"You're already making things better by simply talking to me. That's a start. There are obviously a lot of things still bothering you."

"What if there isn't? What if this is just who I am, deep down? What if I'm just a sad, miserable person?"

"You're not. You're an amazing person. You just have to get past this." I point to his head. "And lead with this." I point to his heart.

Overjoyed that Arnold is speaking again, Mrs. Begay is more than willing to let him come over to my house for the rest of the day. He hasn't been eating much lately, nor have I, so we make sandwiches and guacamole and maintain a simple conversation. I like the idea of taking things slow again. It's almost like we're starting over. A second chance.

Now fueled up and a little more aware of his physical status, I suggest a shower for Arnold while I tidy up my room. But after twenty minutes, Arnold is still in the bathroom. I don't hear any water running, which worries me, so I knock on the door.

No answer.

My heart pounds so loud I don't even hear my own voice when I say his name. I knock again and turn the knob.

Arnold is lying in the bathtub with a washcloth over his face. It looks like he emptied the bottle of soap by the number of bubbles in the tub.

"Arnold?"

I pull the cloth off his face. He opens his eyes and says hey. Then he grabs both of my arms and pulls me into the tub with him. Water floods the floor, and bubbles go flying. But Arnold is holding me. And that means the world.

Eventually, my clothes do come off, and I take a proper bath with him. After which, I give him my robe to wear while I change into clean clothes.

In my room, I debate putting on a record.

"What's wrong?" Arnold asks.

"I don't want to play anything too depressing right now."

"You should play whatever you want. Play your favorite."

I pull out The Beatles album. "You told me it was shit. The last time I played it."

"I did?"

"Yes, but you were high."

"Play it."

"But it's sad."

"Just play it."

Arnold sits on the floor next to me and listens carefully to the music, closing his eyes to hold back the tears. I smile, remembering his crazy dance.

Toward the end of the song, I reach under my bed and pull out Larry's notebook. I flip through the pages. They're all blank, but one sketch remains. The one Larry drew the morning I knew I was falling for Arnold.

"Can you see this?" I show the notebook to Arnold.

"Yes," he says. "It's you and me."

"I drew this. I really drew this."

I close my eyes, feeling the tears prickle up, but I smile and let them fall. None of the other sketches were real. But this one was.

When the song finally ends, Arnold curls his head into my lap and stays like that for a very long time. I play another song and another until we've gone through several albums, and I'm just too tired to hold onto him any longer. But that doesn't stop him from holding onto me. He wraps me in his arms and lies with me on the carpet. We cry a little more. And then we start to talk. Little by little. We talk it out. And finally, when we have nothing left to say, I find one last thing to say.

"I love you."

***

Don't miss your next favorite book!
Join the Fire & Ice YA Books newsletter today!
www.fireandiceya.com/mail.html

THANK YOU FOR READING

Did you enjoy this book?

We invite you to leave a review at the website of your choice, such as Goodreads, Amazon, Barnes & Noble, etc.

DID YOU KNOW THAT LEAVING A REVIEW...

- Helps other readers find books they may enjoy.
- Gives you a chance to let your voice be heard.
- Gives authors recognition for their hard work.
- Doesn't have to be long. A sentence or two about why you liked the book will do.

acknowledgments

I have to start by thanking my family, especially my mom who has read every single novel, short story, play, or comic book I've written since I was a kid. Both my parents have been very supportive of my writing career and have made many sacrifices to give me the education required to pursue such endeavors. I love you both with all my heart. I would also like to thank my husband for his continual love and support, and for keeping our lovely children out of my hair so I could edit. I also have to thank my dog for being my cuddle buddy during all the ups and downs, especially during the querying process.

None of this would be possible without my amazing agent, Jana Hanson of Metamorphosis Literary Agency. Rachel's story would not be the same without her skilled hand. Thank you for taking a chance with me and having my back throughout the entire process, from our first query to the final product.

I would also like to thank my editor at Fire and Ice, Lisa Petrocelli, my cover artist, Caroline Andrus, and Nancy Schumacher.

Lastly, I would like to thank all the wonderful people who shared their personal stories of mental illness, medications, and experiences using recreational drugs.

about the author

Natalie Blank graduated from the University of Maryland, Baltimore County with a BFA in Acting and a BA in Interdisciplinary Studies in Dance and Culture. She writes primarily YA contemporary, focusing on mental health and family relationships. She resides in Maryland with her husband, two children, and zealous cocker spaniel. In addition to writing, she enjoys baking cookies and relaxing on the beach.

authornatalieblank.com

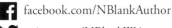 facebook.com/NBlankAuthor
 twitter.com/NBlankWriter
amazon.com/author/natalieblank

Made in the USA
Middletown, DE
27 March 2022

63191008R00137